DEATH GOES TO THE DOGS

ANNA TAMBOUR

MOSS BEACH ODDNESS
2023

To request permissions, contact the publisher at:
editor@forbiddenfutures.com

Softback ISBN: 978-1-7322124-4-2
Hardback ISBN: 978-1-7322124-7-3
Electronic ISBN: 978-1-7322124-5-9

First paperback edition March 2023.
Edited by Cody Goodfellow & Daniel Ringquist
Cover art & illustrations by Mike Dubisch
Layout by ODDNESS

Printed in the United States of America on SFI Certified paper.

First Edition

ODDNESS
www.forbiddenfutures.com

Ordering Information:
editor@forbiddenfutures.com

To Clarence Young, singular inspirer

"I decided right then and there: screw it."

–C.Y.

CONTENTS

THE POWER OF 3

"The Power of 3"
Parsec Issue #1
PS Publishing, 2021

1. The First Little Pig

"Oh, no," said the pig.

"Oh, yes," said the wolf. "Sorry."

"Look," said the wolf. "It'd be so much easier if you'd just accept. Once every telling, I burn your house down."

He pulled out a monogrammed silver lighter.

"No," said the pig.

"Don't get stroppy with me," said the wolf, flashing a gold-capped canine.

"Then don't get sloppy with me," said the pig. "And close that mouth. What do you *do* to my home, my castle, the place I keep my slippers?"

"What d'you mean?" said the wolf, who had started to breathe heavily.

"Take it easy," said the pig. "You must be, what, pension age now?"

"And your chins wag. You keen to be burnt up, too? Please move aside."

The pig's tidy ankles moved not one jot. "Do I have to repeat myself," he said. "Think back. My house is made of straw, so you —"

"Burn it to a crisp!"

"Do you want to go down in history as an ijit? Must I repeat, what d'you do to my house? *Eat* it?"

"You think I'm an ijit!?"

"Banish it?"

"Don't be daft."

"Just try to concentrate. Yes. Close your eyes and say after me. I huff and I puff, and I—come on. I bl—"

"I blows your house down," muttered the wolf.

"Blow is quite sufficient," said the pig. "But why the shifty eye? So you *can't* remember. So you get mixed up. So you're short of breath. So perhaps you purposely forgot. I'm no rooster. I won't crow."

"We don't talk," said the wolf.

"So *that* you remember."

But the wolf had never had a nose for irony. "It's time."

"Rightee-oh," said the pig. "But first, would you excuse me for a tick?"

"Just a tick. Remember, this story isn't just about you. I've a house to burn."

"Oh, *I* remember. Now I'll be just a mo'."

The pig didn't try to shut the door, so as the wolf watched the pig's neat footsteps as he trotted down the spotless hall, not a straw out of place; he looked down also at his own feet, at the swept step, and then around at the front garden—everything in perfect order.

A shit builder, thought the wolf. But, he whistled wistfully, such a tidy neighbour I can only wish I had.

"Here 'tis," said the pig, appearing again in a buttoned-up dustcoat and carrying a new straw broom.

"You want a little dustup," said the wolf magnanimously. "It's not in the story, and everything's in its place here but—"

"Not quite," said the pig, who then beat the wolf to such a death that the step was covered in hairy mush, except for two things that the pig fished out, wearing rubber gloves to do so.

The pig scooped the mush up into a big red basin and carried it past his shed to his burn pit at the back of the garden where at the normal time in this short but eventful story, the scent of burning plantation fir and cedar, rare rainforest parquet flooring, and repurposed ancient oak would have rent the afternoon sky till it could only have wished to cry, "Evict!" but not even in this story's imagination can *that* happen.

Instead, the rank scent of the incinerated wolf was smothered by a unique blend of emissions—corncobs, loose tea, chestnut shells, discarded frightfully stale on-special beernuts, pome-tree prunings, visiting-pigeon droppings stuffed with rose hips, and the slurry from the pig's ginger plant—a divine emanation that rose, curled, and spread like some luxuriating cat, over fake terracotta tile and fifteenth-century chimney pots alike, and made every nostril in the neighbourhood tingle in pleasure at this marvellously organic, truly potpourric miasma.

And the gold tooth? He gave it to DGS, his favourite tax-deductible charity. He had a thing for destitute grasshoppers but he wasn't just some leftist with a soft-as-well-past-al-dente touch to those who never plan for the future, let alone for famine. Grasshoppers are nutritious as well as delicious—and that crunch!

He did regret, however, that he hadn't saved a little something more from the wolf.

So he stuck a note to his fridge in case of another wolf ever calling.

Keep a claw. Would make one grand toothpick.

2. Just Being Neighbourly

Believe it or not, squatters are everywhere.

They were very, very weary, and horribly hungry, and winter was hard on their heels, and this place seemed almost capital, so they moved in during the so-called dead of night under the broken watch of the smashed streetlight, carrying all their belongings on their backs. They had each a bowl for their porridge; a little bowl for the Little Wee Bear; and a middle-sized bowl for the Middle-sized Bear; and a great big bowl for the Great Big Bear. And they had each a chair to sit in; a little chair for the Little Wee Bear; and a middle-sized chair for the Middle-sized Bear; and an electric lift recliner (a constant source of unstated conflict) for the Great Big Bear. And they had each a bed to sleep in; a single for the Little Wee Bear; and a Queen for the Middle-sized Bear; and, because of the recliner another Queen for the Great Big Bear.

Between foreclosures brought on by unpaid mortgages and those initiated by homeowners associations for delinquent dues, squatting in foreclosed homes has become quite the phenomenon.

The Bears couldn't tell if this was a dangerous nice quiet neighbourhood, or an exemplar of the phenomenon, so they tiptoed to their beds.

The next morning, after they had made the porridge for their breakfast and poured it into their bowls, they walked out into the garage while the porridge was cooling, that they might not burn their mouths by beginning too soon; for they were polite, well-brought-up Bears. And while they were away, a ferret named Goldilocks came a-calling.

He and his family of a dozen or so—he'd lost count—were also newcomers to the neighbourhood, having tunnelled in next door just the week before, as the ground shook under the heels of the departing sheriff.

Unlike the Bears' house, the Ferrets' was (though it had a bit of a glass encumbrance what with all the smashed lamps, bottles and glasses) fully furnished, with numerous socks, slithery piles of papers, soft toys, stuffed chairs and sofas, a cute ferret-sized plastic mansion and a fire station with a sliding pole (only slightly smashed), and a cornucopia of a kitchen. So many things, it was a wonder Big Momma Ferret asked little Goldilocks to go next door to borrow a cup of sugar.

And maybe she didn't, but that was the story Goldilocks was prepared to tell if he got caught. He peeped in at the keyhole, for he was not at all a well-brought-up little ferret. Oh, his mother had tried, but she'd kind of had it by his time (# 12).

Seeing nobody in the house, he lifted the latch.

The door was not fastened, not because the Bears were good Bears who did nobody any harm and never suspected that anybody would harm them, but because Great Big Bear knew nothing about breaking in. Though he had for many years read *Popular Mechanics,* he had always passed by the enticing advertisements to 'Earn $25 an hour as a Locksmith', in the process also failing to provide for his family in a manner befitting their otherwise decency.

Middle-sized Bear nagged him incessantly to get them out of this poverty trap and had almost bored his ears off with, "Wee won't be wee forever." As if Wee's ability to get into a place was all that was needed. They were all too polite to come out with naked insults, but Mid was all too eloquent in her unstated aspersions. He had to act insouciant for there was only so much he could do to provide for his family, so he lived in constant fear of Wee Little growing up with neither the right to a decent livelihood nor legal protections to live in ruins.

But that didn't mean he was idle. He researched like a mad chipmunk whenever he had the opportunity. So, for instance, while Mid was out scrounging, gossips said he was lounging feet up in their dive, lost in fantasy pages of another *Pop Mech*, this one blaring from its cover 'Build Yourself a Weatherproof Berry Patch'. Little did they know that secreted amongst those pages was what he was really reading—the key to the Bear family future:

The Wrong Way to Remove Squatters in Your HOA

Beyond learning the proper way to get rid of squatters, you must also know how to remove squatters the wrong way. By knowing what you can't do, you can protect your Home Owners' Association from potential liability.

These are actions that you absolutely can't do in an attempt to remove squatters living in foreclosed homes:

Cut power to the property;

Turn off utilities for the property;

Threaten, intimidate, or abuse the squatter/s in any way, shape, or form; and,

Use violence against the squatter/s.

Mid, uh, Mama Bear knew more than she let on. She knew what he was doing, but sometimes this life was all too much for her who was now just a low-class sneaky nomad, by, she reminded herself, compassionate choice.

For after all, what did she need *him* for? Or any him? She'd always been as independent as her mother, and her mother's mother, and all mama bears from the first to, as proper time would have it, eternity.

But she was a soft touch, and when he came a-begging with no malice in his eyes about her cub, she let him graze beside her in the blueberry patch.

And by the time she heard bushes rustle behind and saw him chuffing the cub along in protective panic, it was almost too late.

When he told her his story in her all-too-easily found den, it was too late. Her compassion, that thing more useless to a mama bear than plastic wrap for freshness—that extraneous-to-needs and able-to-damage-you-if-you-don't-throw-it-away thing—that thing *compassion* had snuck into her heart and lodged there.

She couldn't kick him out to be the loner he was born to be. Not only couldn't she do that, but he became, to the superficial crowd, the crowd most likely to be suspicious and cause trouble, Head of the Household.

If only he'd liked salmon-fishing better. Instead, he'd travelled down to California to get some easy work at BeesKnees Pure Clover Honey. Line workers there got less than minimum wage but they got a two percent discount on as much honey as they could buy. He spent his first pay entirely on honey, and took it out to a place under an overpass that was the closest he could find to a den. On sticking his tongue into the first jar, he pulled back, shocked. Dyed, flavoured sugar-water!

The next shift, he told his supervisor, who took his complaint Upstairs, who then passed Up his details, and by sundown, he was running for his life.

He ran and he ran and he ran. He ran, in fact, right up the bony spine of California, all the way up to the hairy wilds of Oregon, where he met that mama bear and her cub…

...and where they were chased out and had to start the life of indigents, for he was too afeared to go to anyone else, though she told him all about the comfortable life they'd lead under witness protection.

"According to whom?"

"Movies."

"The same movies that say I am a threat to you?"

"No. Those are documentaries."

And so they were this unnaturally enlarged nuclear family, living as stable an itinerant life as possible, and he was always reading, and they were always hungry but with the fixings of three hot meals—three hot meals that were now, in fact, cooling.

Ma Ferret had a wealth of time to read, but she preferred to gambol. The whole family *were* gambolling addicts—on first arriving from England in the wake of the great rabbit famine, such references would often be corrected by sticklers to 'whole family was', but if they continued talking about, say, the tasty hares of the Scottish highlands, the parochial pedants wilted under the immigrants' internationalism.

"I were just norticing wot luvily pockets you have," they'd next say to their abashed audience, for they was always polite, though Pa Ferret did have a smell that could clear out drains.

But the porridge will turn cold as roadkill if the Bears continue to fuss in the garage, tsking at the oil-stained floor, and we are still only up to:

Then, seeing nobody in the house, he lifted the latch.

Actually, he was a little disgusted. What's the use of 'Goldilocks' if you lift instead of pick?

He dropped to the floor and nearly brained himself, hitting his head on its polished surface. The place was a wasteland of cleanliness. The stench of cleaning products made him gag, but he persevered. Ma had heard the Bears break in, she said. And Ma had ruminated over the pickings that the Bears would be treated to. Meaning: *there must be orphans here. Ma will be so proud.*

The Bears had never done anybody any harm, and never suspected that anybody would harm them (in their dreams! Great Big Bear especially was sick of all the times he'd been told how lucky he was, always by those who'd never had to squat, those who'd never had to get their meals from garbage cans, or live on porridge).

So when Goldilocks started casing the joint, he was not well pleased when he saw, not any orphan socks, not a delicious bunny, not a coat with pockets—but three bowls of scarily smoking substance emitting an evil smell. They sat on the floor of a dining room that was otherwise empty except for three unmatched chairs, two against the walls and one mid-room, ready to recline. Its cord was stretched taut as a dead rat's tail.

If Goldilocks had been a well-brought-up little girl she wouldn't have been there. The well-brought-up little girl had been evicted along with the rest of her family.

Goldilocks looked at the bowls of porridge in this desert of a house, and slunk out.

Later that day, he snuck back in to leave three socks.

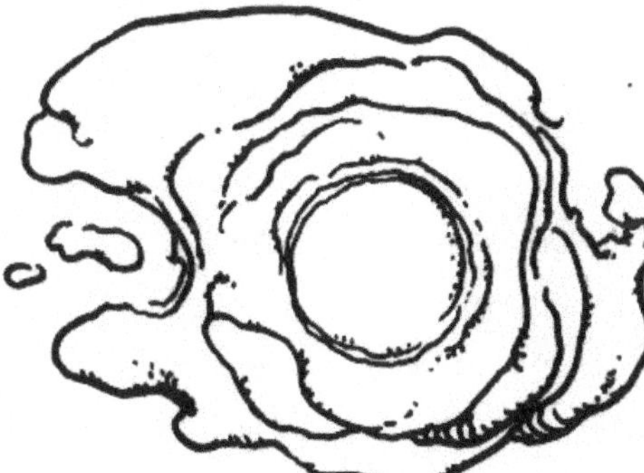

3. How Much is that Teapot in the Sales Bin?

Who would think to rub *this*? It's riven with sharp chased lines filled with dirt, and with that low-slung swell, long spout, and angled elbow, it looks like an angry mother with one hand on a hip, and it has BO. But who can choose their place of birth?

Oh dear. The indignity of being rummaged (and the pathetic, hopefilled thrill). Lifted up high, my spout scoops air laden with fragrances—oatmeal soap, some supermarket shampoo; ohh er! a whiff of *Terre d'Hermès* perfume for men but always in a place like this, worn by a woman who wants to be seen as casually rich and certainly independent; its price is not just for the name, but the story that it's been created by a 'great nose'. But trust me. My nose says—*and do I have a nose!*—it's a mix of citronella candle and spray-on insect repellent with added pepper for irritation. The smell physically hurts my nostrils, tingles on my skin, and if I had a dog, it would make my dog sneeze and run from me. And I'm quite convinced it would ward off swarms of bugs. No one should wear this, especially if you love dogs.

I wish I were consulted re chemical attractants, but no one ever has—though who else but I should know the power, or lack of it re attractants? That cloud of pricy stench, however, has (thank the marketers who made sure it needs constant application) dissipated, leaving room for the richness of the room's atmosphere: must, mildewed leather, tarnished brass and silver, gumboots rife with fungi; a silk chemise that has been hand-laundered but no one can truly get the underarm out. The sad sweet reek of book lice. Wool and more wool and instead of normal dust, a miasma of dog hair floating like a cloud, and—hmm, could that possibly be? It is! There's no smell like it in the world. It's that poorly wrapped toffee (a few dog hairs always sprouting as from a genie's nose) made for a certain charity. The first time I'd smelled it, I retched, but that's only because one needs to develop. But I like the smell of burnt sugar and I love dogs, dry *and* wet, so I was made for this stuff. I've only come across it in passing as I've been carried past in ecobaskets, backpacks, recycled carry bags and cardboard boxes yanked from car boots while the meter's running.

I've been in every shop but this one—the source of that divinity—ground zero—oh my mo' and whiskers—how I've longed to come here—the op shop *To the Dogs* deep in the heart of op shop street, Edinburgh.

"This jersey is a bit steep at fifteen pounds, don't you think?"

"Aye. But I would never buy it."

"So?"

"So?"

"So I'll have it and this. I got it from the sales bin. I don't know as I'll ever get it cleaned up. And just look here. This side has lost its roundedness. It looks like a bloody sultana."

"So you'll be buying it or not?"

"I'm buying the jersey, so you'll give me this bashed teapot for —" She raised an eyebrow invitingly.

"What's it say on the sales bin? All items ten pounds, or charity to customers?"

"No need for such cheek."

"Aye, no need. It's just a wee bonus service."

"Your practicing for the comedy festival here won't get you nearer. I'll need change for this fifty."

"As would we all."

"It's pity's all it is, you know. I shouldn't have got this frightful teapot, but I can brighten anything up. This bit of junk has been in every shop on the street."

I feel the flashing warmth of a different hand and I wish with all my heart—but she'd only touched. No rub. Instead she says, "I'm so sorry for the teapot."

So there it is. I'm up against it yet again. "Fate," it calls itself. I refuse to go so far.

"You're just bad luck," I'd always told it.

Soon as she got home, the old bird fairly ripped me out of the recycled Tesco bag.

"Gimme what I paid for."

I, of course, stayed pat.

"Come out. I know you're in there." I could hear her taking off a number of heavy rings. They clattered on a glass-topped table. I've always hated glass-topped tables. Glass should be used in cases. Putting someone on show is what glass is for, not for coffee cups to mark, old carpet to show up through.

I heard a sofa sigh or cry. It was hard to tell, it sounded so defeated.

Suddenly two hands did rub the teapot, but they did so incidentally in the act of violently shaking it, upended. The lid hung open like a question mark without a dot. Mine eyes saw stars and I passed out wondering whether a human's migraine could equal this terrific pain...

I woke up to a shame unlike any that anyone in history has ever experienced.

She'd de-teapotted me!

Have you ever seen a shelled snail?

If you have, you shouldn't have. If you have, you must know how impossible it is to ever get that image out of your head. That's why evil de-snailers chop them up and then they...

"I have bones!" I screamed (for I'm sure I must, but this wasn't a time to make sure).

"I'd taste like rubber," I added, and I admit, I began to cry so hard, my moustache was soon festooned with loops of snot.

"Why would I eat you, you snivelling flight risk?"

She popped a square of charity toffee into a maw that looked like pictures of an active volcano.

"Now," she said, twiddling her once more beringed fingers. "Gimme my wishes."

"Your wishes are my command," I said, and the one who thinks itself Fate must have broken its face, grinning.

"My first wish—I get three, don't I."

"You know your genies," said I.

"You're my first," she giggled.

"Just my luck," I said, "madam."

She beamed, impervious. "But," she frowned, poking me in a part so private, I can barely admit this even unto to myself. "I know why you've been given back. I know why you've ended up in that bin. You won't cheat *me*."

She lit a cigarette, a Regal Blue, a brand so noxious, the power of smell is vanquished as smell flees the scene, screaming.

I was thrown into a coughing fit. She crushed the thing in a greasy styrofoam dish next to me on the table, and tapped on the glass with her long horrific nails as she waited for me to stop delaying her.

At my first deep breath, she stopped and leaned so close I could see the canyons in her throat skin.

"Every. Single. Wish. I want," she said, "and I'll get, or you'll be sorry. Every bleeding one of the whole blasted three."

"As you wish, madam, so shall it be my command."

"You *are* one of those three wishes genies?"

"I was, I am, and so shall I always be."

"We'll see about that."

"To hear is to obey."

"Too right. Now, you ugly little grub, do exactly as I command."

"Exactly," I repeated solemnly, trying not to look panicked (my nether regions, never having been exposed, were starting to shrivel alarmingly, this table having obviously been, by the corrosive film and toxic gravel horroring its surface, the scene of many a meal of chips liberally sprinkled with salt and vinegar).

Quickly, I intoned the Words:

"You have three wishes."

"Whatever I want?"

"The next three wishes you make shall come true, whatever they are."

"You'll follow my exact instructions?"

I waved my hands in some nonsensical orientalist command, being in too much pain to speak.

"Rightee-oh, then! I don't want much."

"Speak!"

"Make me the most beautiful woman in the world. Make me the richest woman in the world. Make me live forever."

And oh, isn't she? Beautiful, I mean. That's what all the tabloids say, and the plastic surgery clinics.

It takes such constant surgery to stay like this, and to change with every change of what's considered beautiful that her makeup must always cover newly rawed skin. With every passing year it becomes harder to open that up-to-date perfect mouth, that stiff crust of scar tissue, and ever harder to break through the crust of cold lava, to operate. Ever more painful and difficult to pop another vinegar and salt chip in that orifice, and afterwards, to open wide enough to vomit; and she carries on, and on and on.

Never look behind her ears! There are more folds back there than a set of pulled-back stage curtains. No one ever does look there, just as no one ever touches her without being paid handsomely. But she has more rings than Saturn, and when Infinity looks upon her years left to live, Infinity's belief in itself is beggared.

And I? I would have expired on that hideous glass-topped table sprinkled with death crystals had not the girl from *To the Dogs* run after the lady and broken down the door because the lady had accidentally dropped a fiver and furthermore, had wobbled precariously so the girl thought she might not be just a horrible human but a genuinely ill, improbable but possible old dear, a genuine beloved gran.

When the girl broke down the door and burst in, the old dear was gone but there was I, almost at my last.

That girl.

She loves dogs, too.

Take that in the eye, with salt, Fate!

That girl, she *lied*.

That story she told me. It wasn't true. She'd just rescued me but she didn't know if she could trust me.

Of course she could have, but she was right in one way. I wouldn't have believed her.

The truth is, she had only just arrived in Edinburgh the night before and was to fill in that week for her aunt who was out donkey rescuing or something. She'd never been to Edinburgh before, so had never been to op shop street. The other woman working in To the Dogs hadn't given her a moment to look around before posting her to the counter.

I have no idea what she lives on. Her home—I have promised not to reveal it—is full of atmosphere—partly from the many rescue dogs (for she loves dogs as much as I do), some rescue toads she's always kissing (I'm not sold yet. They seem to have a secret agenda.), and her collection of unwashed teapots.

Indeed, she's the kind of teapot collector who gives a bad name to shabby chic. Many of them would be judged disgraceful. And she abhors tea.

I love the nights best here, so many fragrant dogs gently snoring, briarwood cuttings crackling in the fireplace. I've even grown to love the critical gaze of the toads, just as I respect their right to complex personalities. They've challenged us to keep up with the times, to put our morals where our mouths are, to stop sliding into comfortable repetition. As one toad says, swallowing his eyes as he gulps, then throwing out his tongue in the world's most eloquent retch, quite as if we've just offered him a plastic cockroach: "No tropiness from you!"

The girl is getting dark bags under her eyes, but she insists they are her treasure chests. We're to blame, all us rescue genies, and a mixed sense of guilt and joy has grown like a fungus in our hearts.

For we spend the nights taking turns storytelling because she must have, what, three thousand wishes amongst us? Not one of which she's ever called for.

"The only wish I have is that you all are happy," she insists, but that is the only wish we cannot grant.

So we do all we possibly can to repay her, for who could be happier than we?

Did I tell you that she also knits? And we didn't have to tell her that wool is far too harsh for our delicate parts. She spins her yarn from spiderwebs.

WHO
KNOWS
WHERE THE
WASP CAN
WEAR
HER
STING

"Who Knows Where The Wasp Can Wear Her Sting"
Forbidden Future #4, 2019
Oddness

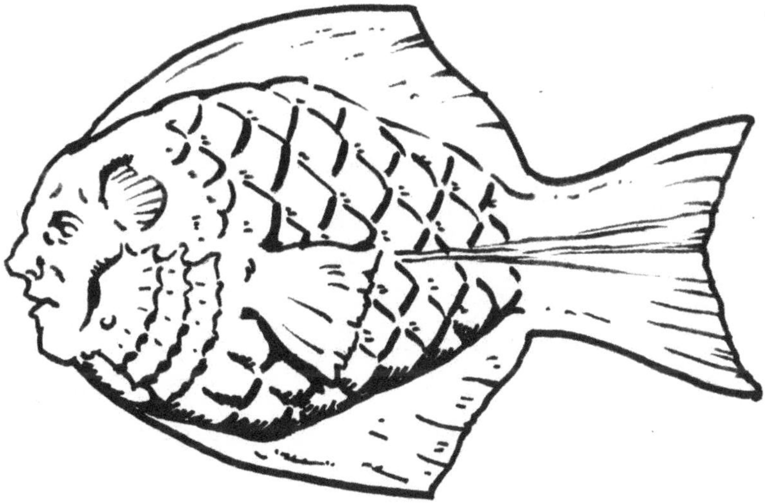

"Next, uh—" The bored halibut rolled his eyes at the ceiling. "Oh, why don't you have pronounceable names?"

"In her eye. Her piercing gaze," whispered Kate* (*the names have been changed) while tentatively rising from the window sill.

"In her retort," answered Petruchia.

They were playing "Who knows where?" to wile away the time while they were waiting, as well as to lessen the fear each had.

They'd never met before, both of them being loners. But the program enforced a degree of, if not friendliness, then enforced camaraderie due to them being assigned the same room. After all, their surgery and treatments were likely to be the same.

"How many did you do?" asked Kate.

"Only a hundred and fifty or so that have a chance, though I stocked them well. Those cuckoo wasps. I kept trying to lead them off my trail."

"We can only try. Better luck next year."

"If we get one."

"We must think poss—"

"This way," said a naked mole rat crossly. The three flew through a maze of tunnels till the mole rat banged through a door and was gone in a scurry.

"Perch," said someone from behind a screen.

The two mud wasps looked around.

The room's walls were plastered with positivism. Before and After pictures of celebrities. All the Before pictures being, of course, of the dead—for whom life's way too short. There's the antechinus male who, like all his counterparts, fucked to death. And that Brainiac Houdiniac, the octopus who starved herself to death caring for the eggs she laid.

It costs a fortune here to escape that fate. But with the power of positive thinking, and flexible terms, even you can afford a new lease of life from the Flatworm Rest Longevity Center.

Kate had revealed the location of a field of genetically modified pansies, their companion flower-spiders having adjusted to suit. Petruchia had pointed out a forest where honeysuckle vines made every tree into tentpoles. There were, therefore, lakes of nectar hanging from the trees.

Anyway, here they were, waiting in a room plastered with horror and hope. They'd perched as ordered, and each couldn't help picking up as many feet as possible. The perch was cold, alien metal.

"At Flatworm Longevity," said the still disembodied voice, "We believe in educating our guests fully about our treatments, products, and services in order to enhance your experience."

The voice came closer, as its owner emerged from behind the screen.

"Our client consent forms provide valuable information about treatments you may be receiving," it droned. Then it looked as them, and not in a way that would win this place any clients in its ads. It regarded them as if it doubted they had brains. "You *have* filled out the consent forms, have you not?"

"Don't you have them?" Kate blustered "We've paid so much, we expected better service."

Nothing in the publicity had prepared Petruchia for this.

Granted, it's extraordinarily pushing things to ask to live a season longer than her own mother. And to ask to live fifty more seasons? That's unbelievable, until you see the claims enough times. And since it costs so much, they must be true.

But she'd been through so many stages in life already. She liked this body.

"Are you an After?" she blurted.

"Petruchia!**" (**remember: not her real name) hissed Kate. "You know you'll have to make some compromises."

Petruchia's wings clattered, but she had to know.

Those limp things hanging. Six limbs of assorted fantastical uselessness. It can no more fly than it can walk up, or hang. Or pounce! How could it, if it's a she, get spiders for her babies? And what's it holding in that useless clamp? A thorn? Maybe it thinks a thorn a good substitute for jaws, or maybe it can never eat again. She felt hungry for nectar. *This thing might be like the mother octopus, forever.* And where's the ovipositor? And where *can* this thing wear its sting? In their place, a wound dressing!

Petruchia remembered stories, tales she'd put out of her mind because she wanted *oh, so much* to live in this wonderful body for more than just one season.

"You were one of us, weren't you?" she asked.

"One of *you?*" the thing laughed. "Hardly."

A flapping knock at the door got the thing up and answering. On the floor was that halibut intake officer. Those two eyes looked up accusingly.

"Haven't you processed them yet? You know all patients should be prepped within two hours."

"Almost ready," lied the thing, turning back to the two patients.

"Sorry," it said. "Halibuts are naturally testy, and that one's going through a mid-life crisis."

"How long do they live?" asked Kate.

"We didn't quite know before, and now we'll never know. But enough of that. You're both coming for the complete job."

"Excuse me," said Petruchia. "But you're clearly a success story. What were you before?"

Its face did something with that tiny hole it had instead of mandibles, and under the thin green skin of two legs with useless appendages, a graceful veinwork of parasitic worms could be seen, pulsating to the beat of its heart.

"I was a shrew," it said. "Haven't they done a marvelous job? I admit the wasp waist is difficult to maintain, and I'm not so keen on the naked mole rat look, but aren't I beautiful? Now, to you."

Never did two wasps fly as fast and as far, though at the end of the trail, they'd reach Death.

Better that by far. That face! A blob with holes, two wet and glittery. And on her head, snail eyes on stalks.

And that waist? Only a shrew could think *that*, a waist.

Who Knows Where the Wasp Can Wear Her Sting",
Forbidden Futures, Issue 4, Spring 2019,
Oddness

HAND OUT

"Hand Out"
Uncertainties Volume 4
Swan River Press, 2019

The first time I saw history, I barely noticed her. Sure, there was that brief burst of irritation. And I might have tripped over her.

She might have tripped you, too.

You've got to look down from what you're doing as you wait for the lights, or you'll trip over them, they're at so many corners in Sydney's CBD.

Not like any normal beggar sitting back to a wall, blanket square underneath, piled shopping cart neatly parked, cardboard sign with sob story to the fore, dog to the side.

No, history is part of a recent invasion that you can't ignore. Always parked on the pavement just where you would stand so you can step off fast, soon as you've the opportunity.

No blanket, no sign, no dog, no shopping cart. No possessions evident at all. Not even a face to look at, though they all have black hair that looks as if arranged by a slapdash crow.

She's bent at the waist—so hard, she looks folded for packing. That's the trick they all have—the only thing sticking out is an arm that looks like a thin branch of an old fruit tree, attached via a clump of a hand, to a begging bowl.

65. May God grant you a year of happiness
66. God bless you and keep you safe
67. My thoughts and prayers are ever with you
152. Love and best wishes for New Year to all at home
153. Best love from daddy
154. God be with you till we meet again

—from the list of statements the interned were allowed to send to their families abroad, Australia, WWII.

88 71 68 Michael Glas

—Letter from Michael Glas to his wife, Alice. They emigrated to England in 1938, where they married. Both were picked up in Churchill's drive to "collar the lot". He ended up in Australia, she in the Isle of Man.

I have buried even the most modest and reasonable hopes. In order to be able to live at all I have suspended my sense of reason and allowed a crust to form around my soul.

—Michael Glas, to himself, 1940.

"When I became sponsored by the Smith Family, I received my first pair of sports shoes, along with a school backpack. I valued the shoes so much. They enabled me to participate in sport, and to assimilate and fit in with my peers." Claire wanted to work with animals and after lots of hard work and persistence she is now a qualified zoo keeper. Share Christmas and support an Australian child like Claire today to achieve their dreams.

—promotional Facebook entry from the Smith Family's "Support an Australian Child" campaign. December 2018.

why [sic] *is so much "Aid" being given to countries who waste it on armies and the rich and our own are going without, homeless begging for sponsors*

—comment on the Smith Family's Facebook site, December 2018.

Exactly. So that's why I contribute. That blonde girl who's the face of their ads says it all without having to say a word. Why comb your hair and wash your face, let alone wash your school uniform, if you're wearing someone's hand-me-downs? Worse, any kid would die if anyone saw their mum buy their stuff in an op shop.

If you feel happy now in your superiority, cut it out. I'm no racist. But those people who sponsor puppy-eyed foreign kids so long as the kids do the right thing back by sending thankful letters make me laugh. The letters are all written in sweatshops—it's the same as when their older counterparts send you emails asking for your bank details so they can park their millions with you taking a commission.

We must get smarter about our compassion, for there's only so much. I know, for I work in fundraising, and it's a bugger to get your attention, let alone make you act.

> *The Germans and Austrians in our midst are in no position to injure us, even if they so desired, as their number is insignificant; but we doubt their desire as well as their power to injure us, because their interests are Australian and not German, and they cannot injure us without injuring themselves. It has been suggested that the local Germans should call a public meeting to express their horror and detestation of the sinking of the* Lusitania, *by way of showing their loyalty to the British Crown. We do not think such a meeting would serve any good purpose. Judging from the sentiments expressed by the people proposing it, the meeting would serve only as a pretext for hooligan outrages on the part of those pseudo-patriots who think to prove themselves Britishers by behaving as blackguards . . . The penny paper patriots now doing their best to provoke the people to deeds of violence should lay to heart the wise and weighty pronouncement made by the British Prime Minister last week . . . to intern all male aliens of military age for their own as well as Great Britain's safety.*
> **—"Aliens in Our Midst: Shall We Make Them Suffer for the Sins of the Kaiser?" Truth, 22 May 1915.**

If you're confused why that's in there, so am I. It's creepy what we get in our feeds these days. If you saw what I saw, maybe it's because Aldi is full of German *stollen* now. Or maybe you haven't seen what just came in on the page. I fuckin wouldn't have put it there, especially in this holiday time when if you're lucky, you're off, having suffered through the office Christmas party.

So if you're off or temporarily still on, please spare a thought for me. This is *the* month of hell for us in the charity sector. Not one of Amazon's thousands of low-paid human drones can imagine the pressure there is on us. My target this year is unimaginably high. The only thing that makes it easier on us is that in the home stretch this year so far, there hasn't been a disaster that sucks all our list up like a hurricane spout.

Driving past a church today on the way to work, the sign announcing early Christmas services hit me in the funny bone. Just imagine being a priest and never getting a Christmas off. I've read of Jews volunteering on Christmas, so what about now? I bet the Jew wouldn't even have to teach the priest to fish.

Ah, booze. Where would we be without you? I tell you, this life is getting too bloody hard. Competition is killing us. Here I am, having shed the old trads, most of which have rusted in their old forms, never thinking to turn a new angle like the Smith Family has. The one I'm in now sounds way cool, and even has a novel form of transport to get the guys in. But for once, the old guys and grans could be right. The internet is a major downer. My company's physical overheads are almost *nada*, other than the catered yacht that is mandatory for anyone who wants corporate and government sponsorship. The office is a dive, which is both good for the look of it, and to make those dollars stretch. I'm paid what I'm worth, which is why I moved to this start-up three whole years ago.

But not only are people too distracted, they're cutting us off and building tunnels that they live in with their "friends". Worst of all, they're getting sucked dry by their contacts' birthday demand greetings. I think it's rude as the devil to be reminded that it's a friend's birthday these days. They don't invite you to the pub. They don't have a dinner party. They don't even bring a cake to work. But they do guilt-gift by asking *you* to contribute to some pet cause—a cause that thanks *them* for rounding you up for the contribution slaughter. And the causes they ask for? Always either super-trad, like PETA, or some pity-of-the-second friend of theirs who put a hand out via the latest Gimmenow.com, which, I swear, are proliferating like bedbugs in the hotel industry.

Ah, booze, I do love you, though you keep on deserting me. Every time I fall in love, really *dig* you, you become an empty vessel. I must get up to meet and greet one of your friends.

But they don't knock on the door.

"Coming," I feel I must say, for while I don't expect anyone, I gotta pee first.

I don't have one of those peekaboo spyholes like they do in the movies. Who does?

So I open the door, poker in hand.

And almost trip over her as I step forward to look out.

It's history.

It was a cold day in June 1915, when an immigrant named Friedrich Striowski, a miner who'd been thrown out of work due to the depression in that industry since the start of the war, volunteered to be detained as a prisoner of war, because doing so meant the Australian government would give some income to his wife and their all-too-many kids.

This was one of those days that only happen in fiction—*old* fiction, too Maupassantic cheesy twisty, too predictably unpredictable to be anything but groaned at today. Ol' Fred had a son who, on the same day, boarded a boat for Egypt along with other colleagues to help bolster the 8th Battalion.

Look, I didn't ask for this story either. And it's not like some old novel that comes out only to become landfill in its youth even as it was celebrated as immortal at birth.

This is the stuff that seeps from history.

She's worse than a broken dishwasher.

And the viscousness can be so thick, it sticks like molasses.

Example: One German who spent much of WWII interned in Australia, painted many scenes, one of which he titled "Sehnsucht" (longing). The camp's name: Loveday. Spielberg would love it.

I could have picked her up like a bag of spuds and tossed her into the street, but she was like those judo guys who practice weightiness. She moved in and plants herself in the most inconvenient places. Where I'd put my feet while sitting on the loo. At the door of the fridge. On my pillow. In the bloody shower.

My brilliant Christmas campaign has so far garnered thirty-four percent less than I make in a month.

The "two guys going to go through India in a tuk-tuk for two cool causes" campaign has, to my eternal shame, creamed me. Both the partner I think of as Gorgeous George and the one with the brains who's had more hedge funds than my mum's had cats, have started to worry me. They haven't *said* anything, but today when I arrived the office sported a new room freshener in the place on my desk where in a corporation I would have expected nothing but empty space for a hot-bunked laptop.

Xmas eve, on meds. Today at work, I know I was let go. Nothing said. It never *is* with that kind. I'm not opening my emails.

So I'm being medicated by the Holy Trinity Grenache Shiraz Mourvèdre. Who could be better to heal a mendicant like me?

I'm past the stage where I'd make a nasty joke about the job prospects of whomever thought up "Be Best".

If only the Holy Trinity had brought friends—cleaning friends, to be exact.

The whole house needs mopping up.

Her stories have seeped into the very pink batts in the ceiling insulation. And if you think she's just stuck on one or two periods, she's a complete sybarite. I know she thinks I'm a prude, only picking up this and that with no discipline or reason. But that shows yet another way she makes having an old-fashioned relationship show as the disgusting obscenity it can only be—she's totally non-judgmental.

She's so everywhere here, she's worn me down. Or maybe I've been lonely. She does beat any relationship I've ever had, by about a million per cent, for she never talks about herself, never asks anything for herself. Is so modest, she won't let me put a cap to her name.

So history seeps her guts. That must be why I was so frustrated at first, looking forever for *relevance* in what came out of her. She's got zilch sense of pitch, no concept of appeal. Never heard of the Three Kings of Making You Want to Sympathise and Spend your hard-earned moolah on them:

- **Appealing to your vanity**
- **Appealing to your prejudices**
- **Appealing to your sense of panic lest you lose out**

"Why're you leaking this at me," I've yelled at her so many times as I've mopped up while she sits folded over as always, like a sopping teabag.

It's a trial keeping the place clean, and it clots so much, it's a bugger to shove down the drain. But some of this stuff *could* be recycled—turned into good stories if the times and characters were changed to something relevant. Maybe I'll write some of them down—become a novelist. No! Better than that. Her most recent hall disaster would make a brilliant film if a romance could be worked in. It'd have to be. There's too much drama and not enough action.

I always knew I was good. You've gotta believe in yourself, I always say. It's also my slogan in my GoFundMe campaign. Who would ever think the money would pour in like it has? I'm launching another today.

What a Type A fucktard I once was. I would have worked for myself years ago if I'd realised how easy it is. Why anyone would want to fund me is a question I can't answer without getting a degree from the University of Insanity, but the Three Kings stroke me fondly.

Will I actually write *"Longing" in Loveday* and its screenplay for a flick with those killer quote marks? Honestly, I don't know. I haven't picked the seep I plan to do it from, maybe a combination. I got a shipment of bottles delivered, and installed shelving along the walls and filling all the rooms, everywhere but her spots where she sits and seeps. In those places, I've installed grilled pans with spigots, so nothing's lost.

Really, it's no trouble, and sometimes it's just a scream. I never would have expected history to have such a penchant for puns.

This little bottle, for instance, is a similar vintage to the interns on the Isle of Man: Karl Lehmann's picture of Camp Commandant Lieutenant-Colonel Sommerset and Officers on Rottnest Island.

You never know when tragedy will strike. I lost the house! Fuckin bank. How does it expect me to keep up the payments when there's no time for me to do anything but collect?

How's *your* memory?

Mine's improving. History is remarkably patient. I can barely remember what happened on a certain day in New York City in the early part of this century, let alone in Shash, Chach, Binkat (what you know of as Tashkent) on a certain day on a certain street in what you know of as 156 B.C. . Let alone those remarkable eleven days lost to most histories when a certain calendar changed in a kingdom famed for its legends and that sticky picky sword.

But she's teaching me.

We'll meet again at a place we know, after the foot traffic ends for the day.

How am I as a fundraiser these days?

Absolute shit.

I keep telling her, "We gotta look 'em in the eye," but she never learns.

AND EVERYWHERE THAT MARY WENT

"And Everywhere that Mary Went"
The Unquiet Dreamer: A tribute to Harlan Ellison,
PS Publishing, 2019

You already know where that lamb was—shadowing her like a creeping white cloud. Its fur was, as you also know, white as snow—very accurately so, even to the yellow pee patch.

Did it know when she was sleeping, or when she was awake? Did it care when she was bad or good?

Mary has been through so very much in her life that, to see her but not to know her, you'd think she would pass this lamb off as a short-lived fan who would soon grow out of the crush or be snapped up and stuck, for its sins, on a transport ship with thousands of others, to be slaughtered on distant shores if it lived through the horror of stock steerage on the high seas.

But day after day, the air was free of whistles from sheepdog handlers, and no one came to roust the lamb. Mary had a habit of expecting too much out of Life, and this time was no exception. Just yesterday she thought she heard a sheepdog's bark, but it was the exhausted fart of a UPS truck needing servicing after a long day of thankless work. Mary might have wondered whether the truck zooming through that red light was the victim of a driver's cruel foot, or whether the truck itself was eager to get home and fed.

Do trucks feed at home? This was one of the questions that could have added up in Mary's head, if her head had been a hoarder's hall. But it was, to all appearances, just a human's head.

If looks could produce. But though she threw looks everywhere, no dice about a sheepdog rounding the corner, or a man in a slouch hat, a belted mackintosh, and a handkerchief soaked in chloroform—and a sheep transport ship patiently waiting where the tourist ships come in.

"This has gone on too long," Mary said. She spun around as only people borne by Fiction can, and in her pinafore and horizontally striped socks à la Alice, she might have been a sight—in some town no one has ever seen anyone cosplay.

Here, even the lamb didn't cause a single pedestrian to move a thumb awry.

Mary bent down to lamb's-eye level. "I've had enough ayou," she said.

She took the first left and then a straight for three blocks, and then mounted the long rise up. Up to the top of "the coat hanger"—the Sydney Harbour Bridge. The traffic was something fierce. Not just all those aggressively fit runners, but a flock of unicyclists and two poets passed before the scene was set—just her, that woman Mary, it, that unnamed lamb, and the man in the moon.

The bridge has been indecently tampered with so much, it's caused countless breakdowns in the suicider community. At the most trying place, a palimpsest of posters therefore greets you from the National Prevented Suicide Hotline ("Depression sucks. There's always a way.")

Mary didn't need no NGO let alone a GO, which she strongly suspected it was, full of misleading enticements to trust their line just to get you in the system she rooted away in her pinafore pocket, and pulled out her Leatherman knockoff with blowtorch attachment for emergency crème brûlée, and blew a hole in the wire mesh big enough for Gilgamesh. (She had to. She'd never asked for dimity ties to her pinafore, any more than puppies do, to be born with the wrinkled lips of toothless old men. Those damn ties flew out in the slightest breeze and caught on everything.)

The little lamb watched from behind, as usual. So now it was on the open, suicide-friendly side of the bridge. Mary bent down carefully, trying to keep her back straight as you're supposed to, even though that's one of safe work practices' most risible frauds. She put her arms around the little lamb and picked it up.

Its fleece—so soft and warm. Its little-lambness—so innocent, so almost entirely white.

Lifting it was like lifting a lambskin bag of iron coat hangers and barbells. The thing defied gravity. In another life, Mary could have compared its impossible heaviness to her mother's matzo balls (but she was one hundred percent goy and seven percent Cherokee).

She couldn't lift the lamb higher than her knees, so there was no way she could have watched to see if it landed on its feet.

Mary had a little lamb.

And other than the period to end that sentence, just what do you, what *could you*, know of all that pain and unasked-for-suffering? There's not even a space. Just Onwards, to the next line. *Its* fleece. It it it.

Not that her theory helped her, but she'd come to the conclusion: There's something about Marys.

That other one was also just a mother whose suffering was also all subsumed by her kid—a kid she'd asked for as much as Mary of the lambbirth.

Our Mary only knew that other one by reputation, which didn't mention all the confusion and shock she must have borne inside.

Where she went after that birth, no one really knows. Perhaps she joined other unfortunate single women trying to make a living in the alleys of Nineveh, or fought them for garbage like their descendants do at sales.

Whatever, our Mary had a little lamb, and for a young woman who had never had a period, who'd never been other than fully clothed—a young woman who sprang fully formed as a nursery rhyme element, having a lamb was—what do you expect?

And how could she, a mere Anglo nursery rhyme Mary, have words to describe the shock, the horror, the, the . . . hmm.

(Which is why she learned German (and why a spell-checker is running a wavy red line under learned as this story takes physical shape is a mystery too far))

So Mary should have known that that lamb—which felt exactly as heavy and sharp as it came out of her before her nursery rhyme firmed up and got its capitals—would be too heavy for her to toss. She uttered one word in German that encompassed everything she felt at that moment, including mullings about motivations for impregnations. The word spread to wrap around her memories of God. She'd only met (actually only seen) him in passing once, but like Neil Gaiman who toyed with her but she got away, God exuded confidence and success, mysteriously so, since what's God done that's really worth worshipping?

This story doesn't have room for the word Mary uttered, but if you know German, you already know. Whether the lamb knew German is a mystery for another time or never. The lamb was always silent.

Mary and her fluffy white shadow wended homeward. (She would have caught the light rail, but Australian bureaucrats are strictly anti-sheep as companion animals, even unto toddlers such as Mary's damn companion. The only sheep allowed in backyards are ones innocent of the knife to come.)

Not a worry. The man in the moon shone on Mary and the little lamb, all the way home.

And as to that place, sorry. He knows where it is, but only the lamb, as far as I know, can shadow her. So her home is indescribable. But for fans, she has a PO Box.

Today, at 04:30 a.m. (when Rowling the Great says everyone successful gets to work).

Mary snores. (*"Mary Attacked by Sleep Apnoea While Lamb Looks On"*—look for it in the *Daily Mirror*)

Which tells you Three Important Things:

1) Mary isn't successful.
2) Mary hasn't changed.
2a) Since she hasn't changed, she couldn't be a fictional character.
3) The plot thickens
3a) unlike bone broth
3b) but she better watch out.

Today, sometime late morning (7.8 years ago, Mary bought a Rolex from a man on the street, for the knell of town clocks is as extinct as the cries of town criers. But though it must have been a real Rolex, as the man said it was, it wasn't a real Oyster, so it didn't work. She never forgave herself for that rash purchase. One sniff would have told her.)

She feels like shit. *But much worse,* given that this is now in the present tense and Mary *hates* stories told in the present tense, almost as much as she hates gerunds, whatever they are.

So, backtracking to a time so recent, you've not eliminated what you last ate: Mary felt very very bad.

Precisely:

Worse than her usual wake-up-and-smell-the-lanolin bad.

Worse than opening her eyes to see that innocent face, facing her.

Worse than not having any butter for her bread.

Worse than having failed last night to toss her shadow off the bridge.

There are three more Worses, but let's get on with it.

You might well ask: Why didn't she give the little lamb the ultimate red necklace? One slit and it'd be gone, and Mary could then have or give away a tasty feast.

Mary fancies herself as a vegan, which might be why the smell of the hot beast, come summertime, so offends her olfactory.

So, though the scene can't be painted for you, smells from last night can be reported—specifically, a rancid sweetness: Mary's tears must have run into her mouth with its unbrushed teeth, and run out, soaking her pillow. (Please don't blame her for not brushing her teeth. She was born without a childhood.)

She woke with a whopper of a headache. *Those dreams again.*

It's like that other fact you know, whether you take it to heart or not.

Eat a bowl of ice cream right before you go to sleep. One hundred and ten percent guaranteed: You're gonna get nightmares.

The last thing Mary ever saw before she went to sleep: the little lamb.

Ever and always.

So every night, Mary's sleep was nightmares.

First one sheep came into view.

Then another.

Then another.

All. Night. Long.

The walk.

The look.

Ever the same.

Utterly predictable.

So should-be comforting.

But the tone! so knowing, so cynical, so migraine-inducing cocksure to come again and again . . .

And they weren't even sheep, she was sure, but lambs in sheep's clothing.

Like Fashion Week.

Her nights have been haunted by countless 'sheep' for as long as she can remember.

But a month ago when foraging for her dinner (she was never given any money, was she?), she was pulling any- and everything she could out of a restaurant skip, while at the same time beating off the ibises who thought the territory was theirs. The remains of a *pho* flew out and spattered their feathers, already that soiled b / w of wedding-reception waitstaff after the last drunken dance to Lady in Red. A half-drunk bubble drink added baubles to the tawdry look of the birds, but didn't turn them from their quest. Then Mary's fingers found something heavy as a fruitcake. She lobbed it over her shoulder, to the disgust of the flock.

Wham went Kurt Goldstein's *Der Aufbau des Organismus. Einführung in die Biologie unter besonderer Berücksichtigung der Erfahrungen am kranken Menschen* onto the alley's tarmac shiny with grease, assorted pink king prawn shells and their land counterparts, a crunchy brown slick of Sydney's cockroaches.

The book lay on the ground like a butterflied pork fillet, soaking up the alley's marinade while Mary successfully pulled a large bouncy hunk of noodles from the bin and ate it, though it looked and smelled like the mop used illegally in both the kitchen and the toilet. A half-full can of Coke tasted curiously worse, till she gagged at the fag stubs. It must have been the cook's.

She was just rooting around for something to get rid of the tastes of her first courses when the door to the closest restaurant opened. *Time to leave.* That's when she noticed the book and pocketed it as she smoothed her pinafore. Nowadays, in Anglo countries, no one makes pockets big enough for books, let alone with titles long as this one, for this was the 1934 edition. In its original German, which was translated into English in Our Year of Portents 1939 as *The Organism: A Holistic Approach to Biology Derived from Pathological Data in Man*, "forgotten" for a decent number of years, found by the French, who can't be taken seriously, and then pulled up into the mass consciousness of Californians at the precise time when consciousness was at the same time, a popular state to look for, and an even more fun place to lose.

At the place she called Home, Mary glanced through the book. She had read a better-smelling edition, merely foxed, long ago, but she'd done many things long ago. So fucking what? she might have said, if she were someone else. Instead, she swore in Italian.

That was a month ago.

Three bags of jackets…

It's still that same morning.

Mary is sitting up in the same place she slept, the same place where she dreamed that horrific Fashion Week of underage sheep, *as she does every cursed night*. The fruit of her womb stands in front of her, its inscrutable head pointed in her direction—a companion animal and yet as companionable as a colostomy bag, only the little lamb is surrounded by a holy aura. But does this side-effect of a migraine make Mary feel blessed, worshipworth, or at one with the Family of Man? Not a prayer. Not a single member of the Family has ever given her a milligram of thought, let alone respect. Reverence is laughable.

"I'll get no help from *them*," she says in the lamb's direction, but not to it. The thing is silent, expressionless. And what gives her the biggest creeps, and always has, from the first wave of its little cotton-bud tail? It doesn't have mortal wonts, even to feeding. Oh, it's always *seemed* to eat when you'd expect it to, but it acts 'Eat' just like a female human movie star.

And it had never needed shearing. That doesn't mean its coat doesn't grow. It grows like grass in spring, all year long, but that growth is a coat that opens up at its chest every few months to be peeled off like a sheepskin jacket minus the skin.

The lamb might be some scientist's Perpetual Coat Machine, if Mary didn't know it came from her, out of someplace in her that has no place in her nursery rhyme genetics. As for artificial insemination, be it God-style or farmstyle, she wouldn't let God's slimy hands get near her, nor was she made with any messy asshole or whatever down there. She's not that kind of nursery rhyme girl, so sticking a tube up her under her skirts is as impossible as finding kneecaps in her knees.

After Dolly was born, Mary speculated that the lamb was an early experiment of a proto-Garvin Institute in Laputa, before the Laputans gave up the embarrassment of experimentation and devoted themselves to theory, which can never be absolutely disproved. She wanted to travel to Edinburgh but quickly had to scotch that idea, not being able to get the lamb past UK quarantine, or away from her. (You might wonder how she came to be in Australia. She was transported—but you've already read about her stealing tossed-out food.)

Shit. It's almost noon already, and reminiscences can't stir curtains.

But here sits Mary.

And here come Three Thoughts.

1) Suicide is out of the question. She just can't do it, not till every bit of Anglo culture and history is wiped from the face of the earth, and who knows if there aren't relatives of Mary who would do anything to keep the family going? Who'd resurrect language itself and all its rhymes?

2) The only way to go is Up!

3) Enough already with the present tense!

Mary jumped up and clapped her hands. Thoughts weren't just Thoughts. They'd come bearing a gift—the answer to What to Do to break her lambic curses.

She only needed to go on a Quest.

Wolf, the's…

"And tell me again. Why should I help you?"

"I didn't tell you the first time."

"That's my point."

That line just words earlier—"She only needed to go on a Quest"—must have read as ironic, but the DNA of this story doesn't include irony.

In the olden days of phone books, the Wolf would have been easy to look up and find. You just had to know which Woods book he was in, just like you'd have to distinguish between the one for Rome, Italy, and Rome, Georgia, USA.

Only problem was if he had a silent number.

Or you could find and follow Little Red Riding Hood, but if so, time was of the essence. She killed him, didn't she? That's all that Mary knew. (She'd never actually read the story, only a review of it.)

Mary must have had unchronicled depths of character, for though she was coming bearing gift(s), she felt distinctly awkward. She didn't want to get to the Wolf mid—his most famous scene—a scene that must take at most, a rounded fifty words.

However, she still had to find him, and as you know by having read it, her quest was a proper Quest.

In the End, it was easier done than said.

She found him through LinkedIn, of course, though of course he'd never joined.

Mary had been given no money, but she had resources. She had a scent to her (One part: fighting off those garbage-grazing ibises, entailing much body contact with their wingpits. Three parts: never having had a bath, nor an ability to change underwear. Three hundred and seven parts: agelessness.) that, when mixed with a Bulgari watch she stole, smelt like the kind of perfume Donald Trump would brag that he gave.

That scent reeking of wealth, and a certain gelled look of agelessness—they were all she needed to step off an Aryan Air flight in Miami, the little lamb at her heels. She almost didn't need her fake Norwegian passport to sail through ICE. No one could do enough for her. And so it was, all across the country. She'd never realised before how much people want to give you when you're rich. She almost forgot her problems, for this was getting fun.

But as you know, fun is the root of all problems. This Quest was becoming dangerous, for Mary wasn't any common-garden character. They're supposed to change. Tragically, they *have* to, whether they know it or not. And unlike with nursery characters who live forever, common story characters are more perishable than watercress. *Change or be pulped.*

Mary had read about compassion. She supposed she should have it for them, but each to its lot. She would always stay the same.

"In a pig's eye, I will!" She felt liberated by this Quest. Alive as she never had, while at the same time, wondering about Death.

I've already changed. I can't help changing more. Will I be forgotten? Will I have an Afterlife? (She'd not considered the third possibility which hovered, salivating—sacrifice on an altar of politics.)

All the while, the lamb stuck to her like her bad smell—in silence.

So back we are, away from that damn Narrative—flies on the wall, holding our noses.

"And tell me again," said the Wolf.

He's at a dressing table, his back to us, but we can see his face in the mirror, and what an artist. That brow lift that makes eyes look perpetually startled. The line of little red jabs around the mouth wrinkles. The hands that cannot lie. We've seen him as many grandmothers, been through the high powdered wig with its sailing boat, the modest mob cap, the Tweetie Pie grandma type with her Ruth Ginsberg collar. Once he was assigned Bonny Elizabeth Parker's grandmother, and frustrated Bonny so bad she hooked up with Clyde and blew her frustrations away the only way she could. The Wolf has been blue-rinsed and pink stretch-panted, bingo-armed and you don't wanna know worse. But today he looked absolutely marvellous—very Jane Fonda 80-as-50, and for once, his natural hair with its grey and gold highlights needed no styling to have the naturally fabulous Look. "You're worth it," he said to the mirror.

So it was with extreme irritation that his alone Moment was interrupted by a knock on the door.

"Yes, Maria," said the Wolf.

"Skuze me," said Maria. "There's a lady says you wanna halp her."

"Let her in," said the Wolf, who could understand why the servant wouldn't know this grandma's granddaughter. What a bitch. They probably went through servants here often as Day goes through nights.

When Mary was shown in, the Wolf was so taken aback, he went out of character for a moment.

Mary might have noticed but didn't show it. She had no subtlety or small talk. Just went for the object of the Quest, like seeing the sword in the stone and swerving the car around, parking anyoldhow, jumping out of the car and running across four lanes to pull that sucker.

"I don't eat lambs," the Wolf said coldly.

"It's not your fault you're reduced to eating girls. You were made that way."

The Wolf ruffled a tarot pack.

"Just look at that lamb," said Mary. "Once you try, you'll never look back."

"I've got nothing against your lamb."

"Lambs."

"Fine. I've got *more* of nothing against your lambs. Look, I've got nothing against you. But can't you see I'm almost on, and you're unnerving me?"

"So you want to eat some innocent granddaughter and cause her grandma to regret the rest of her life? And you wanna be killed trying?"

"What the hell?! Who told you that?"

Mary shuffled her feet. "I read it in a review."

"Reviews!" The Wolf stood up and pointed. (Gawd, if anything's right in this world, Wolf, the's reputation will put Streep, Meryl's in the shade.)

"And magazines!" Mary said defensively.

"I can imagine. D'you know who she's dating?"

Mary opened her mouth.

The lamb coughed.

"Little Red Riding Hood's a spy, my dear innocent Mary. She's killed her parents to get their assets, and now she's after her old gran's."

"But you ate her grandmother!"

"Of course I did. All my life, all I want is to eat old women. Are you mad or just made stupid? No, don't answer the question. I'm sorry."

And the wolf did, all of a sudden, look sorry. A tear rolled down one unnaturally firm cheek.

And another.

Is this overdoing it? The Wolf must have thought so, for he wiped away the tear, but didn't turn back to the mirror.

"May I interject?"

"Of course," said the Wolf.

Mary spun around. "You talk?"

"Of course," said the lamb.

"Since when?"

"Since always," said the lamb, and the sneer was unmistakable.

"But you've never said anything to me."

"You've never said anything to *me*."

"I've said lots of things to you."

"*At* me isn't *to* me."

"And besides," added the lamb, "What would you call what you want to do to me?"

"*For* you, not *to* you. Wouldn't you like to be liberated?"

"Hey Mister Wolf," said the lamb. "How'd you like to be a liberationist of this here little lady?"

The Wolf shook himself like a wet dog or an icedance performer, and all his costume fell away.

His jaws glittered with the foam of slather. He wiped it away.

"There is," he said in his naturally deep, low voice. "A certain island filled with grandmas. I got them out and will continue to, all the days of my life."

"But that's not the story," Mary shouted.

"Not the story you know."

"I would love to hear your story," said the lamb.

"And I would love to tell it to you," said the Wolf. "Please don't mind my spittle. I can't help it."

"If you don't mind my yellow pee patch."

"See yourself out," said the Wolf.

Mary looked at the two of them, and if she had learnt about American art, she would have thought: *But for a pitchfork, they're fuckin American Gothic.*

"But what about all my other lambs?"

"We'll get them, too," said the lamb.

The Wolf wagged his tail.

"But first," said the lamb, "you're a mess. And she's almost here. Let me help you."

"You know makeup?"

The lamb cocked its head.

"Sorry," said the Wolf.

CURSE OF THE MUMMY PAPER

"Curse of the Mummy Paper"
Breakout: Postscripts #34/35,
Nick Gevers, ed., PS Publishing, 2015

We wouldn't be meeting like this—you and I—if we didn't love books, so before I introduce myself, I'll lay these before you as presents. Truly, you needn't jump on a chair or grab a broom.

> *A princess, from the late Mr. Pettingrew's collection, was swathed in forty thicknesses, producing 42 yards of the finest texture. The supply of linen rags would not be limited to the mummies of the human species alone; independent of that obtainable from this source, a more than equal amount of cloth could be depended on from the mummies of sacred bulls, crocodiles, ibides, and cats.*
>
> **—Dr. Isaiah Deck, 1855 manuscript proposing the solution to the great rag (thus, paper) shortage then plaguing the USA's 800 paper mills**

> *An Onondaga county man, worshipful of the golden Eagle and not of the Egyptian Ibis, has put upon the market, 'paper made from the wrappings of mummies.'*
>
> **—[Syracuse, NY] Standard, August 19, 1856**

Does that reassure?

For though I've been known to utter kitten cries and toy with balls of string, this is no more a 'cat story' than the princess mentioned would have been a cat-story lady, or a cat-story lady brought back to life as some world-conquering villain whose only gentle stroke is to a cat.

Both make you creep away from them, warned perhaps by some instinct against sentiment. We flee from love that smothers, from forgetfulness. Not for us, all that petting, nor dishes set down just for us, always decorated with the glued-on bits and bones of unfinished fish, never quite washed because they're 'for the cat'.

We would rather starve than touch that seaminess.

But seaminess doesn't kill, and no cat ever really died—last-flick-of-the-paw death— from that so-common pain, starvation.

And as anyone who knows cats knows: we love good books—from the light embrace of a papyrus scroll to the luxurious bed of an open vellum tome, to a pile of paperbacks. A good bookshop is of course, a palace, but a loving home can be a good abode.

At one time I lived in a beautiful place, not here where it snows every winter, floorboards creak and drawers stick, people rush ungracefully about on hard, unmusical footwear, and the air is a nose-offending reek of 'ninty-nine percent germ killer' and name-brand perfume that no long-time-ago old dung-carrier would have worn. You who know this isn't sentimentalism can call me Keti, for that is what the baker did. *Keti,* by the way, is *fleabane* in your unmellifluous modern tongue.

As to the baker, Niankhum, deserving of a book of psalms to him…

Whenever I dropped a rat at his feet, he was properly appreciative. He never asked where the gift came from. And if it needed a bit more chasing, he kept out of my way, even when the rat jumped into the dough trough or fell into the oven's fiery mouth.

He was also quite a reader. There were no booksellers in Niankhum's town but he had a collection that he treasured. It was quite musical when I settled on it, my purrs setting forth a vibration in the scrolls. He'd pull one from under me and read to us, which always turned up my music.

His wife, who liked to think she was my mistress, was the dream of many cats.

A lap that could hold seven at a time. A face as round and beautiful as the moon.

The baker's wife took care to keep herself beautiful. She rubbed her skin with ground cinnabar, salt, almond oil and honey till it took on the sheen of the baker's finest egg-washed bread. She wore wigs on special occasions but didn't need to, her own hair being so thick that she'd only have to lay on a pallet on the floor and all us cats would comb her thick mane till it stretched out to the door. She made special foods to gain weight, her favourite being milk reduced to cream that she shared thick slices of with 'all my little family'. The other six of us grew so fat, they couldn't roam outdoors at night nor leap atop a wall.

Of all women I've ever known—and what cat doesn't know countless hordes—she was the only one who knew how to wear perfume. And *such* perfume. Her secret was to mix balanos oil, myrrh, and resin (what's so secret about that, you say. That's just what the city of Mendes exported for gold and rubies, nothing special to us.) But this baker's wife added an incomparable something extra. This was her secret recipe:

On a hot still summer day, when the sun was looking down upon everything at once, she carried all six cats up the ladder to the hot clay of the flat roof where a black-glazed platter lay in waiting. Then she carried up and built a mound of cream slices in the middle of the platter. The six didn't wait to be invited. They never noticed her lower a lid upon platter, cream and cats. The dome she had constructed of finest fish bladder looked like a cloudy sky, and the air around them, as the cats ate, grew hotter and hotter till they, if they hadn't been so greedy, would have been panting and scratching frantically to get out and into some cooling shade. But what did those silly sisters and brothers of mine do? They sweated. When finally they had all finished their cream, their coats were matted with sweat. She reached in and took them out one by one, rubbing each down with linen cloths that she packed into a stoppered jar. And in that jar, she macerated her perfume. Like a cat, she knew how to apply it to herself, and as you could expect, knew how to drive her husband wild. Which she did with much more enjoyment, I must say, than any female of my set.

The baker's wife (I don't remember her name, but the other six called her with no sense of shameless flattery, Isis) was not only a loving, but a conscientious wife. She would even make up the medicaments for her husband's frequent attacks of constipation: zizyphus bread, honey, sweet beer, etc., mixed to a paste and smeared on linen that she bandaged around his stomach. That doesn't sound bad, does it? But even though I love the baker—(I don't deny that feeling that I first recognised in that melancholy time when the fire roared in the oven and shot sparks into the inky night, in that time before the dung beetle rolled the sun up into the sky, that thoughtful, sentimental, nostalgic time—the baker used to sit on his stool then, humming faintly. Sometimes he would drop his hand and I would rub against it. Otherwise, I curled myself up between his sandaled feet which were always soft and smelt fragrantly of dough from his stamping.)—even though I did love the baker, do!—there are limits to self-sacrifice. And no way would I pick up the etc. in the medicament that his wife made regularly for his constipation. Cat's dung!

Her cries carried to every house in our town and far over the sands to stir the rooftops in the next town, so loud were they that early morning when he choked on a hard crumb in his cup of sweet *bouza*, an unattractive soup of broken hard loaf soaked in water and honey that I used to turn my tail up at, little did he learn.

His death was so unexpected that the next thing the town knew was the smell of his bread burning.

The baker's wife wanted only the best for her beloved husband, and was quite an organiser. Priests were summoned and scurried to the bakery, where they picked him up from where he had fallen, at the foot of his oven.

They took him away to the music of the baker's wife's lamentations. Around her feet milled the six accompanists. Their high voices would have been far more plaintive if they had known what was to befall them.

The embalming of the baker took the requisite seventy days, and in all that while, the widow hardly touched a crumb, and lived otherwise, on date vinegar flavoured with water. Mice exported grain both day and night while the six lay torpid upon the floor, more useless than ever now that the mice had to climb over them and sometimes had to dig new holes in the walls that were thoughtlessly blocked by a paw or tail or tragic whiskered face.

Indeed, it occurs to me that the 6 reluctantly slimming cats looked like your modern filmmakers documenting a trade route as they lay dilatorily watching fat rats wash their whiskers, themselves watching busy mice lugging the remaining stores of grain, chunks of bread and cakes along the inside walls and out of sight.

Meanwhile, the beautiful widow was in danger of losing her looks, she starved herself so. Still, she cared for nothing other than providing an Afterlife of comfort and joy to her beloved husband. So along with this most unprecedented embalming of the baker and all its costliness (the neighbours did not approve), the widow hired a bevy of builders and painters, and also spent much worry and coin on everything his heart and body would desire in the Afterlife.

Day after day, the widow acted sometimes frantically, but oftentimes as if she were sleepwalking. She worked and worried so hard that her smooth brow wrinkled and her hair grew wild as a bush. One morning, she shoved a wig over it and made for the tomb. For today was the 71st Day. The baker's body was ready and the tomb had been built, decorated, muralled, provisioned; and nothing was missing except her presence to farewell her beloved husband on his Journey into the Afterworld. The ritual required her to arrive on foot from their home, the bakery. The priests would arrive from the direction of their temple.

The spectacle of the priests' arrival holding her husband high was part of the scene that she would store in her heart, ready to tell him when they met in the Afterworld, if she had provisioned him well enough that he would meet her.

As she approached the tomb, however, all she could see was a milling of men. Builders, painters, decorators, the owner of the emporium where she bought all the items he would need on his journey, even to the clay donkey.

'Where is our money?' they asked as one.

The widow was shocked. She thought she had paid them, every one, all she owed. They insisted she had not. Her husband had always hated owing anyone money, and would rather go without than buy something on credit. And she had felt the same. I do believe these men were plotting to destroy her, but don't know finance well enough to be sure.

'Come back to the bakery after this and I will find whatever I can to pay you,' she had just said, when four priests approached.

They bore upon their shoulders a board laden with what I had to assume was the baker, now wrapped and smelling so highly of spice and oils that I wanted to run, but I didn't. I stayed in the shadow of the tomb, watching. (And where, you might ask, were the six other members of the household who the baker had provided, through his missus, with such luxurious lives of feast and leisure? Still at home, those layabouts.)

The chief priest stepped forward, leaving the other three to balance what had once been a man plump as a grape.

'Woman,' he said to the widow, 'Your good husband, Niankhum, arrives impatient for his journey.' And the woman the greedy six called Isis when they were fat, and useless in her mourning state of forgetfulness, answered with a stumbling bow and an idiotic 'Is that my beloved?'

From the shadows in her cheeks and the bags under her eyes, I wouldn't have liked to estimate how long it must have been since she last ate or slept, though she must have cried her fill.

'Beloved or not,' said the chief builder, shoving her out of the way. 'I'll not seal this tomb till you seal my hand with coin.'

'What's this?' said the chief priest, striking his staff against the builder's head. 'May Uytsteth give you piles for your attempt to cheat a suffering widow!'

'Where's our offerings?' said one of the priests.

The chief priest turned to the widow.

The baker's wife rent her hair. She didn't know how she had forgotten to go to the next town to buy those funerary cakes. Her husband had always made them for the people of his town, but now that he was gone, the ovens were cold. Baking was of course, not woman's work. 'How could I forget?' she cried.

It was obvious to me. Every thought of food she'd had since her husband's death had been to provide for him in his Afterlife. Like when she prepared his beer, she thought only of him. She lost all interest in her own needs, and the rest of her 'little family' was just an extension of her, in her forgetfulness.

So call me a mouse if I'm wrong. I am sure that she had paid to the smallest coin, everything she owed the tomb-makers and provisioners, and had paid the priests for the embalming.

But whether she had enough coin left to pay for the ceremony that the priests had arrived for with her husband held high between them, is still a mystery to me.

Whatever, as you say now.

The priests dropped the baker in the sand and stomped off, the heels of their sandals spurting up sand.

The builders trashed the tomb, drank all the liquid and took everything they could carry, even to the last unground grain of barley—all the provisions that is, except, probably superstitiously, the pile of inked papyrus, the Book of the Dead.

They left while the baker's wife scrabbled in the sand with a beautiful broken bowl.

She buried him beside the rubble, her tears rolling off the oiled linen before she tipped him into the hole. I wasn't sorry. The likeness was terrible. His eyes had been warm, lively, and crinkled at the corners. And he stank of resins, rather like your germ killers.

I didn't want to leave, yet was too shocked to make plans yet. I followed the widow back to the sad ex-bakery and those 6 useless cats who were so annoyingly self-centred that they didn't do a thing about comforting her, who needed them so much. They complained mightily however, of the loss of their slices of cream. That night, the wailing was terrible to hear.

The bakery was soon surrounded by old toms, and I don't blame them. She sounded indecent.

Before the pigeons woke the next morning, the front door was shaken by a tremendous banging.

It was old Muhet. I don't know her real name, but everyone called her Muhet behind her back, for she was wrinkled as the plum that loosens your bowels.

'Good morning, Auntie,' said the baker's wife respectfully, though this 'auntie' was but a neighbour, and famous for her nosiness.

'What a sight,' declared Muhet, who rushed past and swept into the bakery, suddenly getting into everything like teeth-grinding grit from a sandstorm.

My siblings scattered. I hid behind a water jar.

'Enough of this mourning,' said Muhet, not even pausing for a polite 'I am unworthy to cross your doorway. A thousand praises on your fragrant...' and she came bearing not a single gift.

She came weighed down, she said, with the demand of the whole town. That the baker's wife marry, and she knew just the man. A baker from ______ (some place I can't remember or she never said, but where misfortune had fallen) was, thank the Gods, free to take over this bakery, and thus, this wife.

And to my surprise, the marriage took place the next day, as if there was no mourning period needed. Where were the gossips, you might ask? Stuffing their faces with bread, now that the oven burst into life again.

This baker wasn't like that last one. His new wife dutifully served him, though her sighs when not in his presence would have made any sensitive cat rub against her leg. Now that she bustled back to work, however, she noticed how thin my six siblings had become (they looked now like healthy cats, not filled wine sacks). They took up their places around the room where she gave them milk. When the baker came in for his midday meal and sleep, he saw them eating their cuts of cream and let out a bellow that could be heard on roofs across the town.

He tore open the front door, and raised a foot to kick the nearest cat out, but his new wife rushed between them.

'Remember Efuban?' she said. Seeing his face, she quietly shut the door. Everyone knew of Efuban, who had been stoned by a mob the day he killed a cat, though everyone knew it had been an accident.

'Remember where your food comes from, your dress,' said the new baker. He stormed off and before the door shut behind him, my siblings mobbed the dish again to polish off the cuts of cream. I might have stopped to say, 'Your beloved Isis is crying,' but it wouldn't have done her good. Instead, I followed the monster.

He went to the temple, met the priests, and soon sauntered back, happy as a full belly.

While his new wife was busy with his dinner, plucking pigeons on the roof, he plucked my siblings off the floor till the floor was clean of all six—all now in a bag, providing a moral about exercise after eating that they have never, unfortunately, lived to enjoy, no matter how many years pass.

Oh, he never noticed me, never knew there was a seventh. Out he went with the bag slung on his back. The noise in the street was too great for anything new to be noticed, though the bag was loud with cries and hisses, six cream-filled cats bumping on his back, tumbling against each other, nose to undertail, upside down and everywhichway. He carried the bag to the temple and handed it to the chief priest, who lowered it into what looked like a secret place under the floor. It certainly sealed their cries.

I stayed at the temple and watched. At nightfall, two priests prepared milk together, fussing over the preparation for some reason, but I'd never watched priests before and didn't know their ways. When they were satisfied, they poured it into a pot that one took hold of. The other priest opened the secret place under the floor and pulled up the bag of my siblings. Their cries were so weak and dispirited, they almost caused me a pang of pity. Like mice they were, lacking all dignity. The two priests nodded to the chief priest. Then one priest carrying the pot, the other the bag, and the chief priest carrying nothing but all looking nondescript as they usually did, they all walked out of town, out to a sandy flat place that was so featureless that it looked sacred.

And in this place sure enough, there was a sort of column, with decorations such as I'd never seen, and when I say that, I mean that it was truly strange, for what *haven't* I seen?

And the priest with the bag of my siblings handed it to the chief priest. Then the two priests took hold of the pot, raised themselves up as high as they could and poured the milk into the top of the column.

Then the chief priest opened the bag and tumbled my 6 brothers and sisters, the cream-lovers, onto the sand.

Instead of running, as any lean cat let out of a bag should, one sniffed, then another, and in a moment's breath, they had surrounded the base of the column, which was crying milk. They lapped and lapped, and lapped in a kind of frenzy. This milk was driving them mad with desire. They couldn't lap fast enough, it seemed. The priests looked on, smiling.

Now I know that I should have pushed them aside to take my place. After all, I am the oldest and wisest. And I should have known that, cats being sacred, these priests would be better providers than any ignorant but well-meaning wife.

I never lived for my stomach, but nothing can slake my curiosity. So I watched from a low point, and no one noticed me. Indeed, out there lit only by stars, I wouldn't have been distinguished from a pile of sand.

'These six won't do much to help our count,' said one priest to another.

'But it's something. We need to do more to satisfy them.'

'And if it works—'

'Yes, there's no shortage of scoundrels we can pay to bring us fresh supplies.'

'But what if we get caught?'

'Who would tell? What's to catch. Look at them. They have chosen to live again as Bastet's aides.'

I'd been so absorbed listening that I hadn't looked at my siblings, but now I did. I had to look fast, because in a few moments, one of the priests had picked up all their still silent bodies and thrown them back in the bag.

The chief priest raised his hands to the heavens, and then rubbed them.

'I do so love,' he chuckled, 'the smell of embalming.'

'I do too,' said one of the milk preparers, seriously enough that he ended up walking a bit alone on the way back.

The next day, in mourning for the missing cats, the baker's wife shaved her eyebrows, earning a beating from her new husband. I know because I dropped in to see how she fared, and could only rub against her legs for a moment once his back was turned. But I had to leave. She had never been anything to me, but I don't like to see a creature that I'm not playing with, suffer.

Back I went to the temple where I almost choked from the fumes while watching the six go through the process of permanent preservation. It was hard in a way not to turn madcap somersaults at the ludicrous idea of cats dying and then being preserved permanently by being dunked in goo and wrapped in something that holds them so tight, they cannot even flex their paws to knead.

But the providing of thousands of mummified sacred cats was serious business to this small third-rate temple in a town so lacking in allure that no one had ever tried to raze it.

My siblings were bundled together with a quirth of others into a job-lot, loaded onto a donkey cart and trundled to out to some other featureless place in which now sat, supposedly forever, a stone image of Bastet. Quite a beautiful image, I should say. You could almost hear her disdainfully purr. She would never have been able to be caught by a bribe of milk. Not that I didn't think (and still don't) the idea of a cat being a God any less ludicrous than the idea that a dungbeetle moves the sun around. Which dungbeetle? I have eaten many. One crunch and they're gone. They don't strike me as any more capable than a donkey, and actually, they are much less able to do anything. I narrowly missed a donkey's hoof one day, and I can tell you: if that hoof had connected, my history would be different.

So back to the statue of Bastet. The thousands of mummified cats were meant, it must have been, as companions to her. Into a tomb went my siblings at the bakery, the Greedy Six, on top of and surrounded by so many other mummified cats that I could almost hear the cheers of rats across the land. Whatever the priests really thought about cats and Bastet, rats would certainly worship any cat that could be the cause of such a cat-plague of religious contribution.

When night fell, so were the stones lowered upon the tomb. So now I knew, as your mysteries say, where the bodies were buried. The Greedy Six, in that tomb that was buried soon enough, by history and sand. And the baker, Niankhum, in a place unmarked, except by my memory. Do I regret that he was left to starve there in the wilderness of between-lives? To be truthful, I am glad. Once the head priest stuck a skewer up his nose and twiddled it in his brain, he was no more the baker I knew than I am a pickled turnip.

Centuries passed. My curiosity got me in many scrapes and more than a few deaths, but that unwraps another myth you might believe in. Why nine lives? Why not five, or a baker's dozen, or 8977? I wouldn't go so far as to say that I'm immortal, but I'm still me.

You've possibly read of me or seen pictures, though I keep out of the limelight, leaving it to those who bask in it. I've sat on poets' papers, posed for painters' portraits, chased balls of scrap-paper tossed by a lonesome limerickist. I've roamed the backrooms of museums where they prepare bodies for a modern Afterlife. I've watched watchmen. I've loved a thousand thousand books, inspired as many tales, but never, if you must know, walked on only two legs (what a waste to use a mere two when we have taken or been given four!). Furthermore, I've never tarried in any place, no matter how young a miewling, if someone called me Fluffy.

As for the Greedy Six? Why shouldn't they be romping free as I am, only caged by the turns of history?

They have one problem that I never knew, that none of them has solved.

Embalming, you see, does change a cat forever.

All that sticky stuff against your fur. It does the same thing as honey to the face. Just try to pull it off, and out comes all your hair. The only way that these cats can come out from their bonds is if they come out—yes, you know already. Hairless. They must wriggle free of their resin-coated winding cloth, and in this act, depilate themselves.

So in addition to greed, they possessed vanity. Such a curse, but they bestowed it upon themselves.

I tried to tell them, but as with their fatal attraction to cream, they would not believe me.

I thought that I'd be telling them for eternity, or as long as we live. Little did I know that there is a way to kill a cat.

Mummy paper. No one makes mummy paper now. Almost no one ever did. But in the 1850s in the busy United States of America, there was a huge hunger for rags to make paper. And likewise, there was at the same time, a huge digging up of mummies in Egypt. Many of those mummies were tossed into the hungry maws of steam trains, but others were sent by the shipload to the New World. And so my 6 siblings became for the last time, sea cats. They took their first and last steam trip and were then treated to the incomparable indignities that ended with them becoming—paper.

Not being, like that princess, liable to clog up the machine as a big-boned body so therefore undressed of what the mill desired—forty yards of linen—being instead, neat little bundles tight as loaves, they were tossed whole into the jaws of the giant crushing machine. In that shadowy wet cavernous place, teeth the size of men thundered, smashing, grinding, ripping the linen to shreds. I saw all six of my silly siblings for one fleeting moment, tumbled from a basket into the maw. The machine crunched down upon them like jaws upon a rat. I heard not a single miew, though who could have heard it any more than anyone could have heard their bones breaking? By nightfall the soup that they were crushed into was: paper.

All the cats, not just the Greedy Six. All of them who I saw tumbled into that frightful broth that day—all of them could have done something through the centuries. Would they have—if they knew their future—torn themselves loose, freed themselves in the shiphold or on the train, or in the carts awaiting to be emptied into the terrible maw of that fateful (if you choose to believe *that*) mill? Freed themselves of their bonds. I ask, but that is my interfering self. I wouldn't choose as they did, but it can't be Fate. They were turned into paper and died as cats, became no more themselves than the breadcrumbs in the baker's soup could again be bread.

And though they can never be recycled, there is a scrap of the paper still extant, I must believe, somewhere. Somewhere?

For as science says: you can't destroy matter.

Such a waste. That a cat can be destroyed is too incredible. I can't believe it, as you would say when something happens that you know just did.

Such a tragedy. So they were vain. So they were greedy. That's only human, you might say. And so do I!

But:

There's a cat down the street here, living like Bastet herself.

A cat so beloved that I would find life cloying.

She's a bookshop cat. She spends her days catching warm rays in the window. And her nights? I wouldn't know. But she has rolls of fat, and is as active as a book.

People point at her, exclaim about her ugliness. But then they enter the shop and try to tempt her to come and let them pet her. They buy books they never thought they'd want, but they do, taking them home, maybe as substitutes for this cat. They become silly in their admiration. They are not themselves.

I would say that she is Bastet herself, if I were a believer. But one thing I do know. She is free.

Her skin is pink as a tongue. She is hairless as a mouse's heart.

God

"God"
Missing Links and Secret Histories: A Selection of Wikipedia Entries from Across the Known Multiverse,
Aqueduct, Press, 2013

~#+* Joe Al "*!*!*" ("The Father") God (October 3, -45BKE --) is an international celebrity / dictator / terrorist / purported inventor / protection magnate / writer

NOTE: This entry lacks appropriate documentation for many of its assertions. Citations desperately needed.

Contents

1. <u>BIOGRAPHY</u>

1a. Early Life

Born to a middle-class suburban-nomad family on the South Side of as-yet (2012) undiscovered dwarf sub-planet 8943-P789, the exact date of God's birth cannot be confirmed, because parish records were destroyed by fire in 1968 and before that, there was no Wikipedia.

What is surmised, however, with only lukewarm debate, is that from early life, God had problems. His mother is thought to have suffered from dermatosis, the side-effect of which was that she did not carry God with her when she gleaned, neither in her mouth, nor on her back, nor in a pram or fold-up walker. The family would not have been of the class to engage a nursemaid, though studies have shown that it is likely that he did have some kind of relationship with a college-age au pair from whom, it is argued, he developed his taste for gold and jewels. She was beautiful, this woman, but she would not have sex with him, no matter how much jewelry he gave her. By the time he was sexually mature, she had left the family. This year of separation, known as the Seminal Year, is the time that Evans and Quiller cite as the year he developed tripolarism.[1] Always a fractious child, he now turned into a contrarian, self-centered adult who hated all women, and one might expect, both hated and wanted to suckle from his mother.

1b. *Juvenile Offender*

God's first offense (breaking) occurred in -32, when he was thirteen. As a juvenile offender, he was given the lightest sentence—a month in a juvenile-offenders' house. His second offense, a more serious one (breaking and entering) occurred a week after release. He served another month in juvenile detention. A week after his release, he burned down his first townhouse and was sentenced to two years' imprisonment in a mixed adult/juvenile prison. (citation needed)

1c. *Skill-sets develop*

Although he worked in the license-plate stamping room as vocational training, this facility is where he is thought to have gained his skill in pyrotechnics, biological warfare, and geological catechlysmics.

Famous in the pen for having a leadership complex, he would take offense at all who didn't humor him, which included the guards, who had to be replaced often due to his habit of destroying them at a whim. This period of his life is when, according to Gulch, Trickett, and Gutapurna, God developed his lifelong habit of creating, setting, and scattering Indiscriminate Destruction Devices (plagues, earthquakes, and assorted Pain, Death, and Destruction).[2]

1d. Gang Leader to Institutional Director with a Global Reach

Known as YHWH, his slogan was from the beginning, "I am what I am." After a remarkably short time, his superb follow-through, never swinging an empty threat, gained him such a slavish following that his troops began to look upon him as "Father," the name he has risen with, and retained, even as his family has grown. Although his armies are uncountable, he has never maintained a personal guard, having demonstrated countless times that he enjoys taking care of himself. He has, it has been theorized, a secret source of power--something so central to his ability to punish and govern absolutely that if this substance were withdrawn, he could go into terminal arrest. (The substance is boiled spinach, an invention without rival in the days before hormone enhancement.) Shortly after his deportation to the planet in blue, after a particularly bad mood, he began to be referred to by those left alive as "the merciful," and he has been called that ever since as an additional assuaging title after he throws some disaster.

2. GLOBALISATION BRINGS CHANGES

Team members are being recruited now on all continents. (citation needed)

3. OTHER HEALTH PROBLEMS

God was born with a film over his eyes, a condition known as Caulfield Syndrome. Although this cleared around age 14, his vision became more and more limited to a small field just in front of him, and dim at that. This condition, known as *Tunnel vision* (Also known as "Kalnienk Vision"), still plagues him.

4. NATURE OR NURTURE?

God is perhaps best known for his role in the evolution of the social sciences. Although Mayhew concentrated on the London poor, who were frequently targets for God's crimes, neither Mayhew nor the great statesmen of his day paid any attention to this lone miscreant who remains as uncaught as Jack the Ripper. No one ever analyzed why they didn't include God in their attempts to guide society toward the social Good, though Patinka Mays Houghton postulated that since the great social reformers have always been the class with wealth, they don't want to waste their efforts on the unemployable, but they do need to reform the work force to their needs. [3]

Houghton, with his *Bow House, Work House* sought to enter the debate. The book--" 'revolutionary thoughtbuster' - Alea Forceman, *New Statesman*"--might have at least been reviewed in *New Scientist*, if Yale Press had published it. Unfortunately, Little Red Press was only known in 1996 for publishing *The Secret Marxism of Bees* and *Stories from My Vagina.*

In 1945, B.F. Skinner (as lead scientist) was the first to draw the link between upbringing and behavior in the newsbreaking paper, "-45 to -40: The Formative Conditions that Made a Psychopath."[4] This study, citing years of animal testing, argued that the evidence was past hypothesis, that God's actions are the inevitable outcome of his neglected childhood (already proven by Freud to have damaged him from breast-feeding age, beyond any self-repair). Skinner died resenting the controversy this paper stirred up. (citation needed) He felt that his findings had been simplified and skewed, that he was summed up as a mere behaviorist, certain criminal elements taking the facts about God's incarceration and Skinner's conclusions to mean that criminal actions should not be punished, but positive incentives handed out instead.

In fact, the paper blamed much of God's personality problems upon his poor vision and stated that God not only has tunnel vision, but can hardly see at all: thus the compulsion, during his mid-life crisis, to get an artificial light source to help him see for part of the time. That this light source would cause him pain is another gestalt that Skinner had, he said later (which led, according to Kcrzseiky, to Skinner's falling out with Sangstromm).[5] The paper further postulated that God suffers from photosensitivity, so that he can only tolerate so many lumens for a certain period of time without suffering halo-vision and the migraines that come soon after. Burr said in a BBC interview in 1978 that he is convinced that God's migraines have never been treated and that Burr's list of incidents caused by these migraines was cut from the paper without his permission, by Skinner, who blamed the JoB. [6]

Today, Skinner et al. are being undermined by advances in biotechnology. Many of the world's most prominently famous scientists are showing how we are "hardwired" and our future "programmed" by our genes.

5. GENEALOGY

God's grandfather on his father's side was a moderately successful traveling sustenance-salesman. God's father, an only child, was allergic to most sustenance, but liked the opportunities he had as a travelling salesman, so he sold something that didn't make him sneeze and that didn't weigh him down with product: encyclopaedia subscriptions. It is not known what their first and middle names were, but the family *God* is not one known on dwarf sub-planet 8943-P789 (which, linguistically, doesn't tolerate an unaccompanied G), though Kgod is common. One theory put forward in the *Pennington Journal of Incarcmigration* is that during processing upon arrival at the blue planet, prisoner number ? (the numbering system is unknown), Name: Kgod, ~#+* Joe Al, was entered in the Book, in the EZ to rite form: God. As the Book was lost in a fire shortly after God's arrival, not even his fingerprint survives.[7]

God's mother's maiden name was Jo-Beth @@@ (Appledaughter). Her family were fruit growers on both her father's and mother's side. (citation needed) God was the youngest child of countless siblings, his oldest sister As-Ura having the independent streak in the family. She left dwarf sub-planet 8943-P789 as soon as she could travel, a good illion and a half years before God was born. She traveled to the blue planet as an explorer, but when she arrived, put down roots, because what she saw was good. She seems to have had a very happy life here, dancing and singing and being quite a popular motivator. Back home, she had never been known for having their equivalent of a green thumb, but here on earth, she could just talk to a plant and it would spring forth, and she was positively dangerous to women who were tired of being fruitful, though she was great company, able to tell a joke and not laugh at her own punch line. However, within a year of God's arrival on the same planet as she'd lived on for so long, she was made the target of God's first great political purge. This was so successful that the only surviving relic we have of her habitation here is the first ironic word in earthly language: "insurance," meaning "promise to protect."

6. GOD: TOURIST, EMIGRANT, MIGRANT?

At either the year 0 or 1, or thereabouts, God got the travel bug, according to his unauthorized biography *I Did It*.[8] Although there are no passports, manifests, or customs documents to prove any assertions, the Earthipodean Society was formed in 1912 to "spread the truth" about God having been judged an Intransigent and deported at age 45 to Earth, "for the term of his natural Life." (citation needed)

Whatever the reason he came, he has made Earth his home ever since, though he is such a recluse that *Time Magazine* put out an all-points bulletin on April 8, 1966, with their cover, "Is God Dead?" Although millions of people thought this was merely a late April Fools' Day joke, others realized that the influential journal was seriously asking people to search. These were the days before milk cartons performed that social service. The lack of a photo or even a police-artist's composite sketch has always made the search for the missing celebrity difficult if not impossible mission, if finding him is the goal.

7. **BIBLIOGRAPHY**

God is most famous for his "Ten Commandments," the document that forms the root of the word "tautology," and from which evolved the English higher-education word, "taught." Five of the ten demands are for unwavering and undivided respect, interrupting general life and other relationships.

Since that time many people claim to have been his ghost writer and others to have carried out their activities under his orders. (citation needed) But he has never written anything else that was such a blockbuster and that was purely his own invention, albeit dictated *à la* Barbara Cartland.

8. **NEW DIRECTIONS, RETRAINING**

In January 2012 God was accepted as one of the new crop of students to be enrolled in London University's first ever crime-writing MA.

9. **SCHEDULES OF ENFORCEMENT**

During the first year of God's incarceration in adult detention, he developed a personal code that he called his "Schedules of Enforcement." After attacking an officer or another inmate, he would explain that this attack was in accordance, and that any disruption to his enforcement of this code should only be so that his chosen lieutenants could act on his behalf. God had much trouble keeping order in the penal system of dwarf sub-planet 8943–P789, but has had no trouble on planet in blue. It is the efficiency and willingness of his large force here that has given him the urge to become a bestselling author of what is hot: crime at the moment, although he considers himself primarily a poet.

10. POLITICAL BELIEFS

As with many of the top conservatives since the 1980s, God has been very influenced by Friedrich Hayek, first being impressed by *The Abuse and Decline of Reason*, and then being absolutely blown away by *The Road to Serfdom*. God, however, finds the reasoning of most people influenced by Hayek to be fatally weakened by the human spirit. The logical conclusion of the need for less government because of its inherent faults is to do away with the root problem: human leaders, each seeking glory for self, funded with offerings from the people.

The Tea Party was formed by thinkers who understand half of the problem. The Wharton_Tea Party site states: "God give us unalienable rights (His rights). God sets moral laws that govern 'we the people.' Governments exist to protect the rights God has given."[9]

God is happy, it is reported, that some of this common sense is finally getting around without his having to pound it into his followers' heads. (citation needed)

One institution that is helping to reform governance worldwide is The Ark-of-Salvation, which sells a book that he is said to have ghost-written. (citation needed)

"This book provides the antidote to the disease known as the 'New World Order.' The Bible says (Micah 4:1–5) that in the end, everyone will come to Jerusalem in the name of *his own god*. This provides the basis for an entirely different sort of 'new world order': one world under **God."** [10]

God is pro-choice. (citation needed)

11. GF

The year numbering system used with God Forevermore notation was devised by God when he was still a juvenile. We know that because these notes scratched on the walls gave him an affection for this writing surface (instead of short-lived paper). (citation needed) No agreement has ever been reached as to the meaning of the system of GF, so no one has ever been able to date God's birth in relation to our system of time measurement. The only thing that's certain is that he was born on the 3rd of October, because he says so. (citation needed)

References

[1] Kelvin Evans and Crody Quiller, *Orders and Disorder in the Pre-analytic World*, Vol. 3, Humanopsychtric Press, Edinburgh, 1999

[2] Sheldon H. Gulch, Manfred Trickett, and A.S. Gutapurna, "One Strike and You're Out: A Survey of Sentences Brought Down by an Advocatless High Court", *JIAJ* (the journal of International Advocates for Jurisprudence), Oslo, 2007

[3] Patinka Mays Houghton, *Bow House, Work House: Why God Has Never Been Reformed,* Little Red Press, Oakland, 1996

[4] B.F. Skinner, M. J. Oldevie, Wilbur W. Sangstromm, and Xavier Burr , "-45 to -40: The Formative Conditions that Made a Psycopath." *The Journal of Behaviour*, Issue 24, June 1963

[5] Josef Kcrzseiky, *The Skinner Beneath*, Veracity Books, NY, NY, 1977

[6] *Scandalous Behaviour: Real dramas in the lab*, an hour-long special report, 2 April, 1978

[7] Ludmila Ogonsky, S.J. Chatterji, and Manuel Bourciez, "ID ~#+*; A Case of Autoformatting Abnormal Characters Highlights Our Need to Address Polycodal Personal Identity Reference", *The Pennington Journal of Incarcmigration*, Issue 1, Winter 2011

[8] J. Turber, *I Did It*, Houghton Miftin, Schenectady, NY, 1969

[9] http://www.whartonteaparty.us/Reports/Meeting%20 Report%208-24-10.pdf

[10] http://www.ark-of-salvation.org/intro.php

REAPER'S BREAK

～ previously unpublished

Countless generations of grandparents have bent over the backs of their grandchildren, put the scythe in a little hand, and held it as they taught the sweep. Mastered, the slow walk, the back and forth sway of the arm and the scythe attached to it as if an extension of the bones, the practiced catch of the fallen—it all becomes as natural and unconscious as scratching your nose.

With that sweep of his, Reaper's a waste of untapped potential. He's worked at golf courses from Hankley Common, England, to Mayfair Country, Florida. He appreciates tools, so can tell you from the vibration of the tee at the moment of the slice, whether the golfer swung a persimmon or hickory wood, an iron, wedge, putter, niblick, or a rabidly wielded heel. The romance of choice—1-wood or 9-iron, lucky stick or pro's special—such agony he had never known but no golfer could have told you with such unerring accuracy, the likely result of that fateful click of the hard face of the club on the skull of the ball.

Sometimes his job's been so fast, he's had no time to notice whether the native spectators miraculously missing being struck were roos under eucalypts, alligators in ponds, or peacocks on the grass, nor could he appreciate the growing acceptability of natives on the fairway who, regardless of the flight of a ball, cannot sway nor duck. Not for him, the time to admire the lizard orchid, the bedstraw broomrape, the marsh helleborine and sand catchfly that it has been written, "make this golf course a botanist's delight."

One of Reaper's call-outs could have been that very course, for the job was bent over a newt struggling in the dry crewcut grass directly in line of sight (but behind a bush) between the golfer who'd just sliced a beauty, and the fourteenth hole. The ball, sounding like a hit by a pro with a silencer, striking that part of a man's forehead beside his eye that has a depression like the top of a hardboiled egg. Reaper rushed to his side—but it was only a concussion.

Nothing was ever said about these false callouts, and of course Reaper never had to report them, but the *knowing* combined with silence left him with an irrational *something*, some feeling, though he knew it must be a cheeky affectation of his to feel anything.

One sun-burnished summer evening, he was at Shinnecock Hills in Southhampton, salt-laced wind riffling the tussock grasses. He swung, feeling a sharp pain in his elbow. The sun *had* shone into his eye sockets. So what? He'd botched the job so bad, his scythe could have been a razor-blade-laden sponge.

How many channels the order came through, Reaper couldn't know, but it came down from the top.

"Unprecedented," says Time. "This calls for the unprecedented. You're going on a little trip."

Reaper's knees make like castanets. He'd been sent to work at many scenes that had started with that line.

"I'll try harder," he promises, a line he's seen used so often, you'd think it was proven effective. He'd never seen it so, but.

"Wheedling unbecomes you." Time is as unreadable as a psychopath. "Don't worry. I'm sending you on a vacation."

"But you *need* me. Or is there someone else?"

"The world will manage," Time says either ominously or wryly. "Holiday, vacation, trip of a lifetime. A break. Something you've never had. Be *thank*ful. And do try to look happy."

Reaper's throat rattles a little—the only protest he dares. For when does he *not* look happy? His smile's a perfect rictus.

Time loses nothing. Reaper's suddenly sitting on the client side of a desk in a small room plastered with posters of bubbling lava lakes, snowy peaks, fiery sunsets; and possibly as a joke, one of those NASA-issued pictures of "Space."

Behind the desk is a sundried guy with hair as glossy brown as a freshly painted bench, his white t-shirt emblazoned with *The journey never stops.*

He gives Reaper a professional smile. "Where would you like to go?"

Reaper has never been asked anything, only told. His jaw drops open so hard, he has to knock it unstuck. His earholes buzz from the sudden aggravation of the searing pain he's developed in his swing arm, what would be classified, if peasants had ever had health cover, as Harvest Elbow.

Reaper can't squint, nor does he make a sound. The agent looks into his eye sockets. "Leave it to me."

"Will I be healed?"

"Time heals all wounds."

"So maybe a spot of golf?" Reaper said at the same time as the agent said, "If so inclined."

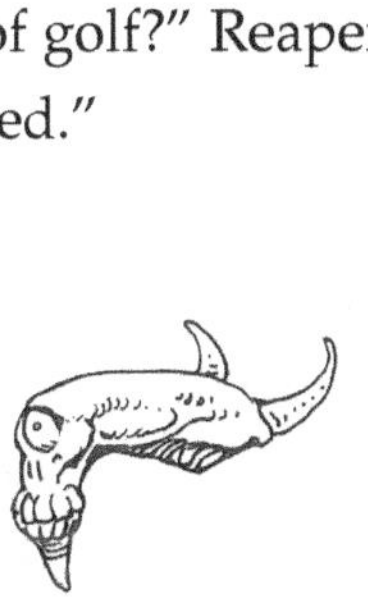

A woman is bent over a dishwasher, dropping cutlery in its basket, a man bent over her back so close, she can't right herself. Her hair is tied back, exposing her red face, eyelashes sopping with the clear paint of tears.

"Yes," she says, her voice trembling.

His voice is beautifully deep. "You're arguing with me."

"I *agree* with you."

"See? Why d'you always argue?"

He winds a lock of her hair around his hand.

"I agreed with you. What you said was right."

"Everything I say, you contradict me."

"But—"

"Shut up."

"Yes."

"See! Stop . . . arguing . . . with . . ."

Here's a fun fact, says a chirpy voice. The man isn't distracted by it, and the woman mightn't hear anything.

Anoxic encephalopathy, continues the voice.

"You talking to me?" says Reaper.

Who else? As I was saying, Anoxic encephalopathy is a form of irreversible—frequently fatal—brain damage caused by obstructing the delivery of oxygen to the brain, is called "brain death.

"Why tell me this? And why am I here?"

I'm your personal commentator, of course. I don't know how good your hearing is, but I doubt anyone but me could tell you her thyroid cartilage has just been fractured.

"My scythe! Where's my scythe?"

Why would you want it?

"Isn't this a job?"

You're on vacation, silly.

"Your idea of fun?"

I understand your discomfiture at finding yourself at leisure. I myself have never—

"Show yourself."

I'm afraid I cannot. But you can turn me off.

"How?"

I must advise you that in doing so, you'll be not taking advantage of the superiorising difference between your bespoke journey, the trip of a lifetime, one that you can tell stories from as long as you live—and the package tours of the masses. Turn me off if you don't care if you know nothing about what you'll see. Turn me off if you don't mind looking—[the voice coughs politely] *in a manner of speaking—like people who go to museums and zoos.*

"But why take me to this? Did you decide that?"

Please don't flatter me. I only serve. But perhaps it's perfect for you who might have no experience of attempteds. As I was saying before interruption, studies of women who were victims of intimate partner strangulation homicide and attempted homicide range from 24% to 62%.

"And I want to know this? You write this stuff?"

Since you're on such a special tour, I'm sure, sir, that you are too well off to take that superior tone. You might instead, savor the irony of the humanlike mistake. Whoever designed your tour hasn't separated attempted from successful jobs. Just imagine your workload if you were sent on false alarms. [another cough] *You haven't been, have you?*

"I've never encountered a disembodied worker. Will I get the, uh, job, of reaping you?"

Is 'uh' a euphemism for 'pleasure'?

"Now don't take it personally. Just get me back to work. This . . . this is for sadists."

Your rush to judgement does not become you. Must I repeat? This tour was planned just for you. Would you like me to find out when she'll be your job?

"Why? Why am I a spectator at this?"

It isn't my job to know, but I presume it's to serve you a slice of life.

"Horror?"

It's the hottest thing. And you, I see from your profile, should know it's life. Would you like to know how many—oh, oh, you can't miss this!

Suddenly Reaper's elbow twitches, but not from harvest elbow. Oh, just this once, he'd love to do a job that he assigns himself.

No you can't, says the commentator. *Unless you can leap the continuum and strangle him with your boney hands.*

"You a mindreader now? And where's my scythe? How can people eat popcorn watching horror? How can they binge-watch? Get me outa here!"

I—I'll take this. The agent's voice cuts in.

"Service," sighs Reaper. "At *last.*"

I'm sorry, says the commentator, sounding, with that low vibrato of worry, like a 1930s recording.

Mm, says the agent, keeping out of sight. *I see some extra work is needed, so I'll make this move for you as a special favor. I see you've never been with us before.*

"Has anyone? Is *anyone* like me?"

We are all individuals.

"That's good, becau—"

And, because it's you, I'll make one more concession. Of course you must choose now. But, given your squeamishness, a vacation might be all too much for you. I was led to believe you weren't cowardly, but you've never been tested. Why don't I cancel this new arrangement and instead, get you in for a spinal readjustment? He chuckles, and in the background, that might be the commentator trying to muffle a snigger.

"I'm tougher than you think. Gimme the vacation."

She's thinking, I really hate this life, says the commentator. *I hate being alive. I wish the fuck I could—*

"I get it!" says Reaper.

I feel your frustration. But there's no need to be rattled. Please refrain from that infernal hand wringing.

"You? Feel me?"

She wishes she could kill him, but she's afeared of getting caught.

"Obviously."

Capital that that's *established. Thus, no need for you to consider yourself a failure.*

"Excuse me?"

I would feel just as bad, says the commentator, *if I were thought of in such ambivalent terms."*

When the visit finally ends, Reaper is confused. She should want me, desperately yearn for me. I—feared above all, or wished for fervently as an end to the unbearable.

Sleep, says the commentator. *You've a busy day tomorrow. Sleep is part of the package. Lay your head down. Now,* croons the commentator, *to sleep, perchance to dream.*

Reaper's clumsy, but he manages to unsnap his head. Immediately, he feels lighter. He lays it down with mounting excitement. To sleep! To dream!

Instead, he can't. His ribs ache as if he'd lost a match with the star of London's Natural History Museum. He'd witnessed for the first time someone who neither wished for nor feared him. *She doesn't give a damn about me.* She's *past* caring.

What if this catches on?

What if no one cares?

What am I if not my work?

Am I being—have I been . . . eliminated?

Reaper can't sweat, but he now fathoms why that accountant, when visited by the clued-in mob boss laughed and said, *"What a turnup for the books"* just before his boss plugged him / Reaper swung.

Bravery. Reaper'd never needed it. Fear? Reaper'd never had it. Excitement? You must be kidding. Time wasn't kidding, however about giving him the Unprecedented with this break.

That woman who needed him so much that he forgot his harvest elbow—*I'm no more thought about by her than dusting under her fridge.*

Reaper's mandible cracks from clenching. His eye sockets ache. *Is this terror?*

His insecure memory leaps into the fray. *This is how it starts,* it says, reminding him of Yeltsin's cockcrowing rant. The man had been so pickled he was brave. He wagged his fat finger in Reaper's face just before the chop. "Live it up on the job," he said. "Never take a holiday like Misha did, or you'll find someone's taken your place."

Reaper's parts make cracking sounds, jaws, knees, elbows grinding.

Feeling. It doesn't need nerves. He felt awash with the stuff. It tangled with his thoughts. Pain. He'd seen so much, but it was, like those patent leather shoes and artificial eyelashes, things others have, like vacations. Until the harvest elbow.

He'd also never had the leisure of idleness, let alone the chance for uninterrupted thought. Soon a new thought breaks into his snaggled flurry: Despite what the agent said, Reaper had not been whisked from that first venue, nor had it been swept away from him. In a way, he isn't surprised. No one had ever given him the faintest consideration till the day of his embarrassing accident. Still, despite all the agent's special treatment talk, no whisking had been done. *Was that deliberate or inefficient? Was I listened to? Ignored? Should I be thankful or angry? Delib . . .*

A distinct crack has him grabbing his head, fitting it on. He feels his jaw and damn. The top back molar is like a tree struck by lightning—bifurcated. "The hell with sleep."

Tomorrow, says the commentator, as if that's a promise.

Reaper's standing in a field of dirt. A woman taps him on the shoulder, and swinging a hoe off her shoulder, says, "She doesn't give a damn about me either." Her breath smells like brook-crushed watercress, though *how can I know that?*

"What beautiful eye sockets you have, Grandma," laughs the woman. "You only had the senses you would need. You have no eyes but you must see. No ears, etcetera."

Wakey, wakey, says the commentator.

Reaper stretches, then flaps his arms. His elbow feels remarkable, but he twists gingerly, and wow, the whole of him feels just as healed, as if—crazy thought— a weight had been lifted off his skull.

How would you like to luxuriate for the day, asks the commentator, as if Reaper has a choice.

"Scuse me, driver. My seat's busted."

Brett Stokowski's made his way to the front of the swaying bus, every step setting off streaks of pain down the back of his left leg.

The driver says something. Brett represses the "What?" he habitually says, said, to his wife. He wishes he still had his TV Ear.

The driver jabs a thumb backwards.

Stokowski takes the hint, feeling somewhat sheepish. After all, his motto "No pain, no gain" will only have to do till he gets through those famous gates.

"Why?" Reaper says. "Who the hell? Where am I?"

You're in mister Stokowski. Now sit back and enjoy the ride.

"But I can't make head or tail of this."

You want me?

"What *you* think? Drop me in the thick of what the hell?"

Straight, or with a little style?

"What's style?"

As if we're playing golf.

"As if we could."

So it was one helluva surprise to mister Stokowski—can you feel his bloat?— that he didn't rise from his slumped body and have a chance to say something to his wife Bobbie who was caught mid imitation pole-dance on the bedroom door as she modeled that surprise she'd bought online for their first real vacation. Actually, a working holiday. He'd secretly saved a thousand C notes to play Caesar's Palace, to really fund retirement. Go anyway, he would have said over the surge of music. Forget what I said about wanting a coffin with escape hatch. I'm dead and I know it. Tickle my body down there and you'll know for sure. And, sweetheart, find that old can of deruster on the garage shelf behind the jumper cables. Open it and use it with my blessing. He'd expected to tell her all that. You with me?

"Mm."

Movies are such liars, he's thinking. I'll never watch one again, no matter how max the screen, how big the popcorn tubs are where I'm going. Will she go to Vegas, he's thinking. Why am I telling you all this? You're sitting pretty in him, so you should know.

"Isn't this your job?"

Of course.

"Do you know how to do anything else?"

Don't be silly.

Reaper laughs, *har har,* such an unfamiliar sound, it creeps him out, but the commentator laughs with him.

"I feel funny, not in a hah-hah way," says Reaper. "Is this what funfairs are like?"

My dear Reaper. This must be because you are inhabiting mister Stokowski, a man of such good intentions, he worried all the time, and worry-ate. He was a job for you waiting to happen, and it's no wonder you feel a touch of the weird, dare I say for I would know even less well than you, being personally disembodied. But hey, why am I telling you about him. Don't you know him? The commentator coughs self-consciously. *You made the house call only last week.*

Oh, Reaper! How red he'd flush if he were flesh. His secret shame: his increasingly low-density memory.

It's no shame if it's your memory, says the commentator. *Mine—uh, Let's drop the class barrier of italics, eh?* "Comrade, will the assembly-line worker recognize the thing she's just screwed the lid down on, the morning after?" says the commentator. "Continuing with our mister Stokowski, and you should really pick up the slack or get the drift before the end of the day. It's not that I don't love this time with you, but I understand that this feeling in him was planned to be part of the Experience. Anyway, when you so abruptly called upon mister Stokowski, it was too late to cash in the trip costs. I hope to God, mister Stokowski is saying to himself. Can't you feel it yet?—she doesn't—didn't? give the trip to Eileen. That sister of hers went—goes?—through boyfriends like drunks go through excuses. This guy, he's disoriented, clearly not noticed and rewarded by Time such as you have been. You must be feeling all this. I've never had the opportunity myself."

"Shh," says Reaper. *This Brett Stokowski guy's even more messed up than me. So disoriented.* "But that's what's s'pose to happen. Time means nothin. Yeah, I can feel him, thank you. I'll be fine."

"Well," says the commentator, with only a hint of exclamation mark. "I'll leave you to it."

One thing makes Stokowski feel happy about—his unbelievable timing. *Bobbie'll have the confidence to have some fun without me. I've still got it, she'll think. I'm so sexy I stopped him cold. She'll never know it must of been panic.*

"Me neither," says the guy next to him, someone so wimpy Brett had ignored him out of habit. The guy could have been a factory-made chocolate chip cookie boxed by Reaper, an honest, hungry shower-cap wearing underage worker, for all Reaper recognizes the job.

"Sorry, what?"

"Like you. It's okay. I used to mumble too. I'll never have money worries again neither."

Someone grabs the top of Stokowski's seat. "None of us will."

"'t's Heaven," someone with a voice that soars over the ambient noise blasts out as if auditioning.

"When we get there."—a former teacher? "This seating."

"Lady, you got natural padding," yells a man who, Stokowski figures, has spent his hearing on a factory floor or maybe building sites. "My seat's torturing my bones."

This bus, thinks someone down the aisle. *It's not going to the right place. I should get out and walk.* "I hear you," says Reaper, leaping easily from Stokowski, who never got a proper grip on him.

"Thorsen. Knut Thorsen, it's me!" says Reaper.

He'd never seen Thorsen in action, nose an outcrop of black scab crumbling from frostbite, grin behind a hedge of icicled whiskers, a grimace of the achieved. Reaper met him years later, when diabetes added new landings of gangrene. The day Reaper arrived, Thorsen's left leg sported an oval ulcer the size of an ancestor's portrait, displaying in Thorsen's case, a tibia so glowing white, it made Reaper feel a bit unpolished. The man was in so-called palliative care, and had refused anything to deaden his awareness. "Shove your damn consciousness relief," he had shouted. Reaper re-whetted his already sharpened scythe, and his sweep would have knocked a ball off the green, but Thorsen was faster. "Takk," he said, as Reaper swept the remains of the explorer's life away.

After that, Reaper could never think his job a thankless task.

But would Thorsen thank him now? Reaper reaches the hero's seat, but *what now?*

"You can't any more than I can," says the commentator. "We have our places."

"If I'da known, I'da brung my pillow."

"How much longer?"

"Anyone hungry?"

"Nowdya say it—"

"Hell, yeah."

"I might have some twiglets in my pocket."

"We'll get ambrosia soon enough."

"I hope not. I'm a meatatarian."

"If only this was a plane."

"God, no. We're going to Heaven, remember. I hope my boss goes to Who wants chicken or fish only fish left."

What the hell? thinks Brett.

"I hear him," says Reaper.

"I know!" said the commentator. "I'm so proud of—"

"Shut up! Sorry. I can't hear you both."

I should be excited, thinks Brett. But I miss her already. He almost feels thankful for the distractions of the painful cacophony and the white-hot pain this trip is causing his nerves from his midspine to his toes—for he wishes against his will for Bobbie to be sitting here beside him. It doesn't bother him when the little shit (who must have been showered with stars in Sunday school, or had connected parents) behind him starts kicking his seat.

Reaper hears all that, including the stuff in parentheses. Brett's thoughts pour quiet but steadily, and often openly enough for lesserfolks. When he says, "Be good. Don't do anything I didn't," the wimp beside him chokes on a sob.

He sits sideways. "I'm so glad I'm dead already. I hope she dances with the Devil himself. Why should all you selfish turds have it in life as well as death?"

For a while during life, he'd wondered about the dancing with seventy-seven virgins temptation, but it had all seemed too chancy changing religions on the dicey story of a payout so out of this world. Besides, Pastor Greiner had said that in Heaven there is no loneliness, just a warm feeling of love enveloping all.

That pain between the shoulderblades again. Nerves, he reminds himself. You've always been too sensitive.

Hoping there will be no points lost for his little outburst of mortal weakness, he falls asleep. Reaper, suddenly relaxed, feels odd, somewhat scratched along his ulnas, as if he'd been redressed as Fairy Godmother.

Not for long. Brett's brain won't stop turning. *I didn't think she'd be strong enough, Does she feel my good fortune now? It's never too late. I always told her. Why else would I have always saved saved saved, worked myself to the bone for that retirement blowout. Now I hope she feel the wins every time I pull the bandits' arms.* His thoughts spin round from hoping she'd join him soon to horror at that selfish thought, back to land on the horror as his hope, till anyone mere mortal would lose their stomach contents from the spin. Reaper does, however, feel a peculiar tingling pain on the inner margins of his eye sockets—*is that my heart?*

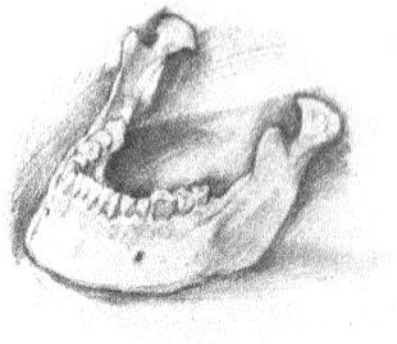

He wakes—such a disorienting feeling. *Why would anyone be born to lose on a regular basis?*

"So you let me sleep through their arrival? I wanted to see him win his first jackpot."

"You talking to me?" says the commentator.

"A simple *takk* should be in order, don't you agree?" says the agent. You've been moved as you've never been before. You've seen old friends, and made new."

Reaper suddenly understands what 'abashed' means. He nods his head and flourishes his scythe in a salute.

"Right," says the agent. "For that, I'll give you a bonus. Now you feel in your bones why you were suddenly called, in cases where a show is turned off by one party, to the chagrin of the one watching. Yet another glorious experience of life."

"Faux life."

"Faux life then. But true faux. Ready for today?"

"Ready or not," Reaper says. He's surprised how ready he is. He'd never before wished to wear a Hawaiian shirt, but today he wishes it, or a pink-striped seersucker jacket. They seem the most appropriate duds for Heaven—not that he'd ever before realized Heaven is in fact, Vegas. But it makes sense. A constellation of old stars you can see every night, all the ice cream and sausage links for every restricted diet you can eat, and everyone winning all the time, with the added false thrill of maybe losing once in a while. He hopes to run into Stokowski, and maybe Thorsen, though he pre-empathizes with Thorsen who would of course, hate Vegas and most likely be trying to walk out—but where to? A chuckle breaks out of Reaper. *The Great Beyond of Vegas is Death Valley.*

"By the way," says the commentator. You'll lose if you get attached. This trip isn't meant for that."

"You again? I still would have loved to see them in their place of just reward. It would have been fun."

"Hmm."

"And what the hell is that supposed to mean?"

The commentator drops the volume so low, Reaper has to strain to hear. "They're just taken for a ride, Reaper. Taken for a ride."

"You can't know what you're talking about."

"Yeah, Reaper. You must know better, and I'm just jealous. Anyway, today you'll have a chance to ask the boys."

These are sure as hell different links.

Gabriel, Nick, Reaper—they make a threesome, Nick and Reaper against Gabriel, two against one as the rules demand.

It's apparent by the third hole that Gabriel revels at this. He should. "Everybody cheats," he laughs. He cheats so openly and loves to cheat so much, he clearly finds golf boring, and being sporting, just a loser's game. The fun for him lies in the blatancy of his foozles, kicks, drops, pilfers, smirks and chuckles. "Doesn't matter," Nick mutters to Reaper. "It's his club."

"Damned right it is. And we love it that way, don't we, Nick."

"Wouldn't have it any other way, Gabe." Nick smiles as if he too, can do nothing less. "I really have to get back."

"Little Nick. Can't run a finger round his ear and do it right, can you?"

"No, Gabe."

As Gabriel drops a ball out of his pocket, Reaper asks him, "How do *you* get time off work?"

"I'm always working. Have you ever heard a word raised in complaint about Heaven? Why, nobody's ever done a better job than I have."

"But you're not there."

Gabriel walks behind Nick and slaps his back. "Why do I need to be when I've got Nick?"

"I should really get back," says Nick. His face has more lines than a surveyor's map.

"To that shithole of yours? Why bother?" Gabriel pats Nick's head. "He amuses me but he's a fuckin shit of a manager. I keep my place clean."

"There's no one there," Nick ventures.

"Good reason! Give me a man who hasn't sinned. And as for women . . ." Gabriel sits in the golf cart, weak with laughter.

"What about, uh, Peter," Reaper calls out as he and Nick run beside the cart Gabriel drove off in.

Gabriel snorts. "Peter? Never met the guy." He tries to gun the engine, but it can't go faster.

"The carder at the gates. You know. The saint who lets people in?" Reaper feels stupid defining the job role of someone so crucial, and so famous.

"Pete! Had to let him go." Gabriel stops the cart, places his ball on a tee, and swings. "Another low I.Q. individual."

"He expected to be paid," Nick mumbles.

"See?" says Gabriel. "And by the way, my little dusky friend. My hearing is, and has always been, great."

"I've never been paid," says Reaper.

"Nor—"

"Gentlemen. Eyes on the game. You're lucky," says Gabriel. "I've got so much, it's a constant worry. Who can you trust?"

It's Nick's turn next, then Reaper's, who is such a natural, he plays with his scythe balanced on his collarbones. But this isn't golf. By now, Reaper has learned the rules of this game. . .

"Man oh man," Gabriel exclaims. "You guys bring out the best in me. But I think your ball is toast, Reaper, unless you'd like to ask the croc in the pond to cough it up."

Reaper has also been unsuccessful taking Nick aside, though he's tried several times. Reaper suspects, using his new powers of observation, that Nick is so depressed, he's past caring beyond the mild revolutionary comments that leaked from him in his first flush of hope of camaraderie and maybe, revolution.

"And that winds up your Day 3," says the commentator.

"No way, Jose," says Gabriel. "I haven't beaten them enough."

"He really *can* hear."

"You can bet your sweet ass on that."

"So let's have a foursome."

Gabriel turns so fast, his ass in all its royal breadth twists like a braided loaf before it falls to attention.

Reaper rubs his eye sockets.

"That never helps," says the woman.

"I didn't dream you?"

"Last night? No. Have you ever dreamt me before?"

"No more than you have, me."

"Just because you hurt me doesn't mean I want to hurt you too."

"I?"

"I've dreamt of you," she says, "since I was so young, my digging stick was a plum tree twig."

She swings her hoe out and down, and again, five times in front of Gabriel's redfaced girth. In no time, her hoe cleaves a long line of the crewcut grass aside.

She walks the line, stomping with her big bare feet.

"Here. Let me take your scythe," she says into the astonishment.

She jabs down the point, dragging a narrow gulch the whole length of the line. Then she twirls it upright and drills in, ranks of holes.

"You know how to cut their heads off. Now you can do my job," she says, opening her bag.

Reaper had of course, never planted anything. Never made life. Just cut it off.

Gabriel? She looks him in his vacant little eyes. Reaper can smell him wither.

"He's below talking to," she says, glancing from Nick to Reaper, and back to Nick.

"Why don't you go home now," she tells Nick. We'll drop in later. Here. Take some seeds."

He dips his horns and takes them without a word, begonning himself in a fling of cape.

"Don't worry about Nick," she tells Reaper. "It's a hard place, but isn't everywhere? Besides, he's got a coven waiting for him in the library. Lean on them, Nick! Catharine Deshayes and lady Janet make the most marvelous toddies, and are great brow soothers. They almost make up for all the violence caused by Gabriel and co's gangs."

"Stop," says Reaper, "I can never thank you enough for this experience. Please pass on my thanks to the travel agent." It all rushed out because he doesn't know when this will suddenly be yesterday and he'll either be in some new place, or at work again. He doesn't give a shit about the travel agent, but he can't say what he feels. It makes no sense.

He picks up his grubby scythe. Its nose needs major surgery but he doesn't care. That prickle of his inner eye sockets—he thinks he knows it but if so, how could anyone have named it with one word?

"I think it is very beautiful," says the woman, "for the poor to accept their lot. I think the world is being much helped by the suffering of the poor people."

"You think *that*?"

Everything Reaper had learned and felt in this unprecedented break is smashed in that moment.

His knees buckle and all the bone density he'd needed to do his job through eons of war, injustice, famine, malice, jealousy, love, negligence, hate, accident, and blame-sloughing fate—it's shattered too.

He tries to straighten himself, but his sesamoid bones have popped off like corks.

The woman sits next to him and takes his hand in hers. He wants to pull away, but doesn't have the strength.

"I was just telling you what I have to put up with," she says. "Life lived as a curse, when all that glitters is the tears of those who have no choice. I've hoped to meet you so many times. I've called for you, hoped *to* you."

"Me?" His hip bones scrape as he turns to full-face her. "What about life being worth saving no matter what? Aren't I disgusting?"

"Honestly, you've seen me with no makeup on—raw unmitigated suffering. Aren't I as hideous as you?"

If only my eye sockets were expressive, he thinks.

She emits sounds that he's heard many times before he's swung: the laughter of abandonment. He's chilled, thrilled, confused.

"But," he says, "We can't stop work."

"Not stop," she says. "Let's jobshare. Have you ever planted a cassava? Of course you haven't. You okay to get your feet muddy?"

Reaper doesn't bother asking to break the break. He's gotten *that* used to the Unprecedented.

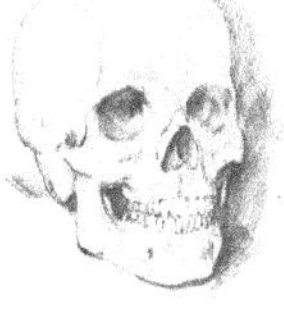

OUT WHERE THE GRAPES OF WRATH ARE STORED

~ previously unpublished

Talk of mislaid praise, you'd think I'd just invented sliced bread. I do believe you are sincere, and I accept your thanks, but your head now. I should chew it off. Me, I could have been just *anyone*. And you don't even know what you're thanking me *for*. Soon, I trust, but—

It's quite understandable, you doing stupid stuff. You should thank your stars you did.

Just lay off touching yourself, missy, and keep your filthy hands in your lap, or you'll go all putrid before we get anywheres.

Stitches? How should I know? Most likely, you'll end up looking like a trainyard. But you're alive, aren't you? And, just being honest, aren't you packing some misplaced vanity? If this had happened to someone pretty—

Not *again*. You're beginning to sound like a cheapskate's jukebox—and *she does it again!* I swear, you say *sorry* one more time and I'll flick you out faster than a picked booger, scuse the crudity. Can't abide the ungenuine.

Alright, and don't be silly. I bet that twister sucked up and swallowed your bag without tasting a single lifesaver in it, and it won't burp out your cash. Besides, when you leave off your blubbering and gobbling, you're no trouble at all. People should help each other.

Alexander. You can call me Alexander. Don't close your eyes! It's dangerous for you to sleep. So I wasn't going to tell you yet. You wouldn't know the physics to understand, but I did it. If you knew Newton's for every action—

Right. You want to tell me what I'm gonna say?

Okay then, to be precise—you'd like that, wouldn't you? I didn't exactly do it any more than Alexander the Great, Genghis Khan, Napoleon or Nelson did. It was all their grunts, as nameless as ants. Just think of me as Alexander, Genghis, Napoleon, Atilla, and or the Alliance zapping the Death Star, or you wouldn't know but the Manhattan Project and Harry Truman rolled into one—but without the recognition.

No, sorry. Phones are down. Enough, please. The day is hard enough without these constant interruptions.

How did I do it, you may ask. It's not like baking a cake. And you'd never know from my little Place de Resistance. But trust me. Those meteorologists who warn: *There's a front coming*. They did it this time, too, didn't they? And no one ever stops them. Not that they could stop themselves if they tried. They're just scientists. They won't tell you what they know. And they can't tell themselves what they don't suspect about this so-called broad front.

You have to be able to research, and only then you'll find the sinister: *Defined by the National Weather Service as an organized and long-lived system of storms producing a family of particularly damaging downbursts.* Organised. A system. Called something like a durango or something but were you told? I, least of anyone, will blame you for reacting like everyone else does, all accepting uh huh with no brain to the forecast of it, and to its progress.

I had put you in the same basket and would have passed by, but was curious what you were looking for. It *could* have been someone's paycheck or a mail-ordered engagement ring. How could I know that scatter of a giant's toothpicks behind you had been your house? You could have been like all the other vultures descending on the pillaged, and ripping them off in their despair and weakness. But I believe you. Those bills and that mailbox are the only saveable things from your uprooted life.

That's alright. Mailboxes and mail are related. Always happiest when travelling. So—shhh. If you talk, you can't listen.

They said *it* will do this. *It* will do that, didn't they? Nodding will do.

It! *I* ripped the steeple off a church faster than a vice grip ripping off fake nails.

I shredded roofs like that wedding cake after it was gotten at by the uninvited guest's weed whacker.

I blew your house off its foundations easy as blowing the foam off one of those girly coffees.

And I did it all—tall, dark and silent at times, screaming to high heaven at others. But who has to tell you that? You'll hear that terrifying silence between assaults, and those eyes-bugged-out, throat-ripping screams to your dying day.

And after all that, the news reports: *It left a trail of destruction.*

Or they pin another it on a Josephine or something even more ridiculous, Isaias, fake names to obfuscate—something to purposely muddle your mind so you can't think. You might as well call your last bowel movement Sally.

But do they ever say who it is? Or more accurately, *what it* is?

Yes, it. It. They always say *it*. If you were in a more together state, you'd know you're just as guilty, though I can't blame you. It's a cultural thing.

Who What When Where Why. Believe it or not, those used to be the five questions that every news story was supposed to answer.

Instead, it's left to us, not you ladies, of course. Us. But nobody takes responsibility.

You comfortable? Turning the vents more toward you.

In the end, as in the Beginning, it all comes down to a man.

I used to hope I'd be suspected, talked of as *alleged*, have my door kicked in in time-honoured manner, get charged, recognised, idolised and argued about as anyone who's done anything worthwhile must strive for as their due.

Realistically speaking, given people's ignorance and the government's lust for secrecy, what could I expect. What do you think?

Yeah. That's so right. So consider yourself lucky, girl.

Thank you. I'm used to everyone else getting the credit, from the so-called durangos and steam devils to the up-themselves tornadoes and those fancy prancy hurricanes with names fit for a cotillion. *Howdy, y'all. I'm Virginie. Love my frothy white dress? And that there's Otto rushing over with a cornfield for my hair. We gonna sweep you off your feet.*

I can't blame *people*. Give a dumb thing a name and anyone'd think it's alive.

And—I can see it bothers you—the contrast between my activism and everyone else's pacifism and—and cowlike acceptance. It's infuriating. Did anyone else stop to help you?

No, no! It's my burden. Really, it's no trouble. Unless you make it so. You don't want to do that, do you? Of course not.

Why haven't people stopped them? I don't mean you, but people who should have done it. Stop them. Why, when they could stop them, when they could protect everyone, would they put up with that—that anarchy that took, say, your home, your street? Why is everyone acting like they were tied down and given a vasectomy?

Your husband didn't? And where is he?

Then he's no loss. I mean, really. I'm allergic to dogs, got no kids. Got so penned in what with restrictions and that. But you've only got to look. No. I don't mean you.

It hit me, as I was just saying. The week after yet another deadbeat little midwestern town begging for publicity was flattened in a most attractive and selective S. I must have been thinking of it subconsciously while watching something called Rocks From Space or something. Meteorites, it said, fall all over the desert, and then the guy bends down and all over the dirt, it's like someone spilled a bowl of Grape Nuts. Meteorites he says. Too small to do any damage. But look at it logically.

What? Didn't you ask for water just a minute ago and I told you then, good things come to those who wait?

If my Bushmaster QRC shot at the speed of light, I'd be had up for killing everything it went through from Uvalde to Cedar Rapids if it followed the curve of the horizon. Lucky I fell asleep while they were talking of those meteorites in our deserts. Sleep is the great revelator.

I woke clear as day, walked out into my patch of yard and looked over the fence to the vacant land beyond town, land as dry and useless as an old hag. In the early spring after a freezing night, the only things out there were clumps of tumbleweed weighed down by what looks like dead sheep till they melt like the Witch of the West, come sun's mid-morning rays.

You like that description, heh? Maybe you bring out my poetic streak.

Anyway, you've got to filter out the sounds of civilisation to concentrate, so once done, I heard my own breathing and a quick, slipshod tapping like the Family Dollar Store girl walking home from work in the winter between the lights on East Leona Street over where it crosses Leona Creek. It wasn't her of course, but the unmistakable tap tap tippytap of an armadillo trying to scurry away. Kids play with them and get bored.

We're never told what we need to know, sure as they stop us from doing what we need to do. So we got to be inventive. And more observant than ever.

I waited till noon when shadows couldn't trick me. If you know what to look for, heavens above, it stares you in the face. A desert isn't a desert because it's dry. It's a desert because no one could live through that barrage. The desert is, I don't mean to frighten you, but it's the simple truth—beaten to dust.

Oh yeah, beaten. Curiously, haha, that Space program skirted the main point, but maybe that's as far as the makers of the program could go. So imagine now: You're looking up Deserts in an atlas.

Now watch in your mind's eye the next—well, any weather report of a tornado, or hurricane, doesn't matter. Anytime destructive winds are involved, isn't it always some meteorologist with glasses or some babe with caked-on makeup who they say is a meteorologist, as if. Whatever, they're always asked to predict as though they're God. And have you *ever* seen one asked the crucial question: Why?

I know this is deep, but try to pay attention. *Why* has no one connected the land deserts with the tornadoes? *Why* has no one connected the vast ocean deserts with the hurricanes? And *why* is desert-making happening?

It's actually beautiful, like a perfect war, the strategic placement of deserts. Their spread is nothing less than how science fiction so blithely predicts mankind's colonising of the universe. As if there's some nationwide hypnotism ray. We've learned, been conditioned by our failures to expect worse. And no one says anything about the victorious Who.

So the deserts, as I was saying. There's all these spreading No Mans Lands, and meteorologists telling us that, as if we'd never seen the satellites' pictures. They do their show and tell and we sit like porcelain figures facing the tv through forecast after forecast. We don't even act like the three pigs when the forecast said the wolf was coming.

Glad you liked that analogy. So we get told Katrina's coming to call—and then what? It's blasphemous, but we sure have acted as if the big Somebody must want us to sit around, no one asking why the it they named Katrina came. We only remember It took five days for the government cavalry to sort of pitch up after Katrina did the dirty on New Orleans. No one ever asks who attacked us, who sent the force.

Exactly. Who and why. If we don't know who and why, how can we fight? If we don't, we'll *live* and die without the dignity of shooting back. Space is all around us, but we don't have to take it like we're children at school.

Here we've got billions, zillions of say, Sallys from Space. They might as well be called that, so little do we think of them once landed. But physics! For every action, there's an equal and—what did I tell you?

Equal and opposite reaction. They land with all that energy, immense energy, incredible energy, energy such as the world has never seen before—and what you expect? Each one lands on Earth and is supposed to lay there like a dead body? It's got to get its potential out. Every meteorite that lands and lays around is waiting, waiting, ignored like rotting grapes of wrath—waiting as if cut off from physics—but none of us escape physics—they're all in a state of suspended potential—from *reacting*.

Instead of recognising this, we lay around when their inevitable leaks lay waste, as the bible says. It's up to us, but no one's seen it. They need to fulfill their destiny.

Our governments are weak as lite beer when it comes to real fight, but I shouldn't need to tell you that.

It was hard, but isn't anything that's worthwhile?

It was almost impossible, but someone had to fight back, someone has to make history.

So, to make a long story short, I became a meteorologist.

That's right. Unlike the fakes on the news, I'm the real deal.

I farm meteorites. Those pebbles that look like a spill of Grape Nuts on the desert floor. At the moment, my operation starts out all primitive hunter gatherer. Once gathered, I store them in a secure facility. That's the simple story as it might be reported. But that's only because the news doesn't respect you. Take a jet plane. When it sits in its shed, a bale of rotting hay is more active. And no matter what you say to it, that plane is going to lay around, cold and lifeless. You can beat it to a metal pulp. Only when you fuel it and then treat it like some spoiled thing will it fly, and only for a few short hours to a place barely farther than a roll of toilet paper.

Not my little grapes of wrath.

They'd *laugh* if they could, at the weakness of those sacks of flesh in barracks, the echoes of promise in all the empty underground silos. What's a plane to them but a variation on the tin man?

Each little meteor was laying around leaking uncontrollably before me—but waiting without knowledge, waiting in their depths of ignorance, their untapped potential, for a master. A master who would recruit each one to make it a part of something.

No longer, the nerve-wracking pussyfooting like at some family vacation with people watching or listening wherever you stop, and you can't even stop on the side of a road without someone coming along to *help*.

No more some Nancy-named tornado *wreaking* some neatly trimmed S of destruction as if it's some Julio who does your lawn.

But the secret of command is mercy. I, therefore, give them days off. That Christmas at Fort Worth where they left racing stripes through fields and then flipped cars like competitors at a pancake-flipping contest—that was one riotous break. That four-hour furlough at your town, another, but not just a break. It was the last. In that, it will always hold a special significance in my heart, one that you might share.

You felt it last night, didn't you? The lack of direction. The lack of pride in those screams. You know, as you might expect, from the beginning with me, they knew that I know best, so after last night at your place, they are more ready than ever.

Direction and discipline! Without that, no one can fulfill their destiny. They've wasted for too long, that equal and opposite reaction. They've spilled their seed upon the ground, and it has neutered them.

It is uncanny, but they seem to have a seventh sense. You might call it the bottled rage each true soldier needs. That and a capacity for punishment. I've found a way to whip that in them till they sweat out a concentrate that you wouldn't believe.

You have to hit it hard—that tapped equal and opposite *plus* energy—and clamp it down so fast, it can't go anywhere. Then you kind of rile it up till it's so riled in reaction yet so penned in, so stirred up and beaten down, it... it's reborn. All other military leaders have had to rely on the crude stimulants—drink and the threat of being killed for not killing. No one else in the history of the world has ever combined their knowledge of physics with military history and human psychology.

So now, today, my grapes of wrath are at the ready, though heretofore unknown, unsuspected, unsung.

You may sit at my right hand as they fulfill their destiny.

At 22:50, you shall be our witness.

You won't see it but you'll hear the roar, as I first stir them to a state of dripping frenzy, then order them to their places. Their battle cry will shake the soles of your feet, travel up your spine, lodge in the roots of your teeth. At zero hour—twenty-three hundred precise, they will shoot forward at a speed that will leave the speed of light gasping in the slow lane. And they will hit as one, point blank in the heart of their Motherland, from whence they were flung. They'll obliterate that mother wherever she is, and earn their medals as clouds of celestial dust.

And then Who? What? It'll be like they never existed, so thoroughly will they be wiped out.

It'll be so beautiful. Who's your desert-maker now, mother dearest to my meteors?

Can you smell it? All their sweat, their eagerness. It clings to me, it coats the insides of my CelestRanger.

Excuse *me.* My stomach never learned to shut up until it's spoken to. You know, I never considered letting anyone get this close to me. All this you can't do this with them, you can't do that. But if you can learn better than my stomach, you might work out fine. I sure could wrap my mouth around a grilled cheese sandwich. Think you could make one?

No! You're not really a cook.

At Denny's? Shut your face!

Better than that? Not possible. I bet you can't make macaroni and—

I'll be a—not pie, too. Not banana cream pie too? Banana butterscotch cream pie! I'm having a heart attack. And up there's a sign for Safeway. Would you believe it? You must be a lucky charm. These things don't just happen. No way. Shoot, no way in heck iced over. This is all too good to be true.

Stop pulling away. It's just my little lie detector test.

You're not seriously saying I'm hurting you with a little squeeze? If I wanted to hurt you...

Alright already. I accept. You shouldn't have pulled, should you. It naturally follows that you wrenched yourself, right? It seemed like something serious. Now look me in the eye. This *is* all like some fairy tale—too good to be true, isn't it? Be honest. You drink, don't you?

Because *all* cooks drink. My uncle—

Don't barbeque me, dang it. I *believe* you. It's just that men drinking are bad enough. Lushes... But they're merely what I hate.

Well now, that's wonderful we feel the same.

You see, so many cooks do it, but it's critical *you* wouldn't be fixing to put wine into my food. Wine is what made Alexander fail.

T. SAGINATA'S TRAVAILS IN DISTANT LANDS; & THE HISTORY OF O, A FOUNDLING

previously unpublished

"I had been for some hours extremely pressed by the necessities of nature... I was under great difficulties between urgency and shame... I went as far as the length of my chain would suffer, and discharged my body of that uneasy load... **[a load of excuses]** *From this time my constant practice was, as soon as I rose, to perform that business in open air, at the full extent of my chain; and due care was taken every morning before company came, that the offensive matter should be carried off in wheel-barrows, by two servants appointed for that purpose."*

— JONATHAN SWIFT *(GULLIVER'S TRAVELS, 1726)*

I, I, I, I. A veritable plague of *I*'s. That so-called *Gulliver's Travels*—what false advertising that collection of puff-pieces is—all for and from a being so self-centred, he told nothing of the being in his very centre—I, the central character in that dramatic scene.

That uneasy load? I was in the thick of it.

It was a great shock, after my years of service, to be, not merely discharged but shot from and shut out like a lender he was ashamed to have depended on—from that, that ignorant blunderbuss of an arse. Me! the sage of the gut. And horror of horrors, not even t'whole of me, but—I can hardly relate this, it's so outrageous. I'd been *sectioned off*. I'd been shed before my time, same as if he'd munched a lot of pumpkin seeds to slice me off, ready for his next squat.

I'm more than the sum of my parts, but that rude separation—it should have been for *me* to decide when travel beckoned, when, for instance, the smell of a fresh upturned field stomped by a healthy herd made me writhe to be freed. Instead, the indignity! Expelled without a by-your-leave!

Not to blow hard, but I must have a reputation (amongst the lettered) for enriching one's life, else why's my name? And my lineage dwarfs Gulliver's, though his sin of omission might be ignorance instead of envy. Let me, therefore, introduce myself: that very *T. saginata* in the title, a name known only to the learned. To ignoble ignoramuses and the envious, I am: a tapeworm.

At least I never did feel I was *his* tapeworm. It is fatal, in my experience, to get too attached.

And those servants—did they rescue me, nurture me, treat me in the manner to which I'd been accustomed? Of Gulliver *and* those servants, let us cry fie on the lot of 'em! I trust your sympathies lie—

Meanwhile, in another distant land some four years past:

One singular spring night loud with fitful showers and the frantic calls of frogs and crickets, one *Aseroe rubra* bent to earth and rotted so quickly, it seemed to melt. Only that morning it had sprung up, garishly red and sex-toy pink, as heavily and putridly scented as an old flirt desperate to be loved, and in no time, its long limbs were glittering with midges, its long throat glutted. Its one day of frenetic life quite as normal to its kind as its voracious taste for flesh, that damned short life with no nymph stage was matched by its curse of common names: *stinking fleshstar, stinkhorned slinker, deathy deapthroat, famished-circle-of-flayed-arms, come-to-me...*

Its reproduction as a fungus is common enough, its spawn spraying far from its arms, its offspring popping up (while it is in its death throes) often enough to earn those names, each newly risen nightmarish creature as putrid and famished and enthrallingly disgusting as the next.

Not *this* spawning. This time, the rain-loaded eyelashes of dawn blinked at a bulge rising from the slime, a bulge that became a pale pole that rose... and rose... and bifurcated and joined itself and split itself asunder, and made peace with its parts again, and rose ever higher, till this Biology's Whim, this Nature's Magick Joke, this tantrum thrown by the Natural Order, was so many times taller than its parent, it could have scooped up that carcass in its hand—yes, hand.

For it now had a hand, and another, and feet that were, oh! not filamented into the earth, but free to move. And a neck and a head, and long wavy hair, and a mouth, and two eyes big as blowflies, and two breasts, and a c___.

And as it was unique but would have no hope of legitimacy as a unique taxonomic Entity or indeed, Person, having no patron, and no Certificate of Death for either parent, let alone the shame of bastardry as they cohabited without so much as a blessing, it shall be designated f, and labelled: O.

Her memories at birth? This falls into the realms of speculation, below the scientific mind, but one must assume: Not of her mother / father whose body oozed between two of her toes. but of the limitless earth below. **O** dropped to her knees and dug, silently sobbing senselessly. Her fingertips felt, and recognised—oh, what a big, beautiful family. *And how old you are, grandparents,* another might have said. Not she.

She wiped her snotty nose and stood, still as a cow chewing cud, while a fresh shower plastered those waves of hair down onto her shining shoulders—a young dumb Venus.

And thus began her life, such as it was—this peerless fruitbody.

As she was drenched, naked, and obviously, from that lost expression, innocent as a new day, it was no time* (*five minutes and thirty-three seconds) till she attracted the attention of a gentleman.

He was passing by in his chaise and four on the way to his country estate. "D___ me, Mister Thwackum," he exclaimed to his inattentive guest. "Rawlings," he bellowed. "Stop this rattletrap at once, and pick up that wayward morsel."

Grumbling, the coachman whoahed the horses who had happily, agreeing with his eagerness to reach the estate (the cook there was generous in so many ways) changed their gait from a trot to a canter as they neared their luxurious stable and the country feast of coal-dust-free feed. And now he wanted them to halt? It outraged the four of them, so it took a while, first to slow, and then to stop. As for retracing their steps, they flat refused for that required turning, a move strictly plough-horse.

Walking was for footmen, grooms, yokels—not a coachman. And so is fetching naked girls, Rawlings fumed, for he had eyes, and they had told him to put lash to backs, spurring hooves from canter to gallop. She was helpless Beauty itself, which could only be bad. But the wily squire, the Lord Chief Justice Allworthy, was too rich and powerful to permit anything bad to happen to *him.*

And I'm lucky to be his coachman, so shut yer trap, man. He put his fingers to his lips and whistled as he had to his sheepdog as a boy, but the enchantress was too far away to hear. He had no choice but to take to the road, hailing her by "Hey," "Wench," and the short, sharp *you've got something comin to you, my lad* of exasperation. Still, the siren did not move.

When he was close enough that he was steaming, his face a hot boiled ham, she was facing the now partly exposed sun and suffering a swarm of midges that not only surrounded her head, but were starting to crawl over her face—her skin delicate as a rose petal, the curve of her lips and their colour, something to die for. He felt a chill and pulled up his collar.

"Come, girl," he said, following that at his next step, with "D___ you, idiot!", for she completely ignored him. "And what an idiot *you* are, my fine lord," he hissed under his breath. "She's not worth a bowl of barebones soup, she's not. Better for you to ride out later with the dogs."

By the time he reached her, he was stomping so hard in his furious temper, the buckles on his shoes were mere platforms for pillars of mud, and his precious, pure white leggings, brown as an arsehole. He grabbed her by the elbow and, shoving down his revulsion at the sight of her bright pink tongue cleaning her lips free of midges, he pushed her forward, shoving her till they reached the coach.

"What now, your honour?" he said to the man whose head was leaning out like an excited dog's, his lips rimed with lather.

"Why, use your faculties, man, or such as what God gave you."

The coachman opened the door.

"Not here, you blockhead! If you can't fold her under your feet for the remnant of the journey, give the piece your coat."

His lordship Mr Allworthy pulled his head back into the gloom and winked at his guest. "God bless deserted country roads, eh, Thwackum?"

The rain decided, at that moment, to loose a heavens-worth. The coachman pulled and pushed viciously as he tried to fit wet, naked, uncoordinated arms into his precious livery—that gorgeous jacket, as effective as saltpetre in catching the weaker sex.

"Like trowsering a fish," he growled, as he missed again. Her wrists and elbows repeatedly folded the wrong way, yet she didn't have the panache of a performer. Her expression wasn't studied disengaged. It was blank page. In his rage, he trod the long blue tails of his most valuable possession into the mud.

"Are you sent to try me, man?" barked his master, throwing open the door. "Can't you feel it's raining? The road will be sucking mud if we tarry longer. Don't button the coat, blast you! Hand her up."

That was some four years ago.

[During that *Meanwhile,* the tapeworm segment extrapolated further but does go on, necessitating cutting, so we meet again here]:

Of *him,* Gulliver, let us speak no more. He gave me not a backwards glance, though the violence of his so-called "need" sundered me, left me afounder, jettisoned, torn from my bearings, my lodgings, my very self.

Of them, the servants—all the gentlepeople I'd been in never stopped mentioning *them.* And every time, a tempest. From sea to bilious sea, I'd been fair to choked by apoplectic anger in more than a few guts, the moral being: *Servants are always servants.* Gentlepeople can dismiss them, flog them, treat them as they will, but I? Helpless I?

It took two of these storied creatures to lift me and toss me into a barrow, then one to drive and one to guide forward from the front, over uneven ground to a fallow field.

"Cor!" said one to t'other, poking me rudely with some sharp object. "Either they grow hogs without legs and heads where he come from, or this must be the yuni verse's biggest white sausage. And it's unnatural, it is, how this guv what looks like a gennelman monster doesn't have no manners. Not for him to chew his food. He swallered this whole."

"Like a mad dog," said the other. "And it doesn't half stink."

"Like that other foul gale."

"Aye, his breath."

"Imagine some mistress giant kissing that door to hell."

While this is perhaps entertaining to some (and if printed could be worth a mint), I could not afford these riches—nor precious Time. Exposed as I was, the air was inhospitable in the extreme—cold and dry—and succour? My source of sustenance now breeched, I was facing a bleak future, me who'd never had to plan, any more than Time. I'd always landed right, so to speak. Always been picked up and planted in a generous berth.

Always eaten of the best, been bathed in the best of nourishing nectars, nestled in the most commodious, warm and silken folds of tender flesh...

And what were they doing? What do servants always do? "You odious vermin," I exclaimed. "Carry, don't tarry!"

"Your ears aren't decorations!" I added, and repeated my demand to hasten, enunciating as richly as the rare roast beef I'd come from to house in the gut of Gulliver some four years past.

But did these blockheads take my counsel? Did they obey? They carried on as if I were a servant too, but from another place, treating me with the utmost discourtesy, worse than dismissal. As if I didn't exist as I'd nothing I could do for them.

I decry violent exhortation but cannot beg off the duties pressed upon me by the necessities of nature, compounded infuriatingly by the nature of servants. So, uncharacteristically, but *in extremis*, I rose up in anger.

Cowards! They ran off screaming, tipping over the wheel-barrow in their clodhopping haste.

Free!

The earth was wet, loamy, scented with cow manure, but being Lilliput, the field was so small, the cows likely to be half my size, my prospects here were niller than nought. I had no choice but to wriggle out of this.

I had no independent means of locomotion, yet needed none. Urgency itself propelled me till I reached a Precipitous Edge, at which I slipped, tumbling into a Waterfall that clutched me till we reached base waters that took me on from there, rushing me along with no consideration till finally, bruised, battered, but unbroken, I was beached upon a bend and the Waters rushed past to their appointment.

Travel is said to broaden the mind. I'd never noticed this amongst the travellers I've been in. Their diet, for instance, is changed only with the greatest reluctance. If a man lives on rare roast beef, a tomato is an apple gift from witches. Travel is for crossing 't's—not seeing new sights. I'd had this confirmed so many times, I could not count.

Yet my travel, ex-Gulliver, had expanded not only my mind, but my senses. As I lay on that beach, I could, for the first time, see. I'd never needed to going down the Alimentary Canal, which has a self-guidance system and no rocky shoals. I'd never needed to in guts. I'd never been afforded the opportunity to entice or perhaps repulse while waiting for my next pickup.

But now, I could not only see, but put together all I'd learned from the talking books of life outside my lodgings.

That enormous thing crouching by the water. A young woman, dripping wet, wigless, and bare of that covering called *clothes*. Those two wobbly things on her front that looked curiously like me—soft and firm at the same time—breasts. So those are breasts, I thought, not knowing why hers should be so coveted while I, talked of only in confidence to a chemist or nursemaid—reviled.

That smaller thing under one of her hands, writhing and screaming—a man!

He was naked as I am. Without his clothes, I could tell not whether he was gentleman or servant.

MEANWHILE, *some four years past minus a few hours, beginning with the sounds of sixteen hooves hitting the road, causing the wheels of his lordship Mr Allworthy's coach to sit up and roll out of their slackarsed rut in the sodden earth, thereby jerking the justice's impatient hands as he stripped the coachman's coat off the foundling.*

" 'Struth, Thwackum" he declared, having pulled the woman upon his lap-rugged legs. "What a stroke of luck this has been. Aren't you glad, now, that I pried you from town? You are a precocious little piece, aren't you," he said, pinching pink nipples till they were cherry-red. "Note, Thwackum. Not a word out of the thing, or a grizzle. That's the spirit, little sparrow..."

By nightfall the rest of the guests had arrived at the manor—as luck would have it, three other bachelors, all old friends.

Neither Allworthy nor Thwackum had hinted by word or wink, so the evening's entertainment was a great surprise, not only in its exquisitry but in the host's generosity.

The toll they paid was exacting and deliciously frustrating. From his heights on the bench, the Lord Chief Justice Allworthy had developed a logorrheic loquaciousness, but no one could claim he was inaccurate, even when he bordered on the showman.

"Behold," he exclaimed, placing her standing before him as he sat. "Exhibit One." He lightly cupped her breasts, and let them go. "Hothouse peaches are hag's tits compared to these. And these nipples."

A groan went up, and a wet patch appearing in one gentleman's tight white crotch might have been noticed but the abundance of breeding in the room dictated that this was not a time for crudities.

Allworthy turned her aft and pushed down on her back so her white bum faced the audience. Pulling her cheeks apart, he remained behind in the position of sacrifice so only his guests could admire the neat little hole, a virgin in more ways than they could fathom.

Modestly, slowly, he toyed with them, stretching this stage out. What a fine wet little mouth she has, those tiny pearl teeth, that mobile tongue... an ecstasy of etceteras. See how this foot can bend around—

Finally he stood her upright again and turned her so her back was pressed to him as he resumed his chair. He reached around her and pushed her legs apart, lightly brushing his fingers against her cunt.

"You little vixen," one guest blurted.

"She must be experienced," said the vicar, spitting the serpentish 'c' in disgust. "Even if she's not a tart, she hasn't fought back, the slut."

"I'll eat my head," declared Allworthy, "if she knows more than a raindrop. So her lovebox is wet. Just look at her countenance."

Indeed, she never smiled at any of the compliments, never simpered with false modesty, never batted an eyelash, nor did she blush with shame while Allworthy's fingers played around that remarkable slit. Lightly covered in a formerly imperceptible down, now those hairs were standing out, each tipped with a crystal-bright bead of syrup. The colours of the flesh behind ranged from tea rose to what hinted to be a brilliant glowing red inside.

"Look in her eyes," he ordered. "Do you see a glint of guile? Or," he hastened to add, looking at the disgusted vicar, "a speck of the Devil's diabolical spirit?"

"She hasn't fought back, but I fold," said the vicar, who was showing quite an unfolding in his southern parts.

"Let's drink to our empty vessel here," said Allworthy, ever the magnanimous host.

The sack flowed with temperance, for no one wanted to be incapacitated before they'd shot their wad, and shot again, and again, those that were up to it.

In all this time, **O** never said a word, nor did she intimate that she bore any hopes for payment, a place, a setup or even a trinket in return. There was no violence or intimidation necessary. Incomparably flexible, she moved nothing by herself, and all by the touch of their flesh upon hers.

Not only was she an unequalled rouser of the heavenly shudder, her sexes (both cunt and mouth)—brought out the most from every man. No other woman could have competed, nor, amazingly, no child. Those beads of lubrication she exuded—that saliva—they not only allowed slip but seemed to invite entry. Each man, regardless of his size, slipped in as if her depths were made for him, and once in, was surrounded by the most deliciously fitting flesh. Indeed, she seemed to hug his sex to her, and to stroke it, milk it, nuzzle it, all the while bathing it in those incomparably smooth, thick juices. Meanwhile, she did nothing to distract, so even the most ineffectual little worm of a prick became a tool to be proud of in her nectared depths.

The library's atmosphere waxed thick with jizz, and all that undress and fumes of alcohol perhaps dampened sensibilities to the point that another scent that rose was either never noticed, or never remarked upon. Nevertheless, as it grew, its exoticism—it smelt like sweet, rotting death—seemed to bring on ever more urges to thrust, thrust, thrust.

When the last of the battery of candles sputtered out at some 3am, the gentlemen were sated. Allworthy sent for cook, told her to take care of the girl, and he and the guests trooped off to their beds.

Cook was in a frightful mood when she took the hussy by the hand. "Not I," she hissed under her breath at the squire's instruction that she give the wicked slut a bit of sup, let her share cook's bed for the balance of the night, and clothe the thing come morn for decency's sake.

"Sup on your character," she said when they reached, down a back passage, a door bound shut with an iron strap fitted to a padlock. Her hand shook as she unlocked it. "Down there's your bed." She cracked open the door just enough to kick the naked, sticky female through and slam it shut.

Cook carefully locked up and fled, up to her bed as cosily close to the heavens of the manor as possible.

O might have tumbled into the hellish place, landing broken on that floor that cook wouldn't deign to look at, not in a thousand nightmares.

But somehow, O caught herself on a ruin of rail, and tripped lightly down the rotten stairs, landing on her feet on the fleshwarm, oozy, rich dirt floor.

In no time, an army of blackbeetles met her feet, legs, streaming cunt, tumescent belly—advancing up and up till they reached her mouth.

Little light penetrated the cellar, but the scents told volumes. A rotten roast joint lay like a stray broken leg at the base of the stairs, a frantic toss against discovery by the valet who'd been given it as a love token by Cook. He'd almost been caught with it, and dismissal would have meant starvation. He'd been wily enough to filch her key and was just as terrified of the place. But that was its saving grace. No one was game to investigate this space.

That rotten meat and its moving crust of maggots made her realise that her own scent was that of an imposter, for she could not compete with that divinity.

The evening had nourished her as much as a newborn calf, its first meal of colostrum, but had given her quite an appetite. After having downed the army, she attacked the joint. The flesh was corrupt in the extreme, soft as butter. Even so, she was not a chewer but one who depended on her slip and juices. So she opened wide, and swallowed.

After that sup, she felt so good, she stood up, stretched, and looked around. Whether her eyes saw or her "heart", she felt a thrill course through her. A heated spring bubbled up in a corner, and along its banks sprouted a gathering of relatives of the fungoid branch. She sat beside them not knowing why, but not wanting to leave. Meanwhile, inside her, blackbeetles tried to swim out of lakes of acid-syrup as they dissolved, and the joint bubbled and broke into disintegrating pieces like a damned ship.

Cook was busy the next morning, picking at a tray of kippers when a scream made its way to her kitchen, a high-pitched but intensely masculine scream that made it all the more terrifying—and another, at another pitch, and *another*, this one, unmistakably the vicar's, accompanied by the foulest load of invectives she'd ever heard, turning, with each new curse, into a voice that could make the Devil himself flee in fear.

She gathered up her rolling pin and a formidable leg of mutton—*and there's another scream, running down the stairs*—dropped them, and lit out, bursting the hinges of the door in her haste, her fat bare legs pumping, her apron and skirts gathered about her waist, the better to give her distance.

And the culprits of this fright?

The squire Allworthy and his guests had each slept the delicious sleep of the dead till the host himself woke to a prickling sensation. Whether his reaction aroused the rest or whether it was a coincidence, both are but suppositions, but each in his own way reacted, to the limits of their vocal abilities, to the sensations of their pillars of pride having thinned like so many heavily licked sticks of peppermint, a process still mightily in the present. These corroding poles, the vicar's most quickly, were dissolving into ephemeral sculptures of exquisite beauty—if only these philistines could have appreciated them. The fat chewy flesh of fingers and one set of toes were melting jelly. And those who'd used their tongues to probe now felt themselves probed by a wash of their own rotted teeth turned quite to a gravelly gruel that choked them till they (by this time cook was too far to hear) could not scream.

Meanwhile, **O**, due to her breeding, would have had to stomach the one-nighter fate of a short life, but for Biology's little trickery. Somehow, she didn't die though she witnessed yet another generation of her family melt and expire. In the space of their lifetime, she felt the bond, celebrated and mourned the tragedy of their minute yet cornucopic lives, for they had to make do with midges.

Her night had been so nourishing, starting with that extended first course, then, as her appetite grew, the blackbeetles, and that maggoted leg of beast. She stretched again, and her right hand brushed the ceiling, smashing through.

She untangled her fingers from splintered oak and sat again for as long as she could, watching a few more generations rise up and melt. Some of her relatives looked like her parents and had their appetites, while the toadstools, for example, seemed not to eat at all. Not that she was capable at that time, of proper contemplation let alone deduction.

Finally, she could fit no more.

Her head burst the ancient manorial roofs, popping chimneys off with such force, the nests of storks luckily vacationing in distant lands were turned to snuff.

When she stood, the remains of the great pile built up for centuries fell to rubble around her ankles. She reached down and picked the little men up delicately as they tried to flee. They weren't much of a snack each, those little tenders. But she tossed each into that mouth

they each, only hours ago, had so much enjoyed filling. And each, she swallowed, so they each all had time to meet again in that beautiful belly, for a time.

Never again did she find as much sustenance as that night and morning, so inevitably, she shrank.

Not big enough to eradicate those who would harm her, she became a vagabond of sorts, forever having to pick her feet clean of the burrs men called bear traps. She was always hungry. The taste of men was, to her taste, vile, but she found the sounds of cows and sheep, birds and bees, women's voices and children's nonsense soothing. She was always alone, always confused, never "thoughtful"—life was too hard for that. She had never spoken a word to anyone, ever. Never known how to make noise of any sort.

She might as well have been a stone, for all the good life taught her.

For some reason, however, she was curious. If anything moved while she squatted, as she had a wont to, she always reached out and touched it, and if it were a man, she pinned him down before she downed him like some bitter but necessary pill.

One day she made the earth shake at a crook in the river when she knelt with the man she was holding, stripped him clean and held him down with one hand while she tossed away his wrappings. His peruque bobbed down the rapids like a drowned lamb.

An old woman and a child were laundrying not three steps away. "Nothing to see here," said the old woman when the girl rose.

"But grandmama, mayn't I greet her? Give her our cheese? Give her our thanks?"

Why she never tried to befriend them was a mystery. Sure, they were only the size of the men, but couldn't she sense that under their silly clothes, they were not just women, but sisters at heart?

"Bide your time," said the old one. "There is a one who needs must come."

"Only in fairy tales, Mother," snapped the young one.

I heard that!

I, *T. saginata*, the tapeworm segment—I, who was so rudely interrupted as I told you of my landing on that beach. I saw that giantess pinning down that foppish lord, his false calves felled by her stripping off his stockings.

I must, I realised, be "the one who needs must come."

I wriggled over to the giantess. All size, in these lands, is cockeyed. Here I was twice the size of the man. She took her hand off him. He wasn't going anywhere.

"Hail, great lady," said I.

She picked me up and *ate me*, swallowing me whole.

I travelled down nothing resembling an alimentary canal, and landed in what other explorers have described before: a tropical haven—an internal Tahiti.

"Halloo," I yelled.

There were numerous caverns, and all the waving fronds and the tossing seas of heavenly bile—bile, how I missed you!—muffled and played back my voice at frightfully distorted pitches.

Yet, from my former frightful state of exposure and exilation, to this—this paradise—I could hardly believe my luck.

This, I thought, for a time.

Soon enough, a lack of stimulation set in. And a fear. This is what I wrote on Day 17— *(tho' wond'ring how this could ever reach an Audience, for she is no bottle and I am no note):*

I fear I will never leave this gorgeous place. Here drinketh I much mellifluous nectar that can only be made to my wonts, and haveth I no shortage of commodious comfort, she, this nameless letterless creature of no culture and no class, has no real arse on her, just a hole for looks, so here endeth, cruelly in my estimation, my singular and Marvellous History. May it spur you to yours.

Come "dawn"—my artifice, I admit—Day 18, the lack of mental stimulation was fair to drive me to an early demise. Therefore, I set myself a goal of reaching the creature's mind by any means, so as to become her tutor, and thereby, expand my own horizons intellectually tho' they were impossible physically, her rectum being just a beauty mark.

Her not having words to interrupt with nor mislearning to correct, and her being hungry, all worked in my favour to such a remarkable extent that in no time* (*thirty-three days) she was able to conjugate Greek verbs, calculate the circumference of the Sun, and plot the best route between the two floating islands of Catagart and Islanor at high tide of the Randum Winds. She learned the secret list of trustworthy wine merchants, and theoretically, I had thought, how to dance the quadrille.

It was she who took to dancing, with me as a partner inside. We made a pair, I must say with no false modesty.

She never said a word but we communed. I know I brought her joy, but I couldn't bring her food. I couldn't help but notice that my tropics were beginning to look bare. The shores of my thick, golden nourishing seas of bile were getting wider, and wider, till one day there was no sea at all, just a shimmer, like a memory of paradise.

And within an hour, so was she as she decomposed around me, till there was nothing for it. I wriggled free of her slime, setting off with the heaviest of hearts.

Little did I know, however, and she had never warned me, but in that dying of hers, Biology remembered her parents, and her parents' parents. So she'd spawned.

Her children cavorted all around me, dancing as if they were born to be performers.

I've lost track, for there is no more need to keep it. But when last I noted my travails, I must have been one hundred years younger. But what does that matter. I've nothing more to tell of travails, for I haven't had any for all this while. What does anything matter, save happiness?

Those days of me knowing how to conjugate ancient Greek, how to curse servants and expect the worst of the weak. They are as distant as my days of life in lords.

After the ant-lion tamer act, it is I, the star performer in this troupe, who is, preceded by wafts of incomparable scent, wheeled on in my own glass-sided pool filled with a felicitous ferment, its billowing bubbles stroking my bellybody as I turn in turn, to stroke their own. And this—this noble rot—I imbibe it at each turn even as it seems to take hold of me, my very senses.

And oh, the drama! Each tumescent hump growing into another beautiful bubble, each tender rainbowed beauty has a bittersweet, familiarly short and pungent life, so our dance is a calculated binge, an act that leaves audience, players, and the owner-managers of this family-run circus all scraped out, crying (I can only cry inside), happy to be alive.

I didn't ask for it, I had no part in the concoction that I am bathed in, but such is my life now, and the manor (and family) in which I am become Accustomed.

It is Marvellous how the old parents who run the show decided how to treat me, since they have not a smear of bile between them.

I love this family, and the travel. The parents are not just two in one, but one set of two—a change in the family that is odd, but seems not only to function, but to bring them, and others, joy. It certainly needs to, for their one child, Insinua, whose own Dance of the Boneless used to bring down the house each night, is now unable to perform under the Big Top, for her nose must view the Big Top now as not big enough to use for a noseblow.

It hasn't shrunk, but she has grown. It is a tragic story, but one that must be told. She'd grown up in the circus and yearned to be like the crowd, so she ran away and sold her stomach fat, that beautiful pad of flesh, for a handful of what he said, that seller, were magic beans. He promised she'd be lifted to a castle in the sky where others would perform for *her*.

So she swallowed the beans and in no time* (*so fast, a stand of bamboo turned so green, it poisoned itself) this freak with a vacancy where her stomach should be, was on her way to smashing through the cumulus. How much she'll grow is anyone's wager, but the bookies refuse bets that before the next harvest, she'll treat the sun like a match-head to snuff between her fingers.

Her parents can but act as they hide their heartbreak, showing only their love and joy that she exists.

Her cousin in the background, the trapeze artist whose hair has prehensile grip, is making a scene only I and a mushroom might be privy to, as she kicks a naked man pulled from her memory of stories told, for she surely has never seen him. I feel a strong pull in her direction—a strange magnetism emotes from—aha! her very core. Eh what—a fluke! Be it from something swallowed or a something.

COVERGUY

"Coverguy"
Weird Fiction Review #10,
Centipede Press, 2020

Horror in the Nursery

Like that Mexican, Jesus[1], many a myth has formed around the details of Alfred's birth and the bonafides of his parents. Some say Alfred's father was an artichoke stripper, but that would mean he would have oozed up from below the border to make it to California for the season. That simply cannot be. Alfred was born not knowing a single word of Mexican.

The gospel is: His mother was Rita Hepworth.

And some even say: Miss Hepworth was no virgin.

It was once common knowledge that the demure but *zaftig* red-head starlet had been seen making with the lox and bagels and Coca Cola with the famed writer / director Mel Slacks an hour after shooting the most famous fart scene in his long career.

1 *Why does Jesus Christ have a Mexican name, was he really born in Mexico?*, Yahoo answers, https://answers.yahoo.com/question/index?qid=20100402011738AALkTLS

S.M. Mention, the renowned expert, has examined every frame of that immortal scene, the one that inspired him to invent the instrument commonly known as the Gassound Ometer, in which he took the principles and technologies of the coloration of classic films, and applied them to both classic silent films and scenes known only through hearsay. With his "beyond modern" technology, he was able to analyze, in detail, everything, down to the merest wind that stirs no branch and a buttock barely moved—all through the magic of sound-chromatified ultra-deconstructionitry. It has been reported that he is now working on "rescentivating" written works, which he modestly denies.

Mention, that rarest of all polymaths—inventor, biographer, critic, and high priest of the church he founded—was the first to poo-pooh anything other than a professional relationship between the popular freckle-faced Miss Hepworth (her real name) and the powerful farce director Mr. Slacks (widely known to be cut from Slacksky). Indeed, before Mention wrote, "Who has Coca Cola with lox and bagels?"[2] Alfred was called their "love child".

Mention followed up his rhetorical question with his unassailable logic, but since some critics of critics speak derisively of Mention's prose, see *Variety*'s cryptic headline: *Nitpicking Critic Nixes Tricks*, and this summation: Mel Slacks would never have ordered Coke with the bagels (and whatever lox is) so the brunch never happened. So he couldn't lead the lady to the next scene (which anyway could only be implied under the Hays Code). So, when Miss Hepworth gave birth to Alfred, she was still a virgin. Not only that, but she was so pure, she did it telepathically, never appearing in the scene.

2 *"Who has Coca-Cola with lox and bagels?"* is the bombshell in Mention's seminal monograph, but to test whether he knows what it means, call him a vantz and watch him swell with pride, for why would you do anything but praise him? He doesn't get within a continental shelf of any persons from that other Book, so he knows their eating practices as well as he knows that of the giant squid. So why hasn't he been accused of plagiarism? Like how to boil water, who would have written such an obviosity? He must have heard someone laugh derisively when he took that nosh at face value.

And so it came to pass thusly. On Day One or Zero[3] in the Church of Alfred calendar, he was born.

Before him, there was no beginning (though there are scurrilous tales of a lookalike posing in the Great Depression as a posterboy for the President who ran on the song "Happy Days").

And now that he is here for all to see, how can there be an end?

Amen.

The Nativity as part of our common heritage

An excellent example is Chapter One: The Nativity in that missionary staple, *Picture Stories from the Bible: the gospel (in full color) as came down to S.M. Mention.* This superb comic covers his whole life, ending with "Tales from the Crypt". Of course, it's all common knowledge, so there's nothing you'd learn there.

If, however, you swear you are:

Under or Over 18

ENTER

The Three Wise Guys

Setting:

A fourth floor walkup manger scented with overflowing ashtrays, work-fogged eyeglasses, and the rotting sauerkraut aroma of 1950s nylon shirts—in short, a room typical of its type in Lafayette Street, Lower Manhattan.

Action:

He appears (not as a walk-on. He just appears [difficult to put on as a school play, but hell, who needs school?])

So yeah, he appears, but he's nothing to look at.

He first appears to two other senses—as a Mel Slacks-worthy fart.

And Now, he appears, still not as a walk-on.

This modern miracle has nabbed the best swiveling captain's chair and, tiny legs waving but unable to plop their heels on the desk,

3 A matter of overheated debate.

Alfred E. Neuman tosses his lanky orange mop from his forehead and emits his first high-power, gap-toothed smile.

Now sit back and relax as everything slips back to the EZ, mostly simple-tense past tense.

There were two guys in the room when Alfred appeared. They noticed nothing. One was making a dreadful racket, laughing evilly as he typed fiendishly (or the other way around with the adjectives. It was so dreadful, it's impossible to be specific.)

The third came in soon enough (zipping up his fly—*and where else will you find that scoop?*).

"Who's that sitting in *my* chair?" is how the next part of some stories goes. Not here, *which is why you should take out a subscription.*

"No parking here, buster," he actually said, swooping down on Alfred and dumping him on the overflowing eagle-nest-size ashtray on the so-far-undescribed guy's desk.

This guy has so far escaped description because he was the opposite of the racketer. The only thing you could hear from him was a regular but very faint sigh, starting out pugnacious but ending on a stoic note, followed by the merest tympanic soupçon of a pop—the aural signature of a trichotillomanicist. In the last hour, his hair count had been particularly good. Forty pulled.

He was of course, the money guy, and if his hair had been monetized, he only had two bits left.

It's the loneliest job in the world, to be the only money guy in a room filled with genius elephants. And didn't those two other guys more than fill the room!

This trio had been working together for years to satisfy America's lusts.

The typing genius was now putting the finishing periods to his newest patent: "The Instamatic Superstove. Come 4th of July, it turns into an icebox—till Labor Day. (completely adjustable for leap years.)"

It was all the money guy could do to get this dreamer to do his hard labor each day, writing down his experiences in crime detection as well as his moonlighting activities. It was like fitting earthworm dentures to get the dreamer to put fingers to the keys, documenting his moonlighting.

"It seems like bragging," he'd mumble.

"Write while they're fresh!" ordered the money guy. "How can it be bragging if only us know it's you? And besides, I let you fib a bit."

"A *bit!*" the galley slave genius always said, his words smothered under his furious typing. (Lipreading flies on the sugar-donut sand on his desk would note that he frequently added, "I wish *I* knew a Lois.")

The poor overworked money guy had enough on his plate, but he also had to make sure the genius guy who was typing got the 25,000 calories a day his superhuman constitution demanded. *And* the money guy had to clean icing off the typewriter keys while the genius was chained to his work. The money guy was only human, but he had an almost superhuman touch, making his cleaning swipes in the line breaks.

The other genius was a professional fashion predictor. He'd woopsed big with the New Look by Dior, when he said that only in comics would Americans want women to wear cinched waists. Hadn't Rosie the Riveter proved that practical menswear is positively *vavoom*?

Now he was a perpetually ill wind. Although his monthly, *Tales from Crypt*, was a hit in all the best cemeteries, cemeteries don't have drugstores, luncheonettes, nor corners as such, let alone newsstands. And the dead don't pay, let alone subscribe. So, inexplicably, this publication which was before its time, was not catching on amongst the living. You'd think, with the boom in life insurance, that every woman and every man would want to look their best when they go to the place from whence you cannot enter with a suitcase, let alone obtain new duds through the power of mail order.

It's no wonder then, that this room was redolent with hope, despair, disappointment, angst, a touch of superhuman sciatica, and that smell that always makes you think the Devil's just scratched *I wuz here* on the glowing lightbulbs after having scratched his balls. (The reason? The typist, who of course must remain pseudonymous, so we'll just call him 'Nate', liked those sandwiches only Schrafft's could do so swell: chopped egg, with the crusts cut off, and cut into thirds. He ate them by the fistful.)

In short, the room, pre-Alfred, confirmed to the discerning, the very motivation of the Universe—every evil molecule of Its undercurrent. It was, in shorter, a scene certain literary circles can't get enough of.

It's no wonder the money guy knew: *Only a miracle can save us.*

And therefore, when the failed fashion predictor rudely deposited Alfred on the ashtray on the money guy's desk, it's only to be expected that the money guy would look up from his despairing hair pull, up into Alfred's face. And it's only to be expected that he saw there: salvation.

Those eyes looked back at the money guy without blinking.

The gap-toothed smile—or is it a grin—didn't dribble. Moreover, it didn't droop.

What did, however, was his right eye, giving him a mien of world weariness with a hint of a wink. Somehow he seemed infinity knowing, with that crucial sense of humor women always say they find most appealing in men.

And then he farted again.

Alfred, the Miracle of the Manger on Lafayette Street, was the answer to the money guy's prayers, especially a money guy who was culturally religious but spiritually agnostic.

Even the galley slave was happy, for what matters what the fuck's in a magazine, if you've got a great cover model? He could invent to his heart's content. His next invention: fake fingernails. Finally the money guy could laugh and say, "Good it's not your day job!"

Alfred is so good a cover model, he doesn't even *have* a side profile. And like the best fruit trees, he was born to put everything into that great head of his.

He never ages, either.

There's no one in the world who's been as successful a cover model. Donald Trump, blubber in your bed. You'll never come close.

And while world leaders treat Trump with the eagerness of anyone who must go to a men's toilet at a World Series game, Alfred E. Neuman doesn't even have to snap his fingers. He's had covers with the most known (dear editor, please don't correct this to 'greatest'). It's not been reported, but he's had affairs that you wouldn't believe. Not all totally consensual, of course. Some, he gave in to out of boredom over politely refusing.

And these affairs! As you know, ugliness is an aphrodisiac—when it comes to men.

But this isn't a tell-all kind of story, even if you are Over 18 or Under 18.

So, yeah. It's time to add up the facts we know—

He's still got the gap tooth. (Which reminds us. Remember that supermodel some years ago who had the same gap tooth? [hmmm])

His red hair is still completely natural all the way to the roots, all the time, and with no hint of a weave.

His freckles haven't turned to liver spots.

His jug ears are still as outstanding as Obama's. And does he care? His answer is the same as always: *What? Me worry?*

He doesn't even fret when his name is messed up, even though these name mixups add to the catechismic certainty[4] of his many pestilential Church followers.

He hasn't needed an eyebrow lift for the one without the droop.[5]

Therefore, he's immortal.

But so's the moon, or near as dammit, compared to us.

His immortality doesn't make him godly, regardless of the magazine founded just for him: *Iconics.*

It's not for us to criticize. But *Iconics* internals would give a gastroenterologist hives. It could advertise itself as *Proudly being for ages 8-year-old boy to people who should lead the world and never do, including women who might forgive half the humor.* This magazine might have

---

4 His name is a cataclysmic subject spawning plagues of arguments who've never known the existence of Debate. But he does that to arguments without lifting a brow. Alfred E. Neuman is so above mortal coverguys that not only has his name been given an extra letter in the official Wikipedia entry. The entry describes him as a "fictitious mascot". If one compares him to, say, the Duracell bunny, the buttrag seller, Charmin; and above all in the cold and flu season, Mr. Mucus—alls anyone can say is: *What is real?* From there it's all too easy to chalk up Alfred, who was there before and will be there after they're turned to history, as the Miracle.

5 Subscriber Exclusive:

The truth. Although Alfred's droopy eye gave him all the aforesaid qualities mentioned, he increasingly disliked his face glowing out all the time, unsymetrically. So he bugged the money guy so much that the mg gave in. After all, what's money? And Alfred was operated on by the best in this great nation, at Mt. Sinai, hospital for presidents and stars. The surgeons did a great job, mopping up their tears stoically. When he came out, his right eye drooped low as ever, and his left looked as if he'd left a monocle in while having a grandma-special browlift. The surgeons had never questioned the open, raise and lift direction. Celebrities ask for the most grotesque things.

So they were privately horrified, but the customer's always right. Only problem was, his chart said Left Eye, so they did it, *but he has no back*, so when he's looking at you, is his left side right or left? Exactly.

Ever since then, he's gone into reclusivity, and the Alfred E. Neuman coverguy you see is a doppelganger.

Some say he's not even that, but CGI.

Say it ain't so!

spawned that saying, "From guts to garters," which is also both silly and way above most people's intellect.

It's this intimidating aspect of intelligent analysis put through the humor mill that added to Mention's certainty that Alfred is God amongst us, and the magazine, His cross to bear. Mention has repeatedly offered Alfred another magazine to grace with his visage for every issue. Mention has told him how trashy is that magazine he fronts for every issue.

Yet Alfred must be content, though the covers of *Iconics*, just as the guts, were created as mere perishables. That money guy was like all money guys. He only thought to the next quarter, not posterity. So it isn't his fault nor Alfred's wish, that the covers became icons.

Not that anyone has ever asked Mr. Neuman. He might want to don striped overalls and take up hog farming up in Mount Judea, Arkansas.

He might want to take flying lessons from 'Nate'.

He might let himself be drafted to run for president, but probably not. Not again. He let himself in for that way back when, when he had less chance of winning.

He's too famous, too seen, for anyone to really know what he wants. And nobody really cares.

He's just a cover guy—putting his face where it counts—to help us choke down our daily grind of hope, despair, disappointment, angst, and maybe that touch of superhuman sciatica.

AND MR. DEATH SHALLN'T HAVE HAD NO B&B

~ previously unpublished

Such Perfect Symmetry

Above Candy Sweet's shop Cupcakes, in an apartment reached from an internal staircase opening onto the back alley, lives Cindy Lux, who runs a home business illicitly called by some townsfolk IFYOL. (Acronyms are banned here, for once you start, where does it end? Lux's business name is long, I Fix Your Old Lights, but it is perfectly in keeping with our town's Constitution.)

Just across the street, you can get your physical from Dr. Pain, one of a limited number of Dr. Pains here. We only allow five at a time. He's Chuck. Next door to him is Dr. Al Pain (Sports Medicine), and there are many more Dr. Pains on the waiting list. But that's nothing compared to Kneebones. How many bone specialists does a small town need? And has *any* Kneebone ever defied their calling and lived to tell about it?

Around the corner lives S.S. Stretch. You wouldn't know to look at him, but he's a serial writer.

TOWN LIMITS

Without strict community standards as well as limits to the number of practitioners in any field, our small town would be prey to organic growth.

We have, of course, many Cooks, a Burger but no King. A few Singers, a Colt but no Derringer. Three Bakers and a Butcher. He sells W.A. Grubb's full-fat sausages. We have no Supermarket (a Mark Super didn't cut the mustard). There's a whole detached garage kitted out with sliding file cases, many of which have yet to be looked at, which means they will not outlast the curling tarpaper roof nor mice. Many of these are wonderfully punnish names, they tell us, in Japanese, Czech, and other implausible languages. Those applications languish along with the Coopers, Knellers, Shoemakers and Smiths, all of whom must wait for the apocalypse when professions smothered by progress might burst into flame again. But we'll probably have our hands full with just a Mann, a Waters, and an Apple.

A Max Booker was refused till he swore he hadn't a novel in him, and was purely a professional bookie.

We've no cheap smut, so one Anthony Weiner got nowhere, though he submitted five hardback editions of his *History of Vienna* and one full-frontal and two full-profile pictures of himself sporting a goatee.

By now, you get the drift. We're just a small wholesome straight-talking town where simple is not only best, but the only way permitted.

NO NICKNAMES ALLOWED

Ordinance 85f78, Clause 78c: "No matter how accurately descriptive, nicknames are strictly forbidden, which means they cannot be used as the means for entry, nor shall they be acquired for any reason, by any member of our town."

THERE SHALL BE NO EXCEPTIONS

The system isn't perfect. Don't let on, but Healey and Feeley Wellness Center has a seething magmic core. Healey recently confessed to me that he isn't really Healey, but Heeley. And that he's good at naturopathy, but has faked his qualifications as well as his name. He's really a political animal who specialized in creating attack campaigns. "I had to get out. I was such a creep. I feel a new man here."

People confide in me. I can't help it, but sometimes I hate this part of my existence. And I dread the future with that partnership, for something's bound to pop one day. I said something soothing, but I wanted to set him straight.

As Cindy Lux likes to say, "There's not no reason our town ain't called Redemption."

Candy Sweet didn't come to be redeemed, but she's also fake. I know from the judge, in confidence. Her real name is Candy Cane, and she's the best dominatrix he's ever known. We're officially full up on dominatrices, so it was he who cooked up the switch. He's no specialist in false identity papers but she was showered with so many from the law enforcement community here, getting in was a piece of cake, or rather, cupcake.

As I say, "Everything will come out in the wash." Everyone here was destined to do what they do by their name. You can't cheat destiny, nor reverse-engineer your fate, no matter what the law allows. Hollywood will expect you to conform to change. Go ahead and call yourself The Rock, but that won't get you in here—*unless* your parents, the Rocks, named you The, and you turned to antisocial crime, busting through bank walls with your bare fists till you got nabbed and sentenced to jail, which we don't have. We don't need to. We're gated.

Pretenders will pop up, but they'll be bogus. Besides, we got the exclusive. No other town will ever get the superstars A. J. Splatt and D. Weedon, authors of that paper on incontinence in the *British Journal of Urology*, to break ground at *its* opening.

We told him we just don't die...

There's so few of us, you see. So we on the Board were confused when a Mr. Death applied. We replied politely (as we prefer to) with a *Refusal 8c./Profession extraneous to needs.*

The next week we received a reply, not with the usual outrage or insults, or threats composed of pasted cutout letters, but with something original and curiously appealing, it was so simple.

"You never know," he wrote, in red ink.

I replied on our behalf, telling him the date and time to come in for an interview.

Besides, given our initial refusal and explanation (8c) that we have no need for his services, the risk was all his. No one comes here to die, and so far, nobody had. You can hardly count the guy who breached our wall, stole a well-stocked boat, drove it out to the middle of the lake, fell out dead drunk and was biblically* dispatched down to his very eyes by the giant carp illegally named Gossip (*It was either the trespasser's Bowie knife that subsequently caused *her* death, or the dye in his red cap.) But since he didn't count, and no one else was planning to die anytime soon, we had no statistics and no prospects for any.

So say Mr. Death came, a confirmed 8c extraneous to...

He'd sit like an insurance policy, unseen and unheard but ready until he expired. Still, the concept of him being here comforted more than a few of us. And for us founders, he completed our vision, somehow rounded out our town.

That old black suit and new crepe sole shoes...

He arrived early to his interview, dressed as we expected—black suit and all. So naturally, from the get-go, he was addressed as Mister Death. I don't remember the question but he replied, "Just call me Death," and gave us a toothy smile.

A ripple of unease . . . nay, horror stirred the Board. One-horse names are far too Western for our town.

"Alright," he laughed. "Kill that idea. Call me Mister." So he got in.

It was Vera Tapper who first noticed something wrong.

She came to me on her shift break at the store. "That Mister Death," she said, "Not nobody should been bought more canned pineapple. Ever. It's indecent." Vera is a numbers woman. Sometimes her words seem grabbed.

"Mister Death and store?" I said patiently.

"Six cans! In [what sounded like 'a Hawaiian shirt']."

Vera was the soul of truth, but she tended to get worked up. Too many extreme headlines running through her hands from the covers of the impulse magazines. But they could have been innocent. Only a few months ago, she would have taken her outrage against decency down to the Station, and unloaded on Captain Copperfield, but she'd stopped doing that ever since taking up with Telly Dobbs, the town snitch.

I told Vera I'd look into it. A white lie. I didn't even bother to put it out of my mind. Confide in me, confess to me. But don't ask me to be a heretic.

So people confide in me. It's my cross to bear, but I do possess a degree of hearing that I consider a curse.

Two days later, the *Town Guardian* came out, its front-page screaming:

Mr. Death Seen Wearing a Hawaiian Shirt...

And that evening, my next-door neighbor was in bed with his girlfriend. I regret to inform you that I could even tell you the exact model and age of his mattress.

"I should never (sniff, noseblow) have gone against my (sob) better judgement," said his girlfriend. "You should see the letters. As if I'm an idiot."

"Why pay attention to ignoramuses," said Tony Dulcet, his words coming out soft as smoke rings. The 'sound of the town", he never raised his voice, and never had to be convincing—with anyone else. Ever since she'd been elevated from friend to Girlfriend, Tony's convincing skills had fallen on deaf ears.

She went on about her bane in life, Lyn Truss.

"She can't help it," Tony said soothingly, which didn't exactly work. So he turned to law. "Look, in some other place, you could criticize her, get a restraining order even, but she's living true to her purpose here, as are we all. She's an antagonist. It's her job to hoist you on your own petard, tie you to a stake, roast you. Shrug it off!"

Ellie, who had gotten F minuses for shrugging, couldn't drop it. "I've filed a petition to the Board. She's not an antagonist. She's a grammaticist, and there's no room in this town for two."

"An Oh-EYE-an shird," he said. From his mouth, the softened syllables poured so sonorously. "Hawaii" should always have a silent 'H' and 'shirt', a softened 't.' The War of Jenkins' Ear was fought for less. You with me on this?"

"With? Oh yeah, just say 'Hawaiian shirt' again," said Ellie Letterman, who had a voice for print.

And you need to know no more. The eves drop.

Next...

Some stuff you had to have heard, unless you're on the outside.

A month or so later. A LOT of noise issued from the normal crypt-quiet work-from-home business, Dead Buried.

When a couple of neighbors paid him a call to inform him, they were met by a horrific sight. Something so shocking, it was like a bolt of lightning to the neat twist of our town's moral coil of fibers. A unknown man answered, hanging onto the door and blocking it with a belly red, broad, and coarse as a butcher's face. On his head was a Santa hat set at a rakish angle. Beside him was a dog with a collar embroidered *Barf*.

"Tell him sorry but town regulations state no relatives," hiss-sprayed one neighbor in what he thought was a whisper.

"And where is Mr. Death?" the other demanded.

"Death, eh?" The face of the man at the door flashed through 'stupid' and 'angry', and ended on 'bemused with crooked grin' and a double-hand scratch at his belly.

He yelled into the house, "You cheeky devil, booking us a fantasy quest. Better get out here."

"What the hell?" came from the place's bowels. "Where's the toilet paper?"

He turned back. "Look, we didn't sign up for games. Just the basic stay. So if you don't mind." He slammed the door, only to open it again.

"Excuse me. Where's the welcome wine?"

Eyes popped. "How would —"

"Then fuck—" (He cut himself off when he slammed the door.)

Within a half-hour that night, Xmas eve, the whole town was rallied to stand outside Mr. Death's place in silent seething vigil—, to Xmas morn, if needs be.

They had nothing against the holidaymakers, but they couldn't let this stand.

As it was, not ten minutes had passed before the B&Bers burst out, wild of eye and word. "Not a fucking drop of wine!" he yelled. "Such pretty quilts on the beds," she said, collaring the nearest would-be choruser. "Covering *coffins*!"

They were off before you could say "holy nite."

Then peace reigned supreme for the rest of the silly season, but Mr. Death's was more peaceful than anyone expected. His neon light, Dead Buried, was off, and he was nowhere to be seen.

Come January 10, Dr. Chuck Pain spotted Mr. Death.

An impulsive and empathetic man, Chuck jaywalked to collar the man in the familiar funereal black suit. Pain had every right to citizen's arrest the miscreant, for before Mr. Death, the town had had a spotless record. He'd soiled the town. But Chuck Pain only saw a man whose face and demeanor screamed 'patient'.

"Come," Pain said, taking him by the elbow. "Come into my chambers."

Dr. Pain was one of those men who die in the saddle. So he understood the damage workload highs will do. When colds went around, he was worked the hardest, just when he was the most vulnerable. Mr. Death had always the same problem, before moving to our town. Here, he'd had nothing to do. He'd been idle as a remote control with a dead battery. This state could only hold for so long.

Inevitably, he, a workaholic as bad as Dr. Pain, had finally been unable to deny his calling, and had taken up his job in the mundane world with the verve of Santa Claus, come Xmas Eve.

Poor Mr. Death. He had no idea how pissed off the town was at him. And how socially out of touch. "Isn't it the modern thing to do," he asked Pain rhetorically. He didn't wait for an answer. "So socially responsible. I wasn't here for the holidays, so some other lucky people can come in for a modest fee. And I do so hate waste."

Pain's eye twitched. He detected a touch of self-righteousness in Death's attitude.

Wretched Mr. Death. Not only did he mix up the uniqueness of our town with not only that siren, modernity, but he didn't understand that if our town hasn't sanctioned an action, it can't be socially responsible. And to add to his pain from confusion was his sickness caused by this sudden bout of overwork.

"I'll put in a good word for you," said Dr. Pain. "But take it easy, eh?" He gave Death one of Pain's famous bedside-manner chuckles, finessed with "You'll catch your life of cold."

As he ushered Mr. Death out, the man in the black suit gave Pain his toothiest ever smile.

"And eat a little something," yelled Pain, with a shudder. There's thin and *skeletal*. Pain wondered if the man was bulimic. *You can never ask them. I've gotta catch him mid-barf.*

IT HAPPENED AT OUR EXTRAORDINARY TOWN MEETING

Cindy Lux stood up. "But you all heard them. They were pissed as drunks. There were no beds, no food. So this is horseshit. History will record, 'Death Shalln't Have Had a B and—'"

Ellie Letterman popped up. "Shalln't?" she laughed.

Someone laughed to the right of her. She looked, and it was Lyn Truss. This threw Ellie Letterman so much, she elaborated. "It's 'Mister Death shall not have had no B and B.'"

Cindy Lux was still standing. She pulled her lips in, and you could see how hard the strain was.

Others didn't bother to hold it in. There was a titter and a guffaw.

"People!" said the mayor.

Cindy sat. Ellie Letterman was stuck, standing up. Her face was the colors of a candy cane.

"Isn't this romantic?" someone giggled. "Our first town fight."

You can't blame Mr. Death. He was quiet as a mouse, only bought three cans of pineapple at a time, and gave everyone, regardless of suspicious look or not, the benefit of his smile.

But the seeds of scandal must have been cast. On the 11th of March, at two o'clock in the afternoon, the most prominent citizen of all, Mayor Instep, former military-parade choreographer, current director of the Creative Real Arts Program, was seen doing something so out of keeping, he would have been excommunicated (given one-day notice to leave). Tragically or happily, depending on your PoV, he took his life.

Mr. Death didn't wait for us wheels of bureaucracy to turn. He picked up the body and before you could say "Bippity boppity boo," Mayor Instep was gone and is now officially expunged.

This was the first proof of Death doing a terrific job. I confess I was so impressed, it made me feel sorry that I had so much work, and Death's permanent holiday was only temporarily interrupted.

But wouldn't you know it? A week later, he got Telly Dobbs—a bit less easy to pick up—more of a shovel, tongs, and suction hose job, if the rumors are right, but nary a complaint from Death, who I recommended for the town's monthly efficiency award.

I almost pitied Mr. Death. He was so good at what he does, he should have stayed on the outside, where he had a lively practice.

Here, he'd had a couple of flukes fall into his lap, but that would only highlight how dead our town is.

Three weeks later, on a blustery Sunday, a little flu outbreak dropped two more into his lap.

And then a flurry.

We on the Board were delighted. He really did have a one-stop-shop there at his small home business. And we had no new complaints from Vera at the store. It could be because the rumors were true. Vera was now moonlighting with Tony while Ellie Letterman was getting the morning edition out.

Now Tony turns up dead.

And *whaddaya know*, as Cindy would say. He's got wounds *consistent with*, as Coroner Bowers wrote, both a box cutter and a long-bladed pair of scissors.

And now both Vera and Ellie have taken a dusting.

Cindy Lux is the *Town Guardian*'s new star reporter. And get this! She's the first successful job-change applicant, and she wrote it all herself. Now the paper will be something truly worth reading. It'll make those magazines show themselves as they truly are. Peddlers of dull lies.

True Rumors is the paper's new banner.

There's so much to say, it's hard to know where to start.

People in our town are dying like flies. All those Dr. Pains are gone with some measles wind. No. The paper said meninjacockis. It's not my field, but it went through them like prune juice, and something else took the next lot out. Now there are no more Dr. Pains on the waiting list. Likewise, we've actually accepted, processed, and are post- all the world's stock of dentists named Dennis.

We've also having to seek for urologists with names you would think they'd be embarrassed by, but instead they proverbially pounded on our gates, yelling "Let me in!" Ploughed down here at the prime of their lives, one after another.

And in record time.

It's all since that fateful Xmas NYE break.

We think it's because he was bored here. Unfulfilled.

And so the hell were we.

It's not that we've lost our principles, or went organic and strange. Or grew, god forbid. Or that there's any churn. No, no one would ever ask to leave. It's so hard to get in. But now, the turnover's terrific.

And Mr. Death?

Our Mr. Death is now the town's celebrity, necessitating a special import of a press capable of printing the front page with four color bleed.

DEATH'S DUMPED THE DREARY DUDS

Nowadays he walks out as he was made to, and all the newbies would call it scandalous if he dressed.

We love him, yes we do, even though he has caused an increase in crime.

Ordinance 85f78, Clause 78c has been shot to hell. And the law enforcement community started it.

It's one thing to want to get your picture taken with Mr. Death. Everyone wants that. But now, because of popular demand, he autographs the pictures *Bones*.

THE DOG WHO'D BEEN DEAD

"The Dog Who'd Been Dead"
Dreaming in the Dark,
PS Pub, 2016

For a reason she wished she'd never learned, her name was Gunzen Rozes, and she hated being dead, a state she'd attained two thousand five hundred fifty-six (counting a leap-day) nights ago (or maybe it was days—too dark to read, but the streetlights were never on; maybe they were only there for the poles).

Technically in all this time, she had nothing to complain of. There was a constant choice of soft food, kibble, huge roasts and corpulent turkeys to drag from tableclothed Thanksgiving spreads; low-hanging sausages, legs of mutton, and chops on trays in a string of untended butcher's shops, a tap that slobbered water, and even a choice of digestive grasses to nibble—heaven to a labrador, *one dog's heaven is...*

So for two thousand five hundred fifty-six blocks of time, Gunzen ate, slept, ate. She had almost sunk to the state of labradorishness, but she could still think *what an existence!* Despite all the food, cushy pillows, lack of veterinarians, fleas, and doggy-lessoned people saying "Come", it was her indignation that kept her from going labradorian—indignation and disappointment at being tossed from Life to Death. *Heaven!* she growled. *No stimulation.*

So she set out to do something about it.

And being a dog who had led in her former state, some twelve birthday-gifted years of idyllic life as the only child of an active couple, she set out to find her way home.

And being a dog, of course she incredibly found it.

~~This is the story of that trip.~~

When she arrived at the front door, she raised a paw to scratch it, and scratched an ear instead. All through her incredible journey, she'd expected to do the expected thing, announce her arrival like dogs do who get 'put out', not that she had ever been in their number.

But now on the threshold, she reckoned that

1) Since she'd never been one of those dogs, no ears inside would be tuned right, and

2) If somehow, they understood, and flung open the door (as she'd assumed they would in her dreams), the shock to Andrew and Katt (she had never wanted to hurt their feelings but she'd always considered 'Daddy' and 'Mommy' in the same category as they considered folk music) might be too great.

Wait in the park across the street, she decided. *Run up beside them when they come out for their morning run.*

Of course they wouldn't know it was *her*. Gunzen never expected that, not with their limited minds. She didn't mind them not recognising her for who she really was. She relished the surprise and thrill they would experience, the tears and joy, as they assumed she were a stray and wooed her gently, then adopted her, calling her Gunzen Rozes 2.

She would spend her new life with them listening to stories of love about her, a life that if she really were a stray, would make her want to tear the throat out of this implausibly perfect being who was now in doggie heaven. She would have shat on that dog's grave.

But this was no time to feel anything about the dog she'd pretend to be, a dog who looked like her. She'd go across to the park to wait.

But first, she needed to pee.

It was that fragrant time after the garbage pickup before dawn, when stray plastic bags flutter soppily, their guts spilling onto concrete as well as the precious few little scraps of grass already so heavily anointed with sprays and markings that this extra dressing is a waste.

She turned around from the front door, for four steps back on the sidewalk, there should have been one of those grass plots with a sickly little tree in the middle. It was gone. In its place was a rack bristling with bikes. She lifted her leg on the nearest one. And yes, she'd had to put up with comments her whole life about 'females' not being supposed to do that, but then, no one made comments about her missing her natural calling of being a mother. It seems you need papers for that. And she didn't have these mysterious papers.

This wasn't the time, however, to reminisce. Things were not as they seemed.

Gunzen went back to the door, bent down so her nose pressed against the dark orifice, where she sniffed its housebreath. Different! She would have run around to the back, scrunching under the gate, but while she was dead, home improvement had hit. There was just more expanse of house. She had to make do with the now curtainless front window, so she jumped up on a concrete cube (where a patch of sunflowers had been) and looked in.

The whole horror of what she saw? This isn't that kind of story.

Cleaned up, however, a glimpse: Walls as naked and pale as the day they were born. Not a book in sight. And in that open-plan kitchen? No food. Nothing at all but bare counters, lots of cabinets, and a frightening shiny hulk of a machine squatting by the sink, looking very male. On top of this Thing a few tiny white cups were perched with the same sinister casualness as the gloves and syringes in a vet's room.

All that trip from the place of the dead that this story isn't about, *to this!*

Run! Gunzen thought. *Run, run, run!*

She'd tensed to spring away when *Bad idea!* flashed through her brain, as it caught the unmistakable growl and crunch of the Department of Animal Care & Control truck prowling maybe a block away.

She slunk across the road and flattened herself in the murk of a bush that stunk of chipmunk.

Gunzen had never been a streetdog. Never run except to play with Katt and Andrew, catching frisbees in this park, or running after a ball thrown on the one beach they could all go to, thrown a tad pedantically by Andrew, who could throw and liked to teach the way, and more considerately backwards or wherever (to give a longer and often unexpected run) by Katt. Being a city dog with parents, Gunzen had never been let out to roam alone. Even her pooing had been always under supervision—that was the one thing she *had* liked about being dead—no one impatiently 'waiting', no poop command, no pursed lips and pointed fingers poising plastic bag. Not that pooping dead was any stimulation.

Running, however. This was stimulation, and running after a frisbee and a ball were two of the reasons she came back. Now she saw the park for what it must have been all along. A tiny patch of grass and a few heavily anointed bushes and tree-posts. The times Katt and Andrew had taken her to the beach were so few, she remembered each one. Suddenly she wanted to run and run and run, just for the fun of it. And it hit her. *They run! They run every morning! As Gunzen 2, I've got to make them* take *me!*

Her tail wagged thinking of it, long hairs catching in low branches, but she didn't care. *Maybe in coming back, I've gone back to my roots.*

With a gnashing of breaks, the dogcatcher beast stopped to pant at the corner, bringing her back to reality. She shook her head till her ears flapped. *Going back to my roots.* She'd picked that concept up from Katt. *I must have carried it like some latent infection. There's so much a dog picks up in life, so much in all the noise, it's a wonder if we can ever forget most of it.*

Yet something lingered till the memory banged into her consciousness, something valuable—and then it almost slipped away—*something back there.* Like all that happened while she was dead, it was easier for her to remember her time when alive than when not.

In that instant of clear recall, she remembered something she'd seen while she was nose-down in a dish of "vegetables and tender meat"—something remarkable, and a thought she'd had many a time in those two thousand five hundred fifty-six (counting a leap-day) nights or days since, back in death.

See Spot run.

He ran as if he was always running, and she never knew what for. She never saw him eat, and now... Lost.

All that counts is now. And you thought you could come here and they'd still be the same except for them missing you with all their hearts. How could you forget that in every dog-goes-home scenario, the dog's people have moved thousands of miles away, always across the country? You've only to investigate. Find out where, and go. They're waiting for you! It's fate.

Of course! A piece of steak. What's Death when up against Fate?

So she investigated.

Mars!

Who would've thought? Gunzen was shocked. Shocked! Her first cogent thought was: *If only they'd been into Space when I was born.* And her cold considered impulse: *I hope they get murdered on their trip, with them being blamed for the only music available off Earth: "Sweet Child o' Mine"—that one song screeching like tearing steel, pounding like a headache, and them with no proper ears to flap over their earholes to muffle the pain.*

She experienced the normal stuff: denial, hurt, and then her rage, suppressed (or repressed—these two words always made her feel a bit stupid, but it was one of these) all those years at being called Gunzen, till she realised something worse.

If they named me now, Andrew would call me Rover.

Then she remembered something else. The life they'd chosen after her was composed by and of people of prejudice. Just like those signs planted all around the city: NO DOGS

One never knows.

This story could relate how the hairless cat next door had told Gunzen all about what happened to Gunzen's 'parents'. But the hairless cat next door, while still alive, had spent all its life trying to get warm and growing a number of chins for its pointed chin to nest in. Besides, Gunzen doubted that cats think, had never had anything to do with cats, and being a dog who had managed to get out of Death free, found investigation, as you would expect, a doddle.

The story of Andrew Wheatley and Katherine Carstairs was a simple tragedy. Within a half-hour of the vet leaving after having administered the needle's kiss of death (on account of arthritis that *had* been quite debilitating—it's amazing what cures Death will affect) 'Daddy' dug a commodious illegal hole in their postage-stamp back garden and buried her there, along with what Katt had thought was her favorite toy, and a frisbee, a ball, her blanket and her 'dogdish'. The couple held each other and cried for about fifteen minutes.

Then they unclinched and promised each other: "We'll never get another dog."

And furthermore: "This gives us freedom." This must be assumed, since by this time, their old-fashioned stereo system with its big black hairy woofers was kicking the walls till they bent like cardboard, Slash's guitar snarling at Duff McKagan's, that barked back like a mastiff held on drug charges briefly, in hell. "Reminds me of childhood memories" screamed so loud that Katt's and Andy's fillings buzzed. (Knowing who Slash and Duff McKagan are were only two of the many inadvertently picked up bites of knowledge recorded by Gunzen's brain, a brain that she sometimes resented. She didn't, for instance, wish to know Katt and Andrew's definition of the perfectly delightful sounding 'riff'.)

In Katt and Andrew's life, three years then passed (post-Gunzen) in Type A activity, culminating in them being chosen to be part of the first manned crew to Mars to actually achieve lift-off. An extraordinary achievement, and one that Gunzen had never heard a hint of, pre-death.

To be chosen in preference to countless others trying their hardest to be picked, Andrew Wheatley and Katherine Carstairs had, according to secret documents, made themselves invaluable in these four ways:

1). Obscene levels of fitness, with remarkably dense bones

2). Equally obscene years of life under their belts (Gunzen considered them too old for the mission. They could fool humans, but to her, they smelt suspiciously as old as the rat mummy behind the heater in the dugout place under the house.)

3). An unbelievably high level of commitment to each other as a couple (Some planners were hoping to learn more about the faultlines of supposedly unto-death love.)

4). High competence in two fields useful to the mission

So now they had moved away as people do, but they weren't even living on a street. *Andrew and Katt: Marstronauts! Who would have thought?*

Gunzen, who now wished she'd been called Froff, for some reason she didn't care to get into, decided that you can never know a human. She didn't want to trust one ever again.

That left her with a problem.

All the dogs she'd met who didn't trust humans but who lived in the city, had ended up in the belly of the Care & Control beast, about which, it's better not to speak, even if you aren't superstitious.

Froff thought hard and long, and decided that, from what she could remember, nothing specific, she was better off dead.

And being a dog who had been there, of course she incredibly found it.

~~This is the story of that trip.~~

However, a glimpse of after she got there:

"See Spot run," she said, running after Spot, while a man and then a woman yelled, "Come, Gunzen, come."

THE DIVORCE OF DEATH AND PESTILENCE

"The Divorce of Death and Pestilence"
Dim Shores Presents, Vol 1,
Dim Shores, 2020

They met at a bar. She ordered a Beyond Proof Absinthe. He, a Crème de Milk.

It was as amicable as a couple's split can be when each is self-made and unbelievably wealthy, and the boredom with each other is also equal.

"But what about the children?" said Death.

"They're old enough to look after themselves," said Pestilence.

"That's what I'm afraid of," Death mumbled.

Pestilence examined her nails. Death's under-the-breath talkbacks was one of the things about him that got on her nerves so much, she was perpetually jumpy in his presence.

"Like them?" she said, holding out two of her hands.

"Glitter becomes you. But why d'you have those stuck-on things?"

"You know I can't grow mine out."

"Oh, yeah. I forgot. Just as you're so peaky, you need blood for your anemia."

"*You* can talk."

"Why do you insist on arguing when you've got no defense?"

"Really. Like when—"

"Don't bother."

"Your supeeweeowity feel thweatened?"

The rest of the conversation went as well as many do at this stage of an amicable divorce.

Yeah, they still loved each other and all, but the talk of the town was: each thought it very unfair that the other didn't move out of town.

"This town doesn't fit you" Pestilence would have said. Death could have shot back, "You're holding yourself back here,"—if they'd still talked.

Pestilence ran a hand up through her hair, looping a finger in a hand massaging her head. "This town is way too hip for him."

Corruption clucked sympathetically. She loved him for his touch, but he also had such a soothing bedside manner.

Greed was working other ends of her.

Meanwhile, Death walked to an appointment. As it is said of some of the world's richest, he lived modestly. The only time he flew or was chauffeured or took a taxi, or boarded public transport was when he had work in the vehicle. He preferred to walk.

And while Pestilence looked the same as she had before the divorce (the blushing cheeks, the super-glossy eyes, her supermodel height and the way her skin fit so well, it showed off her bones) Death was incognito.

For this appointment he was a cockapoo on the way to a children's ward. This was no contemplative stroll. He was being jerked along faster than he could walk. He yelped every time one of his uncut claws caught in the roughly cast concrete. He needn't have bothered. The woman who was leading would have noticed no protest unless it bit her. Nor would she expect it. She was not only the town coordinator for the branch, but the most active member of Visiting Angels. Her fridge was covered with photos of children at the moment they were given, due to the program, valuable minutes of the joy of a companion animal.

Today's visit turned out to be a disaster—

This was a new experience for Death. He'd never been a dog before, and was surprised at the power they have. He found himself licking the spot of an incipient, undiagnosed, operable cancer—the little girl bent over in bed, stroking his head and uttering sweet little-girl nothings—when he heard a high-pitched scream followed by a series of tortured squeaks. Death looked in that direction and saw a nurse burst into the ward and approach at gale force, stopping by the bed with an ear-hurting rubber-burning turn of heels.

The Angel, who'd been trying to stroke the little girl's resistant head, jerked her hands away, painfully pulling at Death whose lead was braceleted to her like the cop and the perp in many movies but no real life.

"I *told* you, Deb!" The nurse's watch pitched and rolled on her heaving bosom. "Dogs *frighten* people. And they're as illegal here as they are in any restaurant."

The Angel Deb picked up and clutched Death defiantly. "They give joy. I'm taking this up with the Board."

"You do that, and explain the restraining order I'm taking out against you."

The Angel's grip on Death tightened so much, Death finally understood a phrase he'd only known as metaphor. The nurse reached out to the Angel, who recoiled. She put Death and the floor and walked out of the ward, viciously yanking Death, maybe to restore her dignity by proving she could make someone else's life a misery.

Death didn't know if the Angel had capable hearing, nor whether his current canine persona came with an extra whoomph for sound, but they were well down the hall when he heard the nurse say, "Filthy bitch."

Death, too, loves a good massage, and he sure did need it by the time he got home.

"She didn't even notice I filled in for her poor little Harpo," he said.

"That shouldn't discourage you. Does it?"

"Before you, it would have."

"But now you can look back and think of all the joy you brought that little girl."

"Joy!" He pulled his head away from two capable hands. "Tomorrow I'm going back as a surgeon. She doesn't need to die."

"Mmm."

"Joy!" he mumbled, lying back. "They've given her up. But that's ridiculous. I can remove it all. I'll be Doctor Wolf."

"Who's he?"

"A visiting surgeon who's really good. He'd know what to do, but they've already written her off, so she's not his patient."

Life leaned over him and kissed his forehead. "This is why I love you," she said, and smiled wryly.

He felt that. She might as well have poked him. "So why aren't you pleased with me?"

"You're so naive."

He rolled out of her grip and stood up, and even as he gasped with insulted pride, he couldn't help but breathe in her intoxicating scent—fresh grass, seedling oysters, rosebuds, cool springs, etc.—all the opposites of his rot and desiccation.

"You're cute, but," Life said. "If they've given her up, this Doctor Wolf hasn't got a chance of getting near her."

"But he can save her!"

"You know nothing about life, do you?" Life tossed her glossy locks. "Hospital protocol is inviolable."

"But don't you care?"

"Of course I care, dear. But you're all exercised about nothing. You think she'll die soon if that cancer isn't cut out. But you're wrong. She's got years more yet. Now let's get those kinks out of you."

He let himself be coaxed down after she reassured him that what she said about the little girl living wasn't a lie.

"You seemed almost fatalistic," he said. "If I didn't know you, I would have thought you *wanted* her to die."

"Never!" Her eyes watered with passion he couldn't see, but it would have made him feel all the more passionate about her.

He sighed with happiness and relief. As her fingers worked their magic on his wretched bones, he couldn't help comparing this marriage to his first. God, he loved Life. He told her constantly but she never seemed to need it said. It wasn't that she was conceited. She just worked so much harder than he'd ever known one can.

"I hope you're not selfless," he said.

Life laughed. "Do you think so when we make love?"

Meanwhile, Pestilence, Greed and Corruption had no misunderstandings in *their* household. Firstly, they were in no time, becoming enormously successful. They'd bought into the town's nursing homes and daycare—turnkey businesses—and had practically no reforms to carry out, making so much money legitimately, in this town, that Greed and Corruption were each worried about becoming impotent, their creative powers not being taxed at all.

Things looked up when, because they were, this threesome, so flashy and unapologetically crass, they were canvassed to run for office. Greed and Corruption were born to it and had already planned their victory speeches and run for President, when Pestilence stepped in. For some reason, she didn't want to. So they had to give the 'want to spend time with my family' excuse, which always just encourages hopeful hangers-on, but this aspect they kept from Pestilence who tended to have a one-track mind and no subtlety. Still, she had enormous power and a drive that neither of them had. And it was she who gave this trio the global awesomeness that they, in their relative pettiness, could only dream of.

Their neighbors admired their style, but could only imitate it to a small extent.

So that little household should have been blissful, but it was discontent.

Death shacking up with Life discontented Pestilence so much, she tried to deny it to herself, which worked as well as that sort of thing always does. Sometimes, Pestilence felt so feverish, she burned.

There was plenty of smoke before the split, as late one Sunday, Pestilence caught Death eyeing Life in admiration.

"She only *looks* younger than me."

"And smells it, too," said Death. "She makes an effort."

"It's just her genes."

"You're just jealous because we're too alike, you and I."

"I'm just so much looking forward to the time I never have to see your scaly face again."

The divorce should have made them happy. They never argue now, for they don't talk. Death and Life live in a house built in the 1920s—cornflower blue with crisp white trim, a wraparound verandah and a swing chair, in a side of town absolutely bristling with street-library cabinets—little shrines to goodness. The flashy threesome had a house built for them in a part of town that was wasted as a public park.

It's got the usual musts for their class: infinity pool, indoor full-size bowling alley and squash court, the wellness spa, and an ironic 1958 drive-in burger joint in the basement next door to a hyperrealistic inadequately equipped emergency ward for role-playing Epidemic.

Each would have hated the other's new home so much, they wondered how they'd ever managed to live together—and for practically forever, too. Divorce should have solved everything —if only everything had been provisioned for. What was needed was this recognition to keep the peace:

One takes the town. The other rides out.

What should each one care that the other was in town? Being separated only increased each other's individuality. Neither had ever been the yang of a couple. It was pointless to compete, yet that was all the talk.

Competition between these two pulled the town apart like two dogs who'd found a rope of taffy.

It hurt jaws all over town. The rivalry between the two households was the prime topic of gossip, though Death and Life never gave interviews and were only quoted in the type of hearsay that only stands up in paid-off courts.

The talk had all the thrills of bad shit happening to someone else, which should have inoculated it. But it also had a strange power. It made people in the town personally worried for their own safety.

Nobody would admit it, but there was a strong sense of panic building. Irrational foreboding. Nothing specific, mind you. More like worrying if the cops are gonna look in your basement, or if the IRS is finally gonna audit you. Or if the musical chairs will stop and you'll be sitting in the house you just flipped while it falls down the market's black hole. Those and the more specific ones: *Is my job being advertised? I can't afford cover. I can't afford to get fillings, so I'll have to get my teeth yanked, but will the dentist take a personalized poem for pay?*

Fear spread like a disease, transmitted by air. Soon many people in the town wanted the divorced couple in their separate households, to clear out of town. People just wanted to go back to old times when the feuds and spite and evil deeds were done on the screen. When reality was fake.

One group of outraged residents met at House of Pancakes for the 10:00 to 11:00 Seniors Pancake Special. They had planned to canvas lotsa plans, and indeed, spoke with the bravado of drunken retired pirates' accountants, about their plans for vacations. They did, however, compose a note that the craftiest of the lot desktop published two copies of and the most adventurous posted anonymously from the next town: *Property valuations set to plummet. Sell now!*

It didn't work.

Nobody could shift them through gentle nudging, and sure as hell nobody told them to pack their bags.

And nobody knew them well enough to act as a falsely sympathetic shoulder.

This threesome and twosome were like that family that moves in next door that you don't know. Every Saturday she must do something to rile him because you can hear them. and it could be very nasty for you if you interfered. And you certainly don't want to make things worse for her.

The town's zoning couldn't settle things. Nor could the sheriff nor the Freemasons nor the book clubs nor the golf club nor the local branch of the NRA.

The chief negotiator from every church in town had as much effect as if the parties were all human.

An intractable situation, to be sure.

So, surprisingly soon, because the situation became the new norm, that feeling of unease that stalked the town, that feeling of impending doom that hung over everyone—was normalized into the general awfulness.

It was getting on time for Thanksgiving.

Thanksgiving is an odd holiday for Life. It's when everything good gets picked. Pumpkins growing so big, they're due for their first teeth, have their life support hacked off. Apples are plucked. Turkeys so deformed they are all breast, suffer their final indignities.

And in the Life and Death household, Death was into his bbq. This was Death's first Thanksgiving, and he was having the time of his life, preparing. His smoker was a work of supreme craftsmanship, and his touch with meat, something else.

Life was all rawfood, nothing killed. So pecans good, peanuts bad (droppeth from the tree vs. duggeth from the earth). Apples are too confusing (is an apple plucked from the tree, alive or dead?).

The menu was imbalanced in terms of deliciousness, but the efforts could have been human, they both went to so much trouble in preparation and expended so much wasted worry re accommodating guests, for when are relatives *guests*?

Death, in his Life-loving reformed state, wanted no one to remind him of his past, so he insisted to her: "The only relatives should be yours. Invite all you want. I'll just slaughter more pigs."

"Great," said Life. She wasn't being sarcastic. She loved his bbq as much as anyone honest would. They first ate it together while binge-watching movies about pigs who talk. Afterwards, Life told Death about her involvement in using pigs as organ banks for people. "People will soon be able to watch their gardens of guts grow, so to speak. No, it's true."

"But will these transplants work?"

"They should extend life."

So a pig could hardly be thought of as something truly *alive*. "Got room for another rib?" "Always! Oooh, crispy *and* gooey."

Thanksgiving Day arrived on time, having no choice. It rebelled, however, as it always does, by doling out black ice, plane cancellations, flu, and enough anxiety and dread to give the world's greatest negativist indigestion from overindulgence.

The Thanksgiving table at Death and Life / Life and Death's house groaned appropriately.

At one end of the table sat Life. At the other, Death.

He'd been looking forward to this day so much. He had cradled an irrational wish: that Life's relatives would warm to him once they knew how sweet he really was. And now they were finally here, on both sides of the long table.

Life had never talked about her relatives. Death had never felt sure of himself to ask. Now, poised with his carving knife over the obligatory turkey, he looked down this tableful of guests, and froze, not as a model for a Norman Rockwell painting update but with fear and shame. He had no idea how to serve out conversation entries.

Just as well. The only way he was likely to catch anyone's eye was if he went fly-fishing for their eyeballs.

"You can only express yourself illegibly," said Literature to Music.

Vengeance and Spite were whispering in each other's ear, their faces a picture of anticipation.

Forgiveness, dressed in a once white dress smelling of a bestselling drugstore perfume and underarm sweat, cc. 1970, ate slowly and deliberately, making Death's skin crawl as the sound of her crunching celery sticks and tearing open apples with her teeth. When her cheeks hollowed, she was sucking clots of apple flesh dry.

Mercy didn't eat at all. Because her sad smile would have cracked? Death was feeling guilty for not having the social skills to put her at her ease, when she said, "I forgive you" as if there were a 'you' she was talking to.

Suffering made Mercy look like a girl who just wants to have fun. Her back rigid against the chair, the metal on it was making loud reports as it turned white with frost.

Not all the relatives were scary. Rhyme was a party animal, fun and obnoxious in equal measures. Drama was a bore. Color made death wish he had more rods and cones, or whatever was needed to see like a bee, an octopus, a human who could see the full human spectrum.

But for the most part, Life's relatives embarrassed him. "Naive," he mumbled. "I sure am."

How could he have expected them to all be wonderful?

"What?" said Life.

"Nothing."

She couldn't object to his obsession with her. That was all good, but he could be so annoying. This habit he'd developed of looking at her out of the side of his face when he thought she wasn't looking—it rather put her on her guard, which irritated her. For what was there she could ever do that she would be ashamed for anyone to see, or that she wouldn't know about. Yet he looked at her as if—

As if I only have eyes in the front of my head!

The thing is, it didn't matter which light he caught her in, she looked beautiful and smelled fresh. He'd tug on her hair when she was asleep. It was not a wig. Her nails with their crescent moons but absolutely no glitter, were as much a part of her as were her teeth. Her breath was fresher than a sea breeze.

Yet at that Thanksgiving table was: Corruption. He was thick as thieves with Greed, both of them eating and what looked like planning.

And it wasn't as if they were uncles who you can't help but have. Or just the two she'd shacked up with on the rebound after Death.

They were Life's.

Her *kids*.

A compounded sound came out of Death: either 'ghosts in my itches' or a geyser fixing to blow.

Pestilence would have been riled enough to imitate, punctuated with spit—but it cut no truck with Life. "Who'd you think I'd invite?" she asked. "The town's dry cleaner, pretending he was mine?"

"Well, I just thought 'Thanksgiving'. Parents, grandparents, cousins. You never told me you had children."

"Who else would have had them?" she laughed. "You slay me, Death. YSN."

He grinned involuntarily, which happened every time she used that acronym she'd made. It stung less than "You're so naive," but it still made him feel as if he'd been born yesterday. Yet there was no denying its beneficial effect: *I feel so young again.*

Death was dying to know who her first marriage was to. She didn't talk about it. Did she have a marriage or was having kids a hobby? She hadn't had any since they'd hooked up, *but would I know?*

That was another thing about her that he loved, when it didn't slightly miff him. He didn't think she tried to keep secrets, but *Life is so much more complex than Pestilence.*

The town's life continued around these households, as any town's life does. A checkout person after a typical day was driving home to the only rental available, given his credit rating, when the co-owner of VapeAway swerved his bicycle in front to teach this carhog a lesson about bikes—they have just as much right to rule the road.

He didn't live to find out if the driver agreed. The mess the car made of him was so definitive and the road so deserted, the driver sped off, the only witnesses being Death and a Great Horned Owl who was cruising by in this area of scattered businesses born to die, billboards that say "You can rent this billboard" and plots of frost-hardened weed skeletons poised like gangs against broken-down concrete.

Pestilence was only kept moderately busy with her usual flu season (more oldies got shots this year) but things got lively at Steiner Elementary, with a lovely touch of measles. Pestilence had fun this year by sending flowers to the parents of the unvaccinated dead. *It's petty, I know,* she told herself, *but I must get my kicks where I can.* She didn't know, however, that all the parents got so many of these florists' Sympathy Flower Deliveries that they rarely opened the cards. The few who did, just chalked up Pestilence's *Thank You* to a mix-up in cards.

What she didn't know about couldn't bother her. What did, however, was the revelation that the measles outbreak wasn't something for her to celebrate but someone Corruption couldn't stop talking about. "You're the activist," he told her. "Skepticism can't *effect* change."

So true. Healthy skepticism was just a stick-in-the mud. But Corruption had taken to praising Skepticism so much, Pestilence knew he was two-timing, stepping out with this creature on the sly, perhaps attracted to Skepticism's fresh-faced glow. *Damn that healthy look! To have this happen twice!*

And Skepticism must have been attracted to Corruption because that measles outbreak, Skepticism was ashamed to admit to herself, caught her by surprise.

Pestilence felt stabbed. She began to worry about Greed's faithfulness, though he seemed so simple, she felt silly.

She did, however, gather enough courage to contact Skepticism and ask to meet for a coffee or something at Domino's. Somewhat to her surprise, Skepticism agreed, meaning either that Skepticism didn't know enough to have jealousy issues. Or was waiting, fruitless plans at the ready, to kill Pestilence.

Skepticism was in no state for either. Pestilence could only admire the job Corruption had done. Skepticism looked as if Pestilence had treated her, only awaiting Death to land the *coup de grâce*. But it was all Corruption's doing, and Death was nowhere in sight.

Pestilence was almost sorry for Skepticism, so was quite happy to talk shop as if that was the real reason Pestilence had asked to meet.

They both had a lot of work in Yemen. But neither could take credit for the initiative which fell as it often does, to that hogging superstar, War, who is so popular that everywhere he goes, he has a minder who keeps fans at bay, and proffers wetwipes to him if he deigns to shake someone's hand.

They bitched about War as everyone does. He's so much more popular than they could ever hope to be. And the most maddening—his success is built on the most ludicrously shaky structure. "He's lazy and gets rewarded for it!" Pestilence groused. Skepticism nodded, unable to answer verbally, what with the coughs and wheezing.

They parted with a hug. There's nothing to assuage jealousy better than knowing your rival is weaker than you. Still, *that sneaking bastard!* Death had never two-timed Pestilence, hadn't even found someone on the rebound. Life had to be a genuine love, found well enough after the divorce for Pestilence to know this wasn't some dalliance of Death's. Besides, Death had never been frivolous.

Jealousy was too weak a sentiment. What Pestilence felt for Life was hate.

She got, with the help of that bemused couple, Corruption and Greed (sometimes she thought they were the couple and she, just the resident cleaner and Mom), a condemnation by the Council, of the premises where Death and Life lived, on the basis of a bad smell that must be emanating from an uncharted sewer gas buildup.

They moved, but not out of town.

She, again all through the offices of Corruption and Greed, got the town dog pound turned into a puppy mill that sold their prolific end-products to the dogfight industry. Life's address and email were published, and instead of a wreath on L&D's front door, dog feces was smeared, till they moved again, this time to the town's haunted house—a place with such a bad vibe that though anyone could walk in through the bashed back door, not even the stray dogs would shelter there in a blizzard. Hell, the place repelled dust itself.

As haunted houses usually are, the place had countless rooms and had been built by a crazy rich person. So it was on Main Street (as it was built when rich people lived in Main Street houses close enough to smell the greenbacks in the banks), much closer to the center of town (with its ghost of a well, and more recent ghost of a pump and horse-watering station) than the house of Pestilence, Corruption and Greed (so far away from the center, you were either poor or rich).

The ghosts in the center of town salivated as they never had before in all their ghostly lives. They smelt smoke, the hors d'oeuvre of a shootout.

Dust rumbled unlucky lottery tickets down the dusty drag. Starlings made filthy whoopee under the protection of the rain-ravaged eaves of the boarded-up Roxy. Joseph T. Johnson, owner of Solomon's Jewelers, hung an Engagement Ring Special banner in his window, with as much hope as the barber next door had, of attracting anyone under sixty. Johnson the jeweler did best with his Golden Anniversary Special, for that always got them in. Trouble was, the only followup you could hope for from those customers was a repeat sale when they hit Platinum, but by then, the couple was usually half dead.

As in all town's Main Streets in the center of town, the discontented tended to look out. Out to the center for excitement.

Maverick Dispatch's hauler was running late from Arapahoe, Nebraska. The driver had to get the load of cattle to Dodge City, Kansas, before 4 o'clock. They'd supposedly broken through the yard just before he had arrived to load them, and once out, they were filled with the joy of escape. He could have left it up to the farmer and his useless sons, but that would mean he'd still be waiting while those cattle went on the rampage, trampling fields and jumping over or just crushing some of the sorriest excuses for barbed wire fences he'd ever seen. He ended up commanding the roundup. The farmer said he was sorry but you could see he hadn't learned a thing. The trucker wanted to hit him when the cattle were finally in the rig. They hadn't been deliriously happy and merely carefree to escape. They'd been starving. He wished he could take off his belt and have that farmer feel his buckle around the ears, but he had to eat, too. And a fucking customer is always right. He did say, when handing over the docket, "Stick to soy ranching."

By the time he reached intersection of Main and First, he was ready to blow. No music had soothed his savage chest. He put his foot down hard when the light turned yellow, and would have made it through, but for the tanker.

Death is always on call, but that was some emergency rush. The ghosts of the town center had been expecting him, but not for this. There was no drama.

Pestilence didn't pitch up. But she did hear of the crash on the police radio Corruption loved as only a fan can, one who'd as "Corinna78" awarded it five stars and a review: "THE best radio station evah! It never recycles 'hits' and always has something up to the moment, but yet classic."

The crash, its fireball, the certain but as yet unknown toll of life came through in a mixture of loud followed by exaggeratedly calm euphemisms on the police radio. Pestilence could hear sirens rushing past as background ambience. She would have loved to rush to the scene of devastation, hide under the boardwalk and watch Death work, but there was only a boardwalk ghost. Absolutely useless, but . . .

But while he was so busy, the opportunity of a lifetime told her to knock. She patted her hair, and rushed out to confront Life.

Life was in the kitchen, talking to a bowl of oysters when Pestilence burst in.

She looked up and took off her apron. "You look terrible," she said. "Tell Mommy all about it."

Well, if the town had only known, it would have voted for a by-pass. This Mother and daughter brunch shot to hell the prospect of that shootout between exes at high noon.

Pestilence was not only confused, but her skin crawled. "Why didn't you stop me marrying Death?"

"Why should I have?"

"Don't you *care* that your husband . . . my father—"

"Where'd you get that from?"

"Did you have a previous marriage?"

Life closed her eyes. The conversation seemed to tire her. "You young ones. Why are you so conservative?"

"So he's not my father? Who is my daddy?"

"You've gone too far. I am Life!"

"So?"

"So what makes you think I need anyone?"

Pestilence couldn't wait to slink away, but didn't know how to ask permission. This was so humiliating. Worst of all is that she'd always thought of Life as being the hag she had to be, but either this was the best case of plastic surgery *evah*, or Life looked frustratingly *vulnerable*. If only Pestilence could knock Life off her perch, she would cover that fresh face with pustules, fill those flowerlike armpits with stinking suppurating buboes. And drag out the result. The bloody cough, the long slow choke of throat cancer that immobilizes while being licked by a dozen cats teeming with toxoplasma gondii. *If only*—the image of her indecently gorgeous, heartless mother dying of multiple causes while being turned into a crazy cat lady was starting to soothe her ravaged—

"Off with you," her mother said. "And if you come sniveling here again, it should be for a reason. Don't you think I have enough to do without your dithering? You think I have 72 hours to find out what you want? You expect me to take a swab? You never did tell me what you wanted."

Pestilence left in confusion, shame, shock, and elation. *Life is a bitch.*

That bit of excitement in the town center came and passed, and the town no longer felt uneasy at the tension between two households. The reason for this could have been that the tension was all on one side.

Life had never given a hoot about Pestilence, any more than she could afford to, the private lives of Joy, Sorrow, Mercy, Compassion, or cockroaches. She couldn't afford to give them a thought once she'd had them, any more than a termite queen can, her offspring.

Pestilence was so shaken, she went into a period devoted to work. There was always so much to do, and she had to travel so much, she actually got upgraded once to Business Class.

A presidential election combined with widespread distrust of everybody got a Doctors Without Borders overrun in a place where she had just planted Ebola. This disrupted her plans, but only insofar as people helped her far more than she helped herself. She came home more rested than she had imagined she would. That was just as well, for the ministrations of Corruption and Greed were beginning to irritate her. They were so chummy with each other, she felt extraneous.

Life never told Death about Pestilence's visit. So he had no idea that Pestilence had harbored any feelings about him after the divorce. So many people say "I felt dead," after a divorce. If Death had

had an ECG just after the divorce, it might have shown that he was more concentratedly himself than ever—in an intense state of Death.

Physiologically therefore, it is no surprise that his attraction to Life was inevitable.

He carried on working as usual, happy enough to get home for her massages, her fresh beauty, and her fragrance—so unlike those of Death and Pestilence, whose body odors had always thought they were making beautiful music together. As she massaged, he tried not to wince at her rather insensitive but honest putdowns that she couldn't help of his naivete.

Much of his work was odd-job quickies. Mr. Otis Bribiesca, 65, self-employed painter and plasterer, had just installed a stuffed Santa peering into a fake chimney on his roof when he slipped. Miss Adelaide Fern Randles, 82, retired teacher, tripped on her landline phone cord after washing the kitchen floor. Rachel Orland, 15, ninth grader with a 4.0 GPA, died on a rainy Sunday afternoon, officially of a heroin overdose, but the dealer had gone short on the heroin and long on fentanyl.

Then there was the type of job that filled so many wards of the public and private hospitals—those passing through the last weeks of a long life. The end was inevitable, the only differences being the Cause officially recorded, Long Enough Life not being Acceptable Practice.

He did his work and went home. Work and home. He was now embarrassed by his early escapades post-divorce when he was trying to aspire to Life's standards by taking on the comfort-dog persona. He was no comforter. Nor was he creative. He had to face facts. He was merely a garbage collector with as little power to decide who dies, as a garbage collector has to decide what people throw out.

Death wondered what Life saw in him. She, who created constantly.

He was trudging home feeling as tired and unsatisfied with his existence as an Amazon fulfillment center worker when something made him stop on the sidewalk and look in the window of a house. A young woman—more of a girl—was sitting up in a hospital-type bed in what had to be a living room. The curtains had been pulled askew so she had a shocking lack of privacy. She was looking in his direction, so he looked behind him. There was nothing there.

Something hit the window from the inside, so he turned around. Her mouth was making gasping fish movements, and she was still looking in his direction.

Not only that, but those mouth movements had to be: "Help."

He'd always laughed at stories where people see Death. Never in his experience of our human lifetime, had anyone ever seen him, much less talked to him.

He walked up the verandah steps, opened the door and up to her bed where she held out her hand. He took it and felt its warmth.

"Please," she said, and her eyes closed in a spasm. A woman in uniform was sitting on a couch on the other end of the long nave of a living room watching a shopping channel on a wide-screen tv. The girl in bed began to talk to Death. She had hardly any lung power, and the loud product-praising ecstasies coming from the tv would have made anything else impossible to hear, let alone the breathless girl, but Death's powers of hearing had improved no end since his stint as a dog.

Still, it took quite a while, for her pain came in waves. She said she'd had all the treatment they said was possible, but it was still going to kill her in, they said, twelve to twenty months. She never specified what *it* was, and he didn't ask. (As for whether they were right, he didn't know because that was too far in the future for him to have received the equivalent of a job sheet.)

Meanwhile, she had palliative care. He could see how well that was working. As she talked to him, the room started to fill. Mercy came and sat at the foot of the bed. Suffering tried to push her way in between Death and the girl, who didn't see either of them, but did have more severe pain attacks when they sat themselves down.

The girl, who must have considered her name irrelevant by her stage in life, told Death, "It's criminal in this state if I even look up how to end this. And I can't have someone else charged with murder . . . (a long delay here while he waited) But they can't convict you."

A fresh breeze stirred the curtains, and Life appeared. "Just what do you think you're doing?" she said to Death.

"I don't know," he said, for he didn't. "She needs my help."

"What? Don't be ridiculous. She's not dying now." She bustled in, plucking his hand away from the girl's. "Bug off."

"But—"

"But nothing. Life is above all. You most of all should know that, or haven't you learned anything? She'll live as long as I damn well please."

"But look at her."

The girl reached out to him, crying, mouthing *Help*. He snuck his hand forward.

"Get away from her!" screeched Life.

Her delicate nostrils quivered as a foul wind fluttered the curtains.

"Get away from her, you bitch," growled Pestilence.

Life jumped back, stepping on Mercy's toes, who hit Suffering mid-skedaddle.

They fell in a snarling knot.

Pestilence blew it away with such force, the shopping channel yelped once, and shut up. The blessed silence was cut short by a whimper, yelp, then silence—of Suffering, Mercy, or who knows—Life herself?

Pestilence turned to the girl. "This'll be quick," she said, and gave the girl a kiss.

Death got an odd lump in his throat.

"And as for you," Pestilence said. "I've never stopped loving you."

GNAWER OF THE MOON SEEKS SUMMIT OF PARADISE

"Gnawer of the Moon Seeks Summit of Paradise"
Sprawl
Twelfth Planet Press, 2010

We have had a few Trials, & plenty of Flogging, but I believe the Devil's in them, and can't be flogged out...These thefts are generally, of Provisions, and a very aggravating Circumstance in them is, that the Foragers are allowed as much of Salt Beef, Pork, Peas, Flower, Rice, Bread & as good in Quality, as any officer on the Settlement, but still they cannot be contented... The Sheep die very fast from some Cause.

George B. Worgan—*Journal of a First Fleet Surgeon (1788)*

"Remember the eel," Griff refrained from saying, but in his dry, tinder-lighting way, he didn't have to. Not saying was reminder enough.

But this was different. How could there be anything but magic in this adoption, nay—sheltering—of the mythic?

Of course he didn't say me nay. He even went out of his way to make them comfortable, so much so that we and Green Valley must have made headlines in some *Extrasupernatural Times.* As the population expanded here in the Valley, and the complications grew ever more gnarly, Griff never once reminded me—his gentle silence as large as the skywriter's loops in *You'll be sorrrrry!*

And it wasn't like the eel. I don't deny that the episode of the eel was a romanticism of mine, a lack of judgment. And a painful lesson. This, even that vain old pest, 'Queen Titania' with her *A dab a yoor owld budder what you trow out de winder if you pleeez, Maarm,* was throat-catching joy and wonder. And with sufficient caution, there needn't be dread. It had been seven years so far, and nothing really bad had happened, yet.

I dropped the letter into Griff's lap. "And worst of worst," I said, ripping the wall calendar off its nail and tossing that in for good measure, "Is the fact that—"

"Give me a mo', please," he said. The calendar slipped to the floor while he began to unfold the letter onto the open pages of the book he'd been reading.

That first day, when they came, I remember better than yesterday.

After her dinner on the balcony, Rosie barked once. I looked out the window: the hair on her back was raised so high, she looked like a Polish paper cut-out of a wolf. It was that inky time of dusk, too dark for her to see much but she turned her head back to me and looked ahead so that I could get her message. At first I couldn't see, but there, flitting between clumps of tea tree, were what looked like a group of shadows, as indistinct as wallabies but clear enough to see that they definitely didn't hop. Against the brown of the paddocks, they stuck out, in that monotone time of day, as a different shade of grey. They barely topped the arthritic curls of dry bracken fern in the back paddock, and seemed to be moving towards our sliver of creek.

"Come in," I motioned to Rosie. She raced herself to my side, so eager she was panting in little gasps. Griff was ready, having silently watched both of us. We opened and closed the downstairs door making as little sound as possible, and we ran after them, down to the first paddock, over and through the fence, Griff and I trying not to be too cloddhoppy in our gumboots—both of us imitating poorly the quick, silent, almost flattened slink of Rosie, a red kelpie who had sheepherding bred in her as instinct. No senseless barking from this dog, no silly run. When Rosie was within a leap, they dropped into a defensive scrum, bums out like a tattered flower.

Griff and I stopped where we were. Rosie stepped back a pace and sat at my side, her left paw on my rubber-shod toes.

"Come," Griff said. He turned around and began walking to the house. I was too stunned to do anything else but follow, but I looked around.

They were just behind us, following.

Rosie bared her teeth, and ran behind them. For some reason, she didn't trust them, but she was a herder, not a killer unless the word was given.

Griff was studiously not looking back, so I followed Rosie into the pushing position. They didn't seem to mind.

Just short of the verandah, in the invisibility that backlighting from the windows gave him, Griff turned and faced everyone on the piece of the pasture we call "lawn". I motioned to Rosie, and we went around them to stand beside Griff.

"Youse have a nice place," said one of them.

"Aye," six agreed in several keys that didn't make a sextet.

Griff ignored the compliment. "What brought you here?"

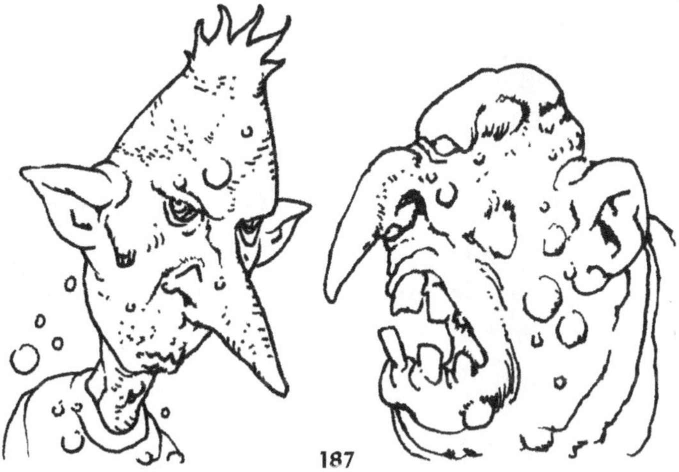

"The drought," said someone. "Thee our dongues."

All seven stuck out their tongues. "Okay," I said. Opened mouths in harshly lit darkness are always horrific.

"Thanking you for your graciousness," said one of them in a sing-song, I couldn't tell who. They were all of a group, bobbing, smiling, sweeping off hats. "We saw your green field and this bright silver creek," said another.

"In the dark," said Griff.

"We'll be good as rain."—a wheedle from the one on the far left.

"We're leprechauns!" said the smallest one.

His hat was torn off his head and he was slapped with it. "Fie, Griff," said the slapper built like a miniature bouncer. "D'you take this master and his beauties for a dunce-lot?"

The one they called, oddly enough, "Griff" (but who the shadows were either kind to or who was really pretty in a petulant, full-lipped way, so I'll call him Byron) hung his head.

Rosie yapped once, took her foot off me and poised, just waiting for my "Go" and she'd nip them anywhere I wished.

"Uh," I said. She stepped back and sat, this time with her bum on my foot, so she was just that little ways forward.

I was pinching myself so hard, I knew my head was clear.

I patted Rosie's head.

"Don't mind her," I said to young Byron. "She doesn't know that leprechauns bring luck."

"Our ancestors is First Fleeters, since you asked," said Bouncer, though we hadn't. I was too curious to begin to ask, and *my* Griff (what a coincidence!) too infuriatingly reserved.

A leprechaun who might have been just past his teens rolled up a trouser leg and bent his knee so it caught a bit of harsh light, just enough to show the bulging and the crevasses. His knee looked like a tree bole, it was so thick and scarred. "Stowed away in a hogshead, missus."

Missus!? I didn't feel old.

"I thought you said your descendants was First Fleeters," Griff said with a smile.

"Yar, your honourship," said Bouncer, giving the young one a dig in the ribs. "He got that knee at the Westfield Shopping Mall in Sydney. You know it, don't you?"

"They sell knees, do they?" said Griff.

"Waddid I tell you, Tom," said one of them from behind. He stepped forward. "Not to put too fine a point on it, me name's Aloysius. Young Twiddlefoot here was showing off his heels, jigging atop the sign."

"Gravy to that," said Twiddlefoot. "On your grandpa's teeth it was. I was at that high school in Emu Plains, a skateboard flip."

A bark of a laugh came out of Griff.

"I knowed you'd have wit," said Twiddlefoot.

"You knowed that, too?" Griff scratched an eyebrow. "It's alright, Rosie."

Rosie's grrrrr wouldn't turn off. Her fur was vertical over her spine. I stroked her back and it was clammy, which is surprising since what would she know of supernatural versus normal? To a dog, every stranger is just a new combination of smells and shape, and her first duck met wouldn't be any stranger than these leprechauns.

"Me name's Billy," said Tweedlefoot. "We's vegetarians."

"Don't let Tweedlefoot give himself airs," said young Byron. "We can live on a look and a sip."

"A look and a sip," came the chorus.

Griff rubbed his chin. "If you're very good... you can stay for a day or two. Down there." He pointed to the creek. "Where I can see."

Like a pack of cards that shuffles itself, they lined up in a kind of order that must have meant something to them, swept their hats off their heads, bowed as low as their various states of legs would allow, and skipped off. In a heartbeat they were lost in the tussocks, then lit up by a raucous trill of pennywhistles.

"Come, Rosie," I said, and though she came along with us at my side, she made it clear from the grunts she uttered just softly enough not to be considered disobedience, that our stupidity of trust was dangerous, but she'd protect us.

We walked back across the paddocks and up to our house, built on the small rise that overlooks them and the tree-fringed creek. I couldn't shut the door, and I couldn't settle down, and neither would Rosie.

Griff was exasperatingly calm.

"It's a pity," I said finally, teased beyond endurance, "that dogs have no sense of the marvellous. If she only knew: leprechauns!"

"If they're First Fleet descendants, I'm Captain Cook."

"Who cares when they came?" I snapped. "They're here. And they picked us to shelter them."

"They smelled Rosie. They're not leprechauns. They're cluricauns. Or they've got it in them."

My lip curled. "You're too learnéd, doctor Bartlett, with all your ethnogodological studies. Leprechauns too common, or too close for duh loiks a yuh?"

I motioned to Rosie to come, and was just leaving him to his infernal books when he cleared his throat in that way he has. I hate it but I can't ignore it.

"Sure they're leprechauns," he said, "but just as you're from one stock and I'm from another, blighted one. A cluricaun is a breed of moon-loving leprechauns."

"So?"

"They favour that light for their riding on the backs of sheep... and dogs... to the death. Not theirs, mind you."

"Oh, Griff!" This was too much. My stomach felt kicked. I dropped to the floor and hugged Rosie.

"You're smarming doesn't work on her, you know."

I stood up, embarrassed by both of them. "What are we going to do?"

"I'm sure they're reformed. And you *do* want them here, don't you?"

I nodded, unable to speak.

"From my head in the clouds, I'll keep an eye on the both uh yuz."

So ever since then, more and more feral supernaturals found Green Valley. I say feral because none of them belong here—in Australia, that is—they're as feral as cane toads. We all want to meet a bunyip, but no indigenous supernatural visits.

I grabbed the damn letter off Griff's lap. Giving it to him was a politeness, since I'd just told him what it said. I needed to point out to him who never remembers anniversaries, preferring New Year's Eve to surprise him:

"Not only is he coming at four o'clock tomorrow, but tomorrow's sundown starts the Night of the Waxing Gibbous Moon."

At that, he ran out of the house. He always comes through in emergencies. This was. The day before the night is always a raucous one, with spirits so keyed up that I've always worried lest we get a casual visitor. He went down the hill to the west, and I went east towards the creek. That was 11 a.m.

At 1 p.m. by the crook of the creek, the meeting met. Present were Griff, myself and Rosie; and one wombat, the only one who consented to come out of his hole in the rude glare of day; twenty-five leprechauns (including the original seven good-as-gold reformed cluricauns), eleven elves, an almost blind boggart, a couple of German elves who were so happy of a home that they didn't even enjoy bragging about their terrible pasts, one hag of a fairy who insists she's Queen Titania, three wraiths; and in the creek, two nymph sisters, a flighty water dragon and a slick-back skink. A lonesome snake-neck turtle and a rowdy cabal

of yabbies clacked their giant claws. Towering above us, and the eucalypts if he'd have cared to, was Henry. He'd be hurt if I called him "the troll", though he still has cravings for bread made with human bones. Watching from the stands, as it were, was the usual rabble — including, in their own way, the witchetty grubs.

Rosie sat beside me, her foot resting on my gumboot. She gave me the strength that nothing but a loving dog can, and I like to think that I gave her some, too. You can never tell if a cluricaun is *truly*, forever and ever reformed.

The female caretaker (me) read the letter.

"Dear Sir stroke Madam," I whispered to get their attention, then opened my diaphragm and projected, bold and black as the type: "Noxious Species Act two thousand and five, Notice to Enter and Inspect for Introduced Species."

The nymphs screamed and clutched each other. Griff cleared his throat but there was no need. I wasn't trying to stir up nonsensical fright, so I dulled my drama instinct and intoned the rest of the letter in as exciting a manner as the man in the phone who says "At the third stroke... it will be three. Forty-three. And fifty seconds."

The notification pinned the Valley down to some numbers on a master plan, then ominously, to *ongoing responsibility and committment* [sic] blah blah *enter your premises*, then the chilling *Thank you for your cooperation.*

Well before *cooperation*, the meeting turned into the normal pandemonium of get-togethers at the Valley. The water dragon and skink were having a who-can-open-his-mouth-wider contest, a yabbie was trying to get the turtle to play the yabbies' favourite game, snap; and Queen Titania (or Q.T. as Griff and I call her privately) was leaning over the stagnant pool with its metallic mirror of eucalyptus oil, doing facial exercises though she is wrinkled as a dried chili.

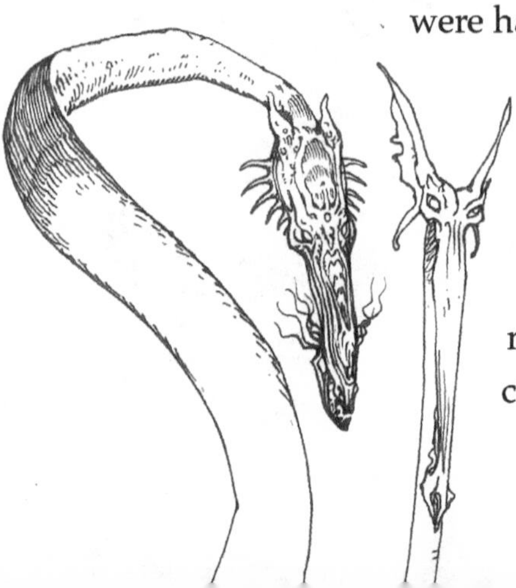

"Hear hear!" said Griff.

I waved the letter. "It's signed, 'yours faithfully'! Hilarious!"

"You're wasted here," he said. "Hey, Fey and Feyette. She didn't *mean* hilarious."

One of the nymphs, Fey or Feyette (we named them, but never could tell them apart) had swallowed mid-giggle, and choked. Her sister patted her on the back, while hiccupping. The wombat was already walking away on his short bowlegs, toward his closest hole and sleep.

I wanted to kick Griff, I was so embarrassed. The meeting was a fiasco. Why had I taken drama classes?

He turned to me and shrugged.

"Can you fell a tree in the road or something?" I asked.

"Who signed it?" said Henry, stretching his arm out till he could have grabbed the letter if he weren't such a gentleman.

After reading, he sniffed. "John Smith."

"Some people have that name," said Griff.

"As I am Thor," said Henry who had asked to be called John Smith when he arrived, because he said he didn't want to be known as the usual: *Tungl Sjötrungnis*. We had to look that one up and I wouldn't want it either. Gnawer of the Moon.

Henry understood the letter.

Henry got what I couldn't get: the meeting's attention for a while. He handed me the letter, now scented with his dry rankness—rock lichen covered with snow?

"I'm sorry," I said to everyone, "We'll have to move the Night of the Waxing Gibbous Moon to another time."

"Wax facts," said a leprechaun.

Griff coughed.

"Moon's soon," said another leprechaun.

"Bibulous bib," said another.

The nymphs drummed their hands on the pond.

"You're too late," said Griff.

"Why do you have to state the obvious?" I turned on my heel. Rosie was at my side. I was crying and I didn't want Henry to see me. This wasn't the first time that I wished he fit under my bed, or perhaps in it. I am ashamed to say that I stomped home trailing a confused Rosie, and went to bed with a box of chocolate prunes, ate the whole box and fell asleep dreaming of stroking Henry's lichen-encrusted shock of hair.

The Night was Griff's idea back when only seven leprechauns (ok, reformed cluricauns) lived here. "Nature outs," he'd said. "And the supernatural. If they can't let rip sometimes, then what good's a sanctuary?"

"Are you out to lunch?" I said. "What if someone hears something, or comes down the road and sees? We are in a valley just off the highway. Remember?"

"There's always that chance. They can't wait to see what's to the side in the forests in the dark as they drive between cities on this featureless road. After all," he yawned. "It does get boring in the stretch between McDonaldses. And drivers are always on the lookout for a turnoff to a dirt road that might lead them to someplace they can get some real home cooking."

"I'm serious!"

"So let 'em eat Rosie," he had shrugged.

Griff woke me. His face was a frightful scene. "Shave," I told him.

"Do what you can to yourself," he said. "And see if your boyfriend has any bright ideas."

"Don't call him my boyfriend."

"Whyever not," Griff grinned nastily. He never could hold his moonshine, and the brew made by leprechauns dissolves corks.

"You don't have any bright ideas," I pointed out. "*You* wanted the status quo kept up. So *you* should sort out the problem of hiding them all today."

"Why don't you turn your wiles on the inspector?"

That hurt. "Why don't you?"

"Please. You could wear a dress."

I sat up in bed and really looked at him sitting on the side clutching his head. I sorted through what he had just said, the dear. He really thought I could seduce the inspector. Sometimes Griff surprises me, he is so wonderfully unworldly. I put my arms around his waist and rested my head against his back.

"I don't really love Henry, you know. I just appreciate him."

Griff turned and kissed me, sweet and slow, only releasing my lips when he was finished. "I should have helped you put it off," he said. "Seriously, why don't you see if Henry has any ideas?"

So I threw some clothes on and ran out to find him. He was busy tearing lichen from his head with one hand while soaking wads of it in the creek to make compresses that the fairies swore by, but the loudest sufferers scorned. "It hurts less if you keep still," he said, the picture of calm reason. Around him, the paddock was as noisy as a fair, and as active. Moans, cries, and the stamping of little feet rent the air. Leprechauns don't get the concept that jumping up and down in rage over feeling sick never helps them feel well.

Rosie gave Henry's leg a friendly lick. He stopped that horrible ripping from his head, to smile at us.

"Could we talk?" I yelled up to him.

"In a manner of speaking." He has a very dry humour.

He lay down on the ground, making sure his feet didn't flatten any bushes. We discussed the problem of getting everyone hid, and that didn't seem half the challenge of getting everyone to quit bloody stamping, moaning, singing—to be, as Henry said, "quiet as a pin." Unless they were, even the doziest inspector's curiosity would be pricked, and then... Neither of us discussed the problem that was bothering me the most. I didn't because I was feeling too emotional. Hangovers from chocolate-eating do that to me. There was no place that Henry could hide. He had only been able to smuggle himself to Australia because a once-in-a-lifetime opportunity arose.

For many years, Gnawer of the Moon Tungl Sjötrungnis—this chill-bitten, damp and lonely troll whose borne fate was to live in supreme discomfort, blaming the moon—for untold-many years, this creature of the dark Norwegian forest had raged against his fate, earning a fearsome reputation. His first serious dreams were of Polynesia, and he spent moons yearning until he learned how small each island is, and how cluttered with palms. Just lying down would be like sleeping on a porcupine. So Polynesia was out, dashing his South Pacific dream.

Then he learned about Australia, especially the special quality of its sun. Stronger than anywhere else, he read, and so many artists in colonial days came without being sent. They sought more than the exoticism of animal and plant. They came to capture that unique brilliance of light, on canvas. Indeed, the strength of this sunlight is so great, he was thrilled to read—*it can change skin cells.* But now that he was seriously contemplating emigration, getting to Australia was a problem. Sure, in not so many strides, he could have jogged to Siberia, leaving only footsteps where there was forest. But even the largest troll can't stride across oceans, and he'd never learnt to swim.

All his learning was accomplished from the books delivered each week from the local bookmobile. He read them and left them in the delivery / pick-up box made from a dumpster. The librarians used him as an example to the children. *If Tungl has a thirst for learning, everyone should, since* (and this hurt Tungl, not that he showed his hurt and anger in any way) *someone so ugly, and with such shocking habits in his heritage should make even the pug-nosed lazy boy a model of beauty, thought and genius.*

One day Tungl heard timbercutting machines almost underfoot, and soon his dreams were more alive with light and sun than ever. The Norwegian mining-equipment company

Skarpnord was setting up a building site—one so big they had to flatten a forest for it and build a special road down to a special dock for a specially fitted out ship—all because Skarpnord had won the contract to build a very special (and technologically ground-breaking) extraction plant for Abednego Resources, owners of the humungous yet recalcitrant Father Christmas laterite nickel deposit in Western Australia. A big part of the golfing-resort-hotel-size heat exchanger system that Skarpnord was to build, was a drum about the size and shape of a wasp's abdomen, if the wasp were the size of a soccer-star's beachside cottage.

All of this massive plant was to be loaded from their factory site onto purpose-built road transporters so big that Tungl wished they'd been around to play with when he was a toddler. Just one tyre of these rigs could flatten a town hall to the thickness of rye crisp. They would board their ferry for its two-month sail halfway around and down the world, to a new heavy-duty mining port in South Australia. From there, on huge roads built for the project, the plant would be trucked all the way to the Father Christmas deposit, a distance estimated to take anywhere from three days to two weeks depending upon what fails, since something had to fail and everything about this mining project was stretching the limits of what was known—everything except the amount of ore in the ground, which was almost unbelievable.

Tungl learned all about this from his little radio, something a visitor to his forest conveniently left behind one day, when Henry sneezed. Everyone was so proud to speak of this project that would earn Norway so much money—and besides, there needed to be much urging and announcements of the high pay to get enough skilled tradesmen to want to live for two years in a place where the company was the only source allowed, of liquid companionship. And very stingy at that.

Two years passed and the project was not finished. Specifications had been changed and parts had failed in testing. But by the end of the first year, the trees in Tungl's home forest relaxed their limbs and spread their roots, quite recklessly, as this middle-aged troll trusted that Skarpnord would succeed.

"The sun will dry out my scrofula," he sang, "and proper hair will grow on my head. O, I'm leaving to where I can shed my rags and walk about the clean, uncluttered-with-forest outback, wearing a tan of gold."

For he had been spying on developments. One advantage of his shivering, damp, lichen-infested state is that the soles of his feet were soft and silent as velvet from the fungus that grew between his toes—and grew and grew till he had to wrap it around his feet and tie it in a soft bow at his ankles.

So finally, one afternoon he spied the great wasp-abdomen-shaped drum being picked up by a crane that even he, a giant troll, thought was pretty big. Two tense hours later, the drum was in position and tied onto its special transport rig.

That night he crept up to it and crawled in. It was surprisingly comfortable. He fell asleep with his head cradled by its cool, dry inside.

He woke feeling as if he had eaten a bad man. His stomach rolled. No, it was his head. He pulled a periscope out from his rags. He'd made the thing from some parts he'd borrowed from the Skarpnord factory (the loss of these pressure vats had cost three months and litigation that is still making lawyers smile). The troll looked up through the periscope. The open end of the vat was pointed halfway between ground and sky. He expected to see top of the hill that looked down on the building site, but saw only grey clouds—and they *lurched.*

Tungl Sjötrungnis beat his head, half in anger, half in superstitious dread. *At sea already! And I never said goodbye to the land of my fathers (cursed though it be).* He would have cried out, but didn't dare. Not that he was afraid of any man. He feared, rather, that if he showed himself, the ship might never dock. He needed a happy captain and a calm voyage.

He never got a calm voyage. Gnawer of Moons they aren't, any more than they are Sea-Legged. By the time the ship docked one dawn, the troll was rolled and coated in eighty-seven days and eighty-eight nights of sickness.

That night, the moon threw shards of light into the tank. The air felt wonderfully dry and warm. His stomach was sore but quiet enough that he was eager to leave, to breathe and drink in this sun-blessed land. With both hands gripping the open edge, he pulled himself up, but he must have jerked, for all of a sudden the load shifted on the rig. He was thrown back into the bottom of the round-bottomed vat, his head banging against the side. Something outside snapped, and the vat rolled off the rig. His head ended up under his feet, but he straightened his legs and threw out his long arms. These, as long as railroad carriages, ended this stage of his momentous trip. He pushed the vat off him, and kicked it away in a fit of release.

"I stink!" he said, and strode away toward a hill that he saw to the left. It looked under this new moon, wonderfully soft. "If I can't find a lake to wash in, I can at least give myself a powder."

And so began his new life where the light is marvellous, where the fungus between his toes dried up so much that by the next full moon, his feet in that desert were hard as an iron frypan, and cracked and sore. And before he had counted the unfamiliar stars, Tungl missed his old home.

There, he was a natural part of the landscape and history. In this new land, he had always to hide. Hide from the hunters.

It wasn't fair. He hadn't eaten a single person for many years, and hadn't started up the habit again. His nose still dripped, not because he had a cold any more but because he was so sad, and so hungry.

Under the pitiless sun, he curled against a hill, hoping to blend in to the landscape. "No-one provides for me here," he cried out, and his voice sounded too loud in this strangely naked land.

Somehow when he made those plans back home, it hadn't occurred to him that in this new land he would find no tubs of *Rodgrot med flote*, his favourite berry pudding with cream; nor piles of butter-dripping *lefse* made as he liked it, thick as a woodsman's coat and long as a beechtree log. Nor could he, while propped against his favourite hill back home, pick at a great stack of books piled high as a cabin—all left for him by the good people who know the forest and what is good for them. Someone even knew that he liked his *Tysvær Bygdeblad* delivered fresh daily.

Instead, he learned that his landing as a stowaway would not get him anything but trouble. Some introductions here are better than others. Such strange prejudices about who belongs here and who is vermin. He stole a ute and used to put it to his ear to listen to the radio, and learn. A giant hole is dug for a tower, and that is good. Mountains are cut away and sold off and that is good. A rabbit digs a hole for his family and that is bad, so he and his family are hunted.

Then there was one of those tales between the lines that Tungl gleaned from an upbeat science report: *Sydney's native bush rats were unintended victims of a campaign to exterminate foreign black rats during a plague epidemic in 1900, according to new research by scientists who plan to reintroduce the native rats into bushland around Sydney's harbourside suburbs. A prestigious suburb on Sydney's north shore will be invaded by native rats in an attempt to wipe out its weaker rodent cousins.* His ears burned but he not only didn't change the channel, but made himself listen to the end and past it, to the callers' reactions. The only upside to this horrific incident was that it made the giant troll stop wishing he were small. The reporter's voice was high-pitched with good-newsiness. *The natives are harmless. Unlike the newcomers, they don't carry disease, and only eat bush foods.* There was not a word of sympathy for the community of rats whose founders landed in the 1840s. Tungl ground his teeth as he thought of the natives' taste for city foods back in 1900. Like all humans salivating at chocolate, and all trolls drooling at bread of human bones, Gnawer of the Moon had never known a rat who preferred the wild and hungry life to bread, cheese, and the desserts of modern life: boxed foods, soap, and electrical wiring. The report got even more shocking when it named the rats to be displaced: black rats and Norwegians. At that, Tungl's head felt clonked by a felled tree. "I'll *never* be accepted," he moaned. The after-show callers were enthusiastic and talked so knowingly, like the one who said, "Generally the *native rats* stick to the bush and have a much nicer disposition than the *introduced* rodent species that we find in and around town."

After that, Tungl made extra sure to keep away from people. He tried to forget the report but couldn't cleanse his mind of the chirpy sound of the words *trap vermin*. He wished he were brave instead of wandering hopelessly, hungrily, always looking for safer places to cower and hide.

He scrounged the outside of their settlements and thus met his first otherworldly at the above-ground tip by the underground mining warren of Coober Pedy, when his bare leg was stung with the sharp-edged, licked-out lid knifed from a tin that once held Champion Salted Sheep's Tongues. "Schmeckt!" he heard, and he reached out and caught the little gnome, who turned out to be so hungry that he had thrown caution of people to Chance. They travelled for a while together, meeting many others who don't "belong" in this country: thurses, colt-pixies, goblins, lanthorns, unintelligible korrigans, boggleboes; and in South Australia, lots of German kobolds. Tungl soon found whole camps of assorted supernaturals, otherworldlies, call them what you will, it's not what they call themselves—squatting within smell of the two ends of a typical one-main-street town. Out past the petrol station on one end, and the place that sells takeaway chicken on the other.

But these are dangerous places, where bragging and thieving is rife. Fear imbues the shiftless residents with a lack of honour, which repulsed the discriminating troll. He recoiled, also, from the main topics of conversation: how horrible, ugly, and uncivilised this new country is compared to the old home wherever (their talk put pause to Tungl's nostalgia), how unfair the prejudices here; and how ridiculous and inferior the supernaturals here, mainly the hated Bunyip—a running sore of a topic. No-one had ever seen a bunyip, but they hate bunyips with a hate born of jealousy. The leprechauns hated them the most, as their leprechaun ancestors had been the most cherished "back," as the ones who cursed their ancestors said in their sad lilt, "back where we-uz belonged".

But the Norwegian troll couldn't really look down on the leprechauns. These hadn't made the trip. He had. They had been handed fate, and usually made music from it. One heartlessly hot day while he hid in the ravages of an old gold mine in southwest New South Wales, he heard the lovely trill of an Otherworldly pennywhistle. He halloed back in the jingo he'd learned on the road.

"You've as much right here as I," he called softly, but not too softly, for he'd learned that leprechauns are as bold when unthreatened as the little native rainbow lorikeets who leprechauns resemble so well, even to the range of screech and jingle that both are capable of, as music.

Petrus, for that was the name of the leprechaun, danced right up to the giant's feet, bold as a lorikeet. He was almost pathetically grateful for the company. "For a talker like me to have no audience," he said, "is as bad as a tree having branches with no leaves."

Tungl Sjötrungnis ignored the fact that in this dry country the average tree is a stick with mostly naked branches.

Petrus talked, and talked, and soon had talked so much without Tungl once interrupting, that the leprechaun stopped and said, "Now you big ugly lichen-ridden troll. You've earned my respect, so listen and I'll tell you something true."

He talked of a valley where they could escape to. That was where he was headed, an exclusive place known only to a few. Where even a troll would be welcomed, where the likes of them would not be hunted. Where they could eat their fill and a troll could stand up in the middle of the day and beat his chest, "if that so be yous's pleasure."

The leprechaun was a compulsive liar, so Tungl had not believed a word of his story about having met and charmed to dance, the fabled meat-eating kangaroo. But this story of Green Valley was different. Petrus started out telling with typical irrepressible overembellishment, but ended in a speech of such down-to-earthness, such serious and unpoetic reason that Tungl believed it all so much that while listening, he shut his eyes to see the sun shining on this sanctuary and he felt the warmth of welcome. His heart beat faster, so eager was he to get there.

He was just trying to figure out how he could interrupt to thank Petrus for the invitation to accompany him to Green Valley (though accompany wasn't quite the word, as the leprechaun's idea was that the troll would carry him in his pocket "whilst we make tracks of a night" and that Petrus would slip out and steal for them, using the leprechaun's ability to be invisible at will) when the leprechaun jumped up in fright.

"Sorry, I haven't eaten for a long time."

Petrus took his hat off, wiped his forehead with a polka-dot handkerchief. "We taste bad," he laughed, and pulling a hot cross bun out of his pocket, held it out. Tungl smiled and shook his head. "A crumb to me, but a meal to you."

"I've a dozen of them," said Petrus. "Have six." So Tungl did, and as soon as night fell, they started out for the promised sanctuary. Petrus was an excellent guide and as wily a provider to his adopted friend as a real, not fairytale fox.

The only aspect of Petrus' personality that annoyed Tungl was the leprechaun's avarice for gold. He loved talking about gold's beauty and its smell, how he wished he could build a house of gold bricks "wid gold bars on me winders". How "I tink me mudder ate gold bambrack when she were carryin me." At these times he'd go so soppy, he'd cry, and he'd lay such a thick brogue on his tongue that the Norwegian was tempted to answer, "Leftse u! Sjöt junking wörden örd?"

Gnawer of the Moon never talked about the hoard in the tunnel in his mountain, tributes to his family over fourteen extremely long-lived generations. Gold had always bored him, so much that he forgot it when planning his emigration. He had packed a knapsack with dried herrings, a change of clothing, and a pile of food for the soul. That pile embarrassed him even now. He had filled his pockets with that last delivery of library books. He still carried them, but after that sick sea voyage and such hard travelling, even if he were to sneak up one night to the Norwegian Embassy in Canberra and drop them lightly on the roof, the books were in too shocking a state for the library to ever accept them back. Of all the impossibilities he felt about going home, this was the greatest—his shame.

This is probably the reason I fell in love with this brutish-on-the-outside sweetie. He unburdened himself to me shortly after arriving, and it all was because he felt the fear in Rosie and wanted to assure me and Rosie that he would protect us, and wouldn't let even one cluricaun revert to type. He knew their tendency, just as he had learned, to his cost, the irrepressiveness and irresponsibility of leprechauns in general. Petrus had been good to his word, as far as he could be. He had directed his new troll friend to Green Valley, and their first days had gone very well. But Petrus had stirred up the gold avarice to such a pitch that one day I found a clutch of leprechauns in my pantry unwrapping and turning inside out, the wrappers from a box of Red Roses chocolates. "I swear it's real," said one. "Pinchbeck!" said Petrus in disgust. "And you say she's not got a proper jewel box?"

"Not with gold," I said, causing a chorus of "Gravy!"

But Tungl craved no gold. Learning, yes. He was too shamed about the book theft to ask us for any, though Griff's library lines every wall and occupies more of our "living space" upstairs than we do. I like to say, "We camp amongst the piles," but Griff doesn't hear me.

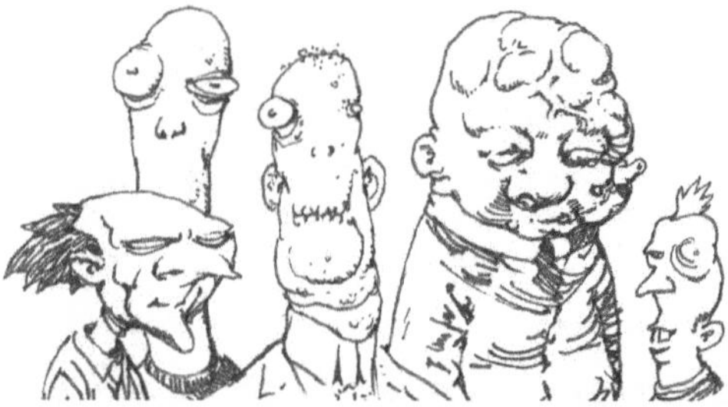

Anyway, here we were, and it was 3:00 p.m. already. The inspector was due at 4:00 p.m., the time that every weekday, Griff takes a break for what I'd called "your sacred hour", so I had to deal with the inspector by myself. The Night of the Waxing Gibbous Moon was due at dusk, 5:36 p.m. by the chart. But that celebration would never come because everyone would be nabbed in what I could only imagine as a holocaust of unimaginable proportions.

So far the only ferals declared Enemies of the State were the ones that the inspector would tick off on his form as our land being free from, the newest uninvited "introduced species" being something so mundane it made me want to laugh: Parramatta grass, an enemy because it is unpalatable to cattle. So are those houses being built on the dairy land near Kiama, but those houses aren't declared feral.

Anyway, as I was saying, here it was now, 3:45 p.m. already as the time flew, fifteen minutes from Hour Zero. And though most of our residents had the ability to make themselves scarce if not invisible when they have their wits about them, they lose powers when they're emotional, and now they were so festival-oriented and stuck in their newly-acquired tradition that not a one could pull the slightest trick, let alone disappear. Green Valley was as loud as a circus, a cacophony of commotion, and I was one crying wreck.

Henry had resigned himself to his fate, and was trying in his own way to make me feel better. He patted my head. "A true friend is life," he said, which only made me cry more. Rosie looked at both of us with eyes that even a scientist would identify as intelligence.

A car horn sounded. I jumped and saw Henry involuntarily cringe. The manic dancing and yelling around us might have slightly dampened. Henry and I looked to the road, though Rosie looked toward home. The horn blared again.

"Hey," yelled Griff. "Get your arses up here. Tell the queen I'll give her a looking glass. Tell her anything but rip her away from the creek, and those dozy nymphs. Hoy, you leprechauns. I've got gold." He waved his arms like a maniac. The leprechauns needed no second invitation.

Henry gently scooped up the ancient fairy, who only stopped cursing him when he placed a blossom crown on her shiny yellow skull. I had meanwhile organised everyone else. The troll loaded everyone around him, his scurfy brows creased with care and responsibility. In three of his strides we caught up with the leprechauns at the top of the hill.

"C'mon!" Griff said, running to the back of the house. He had opened the roller door to the ground floor, not our living space, but what we call "the dump"—piles of books he hasn't read in ten years but that he might refer to, a set of blacksmithing tools, the laundry, a few pieces of my craft equipment.

"Everyone in, and stand against the wall," ordered my normally mild husband.

Henry unloaded everyone with speed but the gentleness of a mother crocodile, even querulous Queen Titania. "You be good," he said to everyone. "I'll be on my way."

"Where to?" Griff said. "I've cleared the place for you."

And he had. He hadn't turned on any lights, and the contrast here to the bright outdoors was stark but I couldn't see any piles of junk.

"Crawl in," I said to Henry.

Like a lurcher fitting through a cat door, he just managed to get in, and stretched out where Griff directed. Griff ran behind him and rolled the door shut. Everything had happened so fast that everyone was silent. It was so dark I could read my watch by its illumination—3:55.

"Where's me mirror?" asked Q.T. in a voice like a cockatoo.

"Good things come to those who wait," said Henry behind me. I turned around and gazed at him, trying to remember every loved bit of lichen. In the darkness, I could just imagine his expression. A peaceful half-smile? I could just make out his form, propped up by one hand as he rested on his side like some Nordic buddha.

Any time now I'd hear the car of the inspector coming, but in five minutes it would be sacred hour, Griff would be upstairs, and who could keep this mob from breaking out and wreaking their own ruin? Griff had no gold.

I exploded. "What false saving!"

Griff turned his back.

"That's right," I said. "Go upstairs to your beloved genie, and I'll go out now and make myself irresistible."

"Where's our gold?" "My mirror!" "I'm scared!" sounded all at once.

"Shut up!" said Griff. "And close your eyes . . . Now open them."

He'd flicked two switches. The room was bathed in the harsh shadows of one fluorescent tube, and into the silence cut, "Now you can have Bessemer cookware for half the normal retail price."

"Griff!" I burbled, unable to contain my remorse.

"Get out and charm the pants off the bastard," he said gruffly. It was 3:59, and as I ran out, I heard both the bump and grind of the *I Dream of Jeannie* opening music, and up by the highway, the slow bumping of someone driving like a careful old codger on our dirt road.

He was young, freshly out of uni with an ecology degree, and he was charmed by me. I had the important parts of *Noxious Weeds of Australia* memorized (acting classes did come to *some* use). And I told him of the time I found a patch of fireweed only the year before and —horrified—plucked it out and burnt it. He was, despite his age, like most inspectors—too lazy to walk anywhere—so he inspected from where he stood, leaning on his immaculate 4WD, close enough to the house to hear the sound of loud television music. By loud, I mean just that. It roared like TVs in homes where people leave them on all the time.

It was as obnoxiously loud as duelling TVs in public hospitals, but as normal. "Come to Summit Ridge," I heard while the inspector talked of a dairy farm he'd just come from. He'd put the place under heavy penalties because he'd found some Parramatta grass.

"Summit Ridge," I heard again, while he talked about his difficulties finding some of these ridiculously placed properties. "Summit Ridge Estates," I heard with half a mind, wondering what was keeping the mob inside from breaking into laughter at that ad. But my guest was having such a good time talking that he was getting downright flirty. In the background was the constant patchwork of zany noise. Then suddenly the inspector stopped talking, put his hand up to his ear, and my heart jumped to my mouth.

"That isn't *Bewitched*, is it?"

"Yes," I giggled. "It's my husband's sacred hour. A genie followed by a witch."

"That old stuff. My parents love it too," he said. He scribbled something on a form that amounted to a pass with honours, and shoved the clipboard at me, pointing to the place where I needed to sign. I pulled my pen from my pocket and barely touched the paper before he tore off my copy, handed it to me, said, "See ya," opened his car door, turned the engine on with one hand and slid behind the wheel. He was on his way so fast that you'd think he was fleeing the scene of a crime.

I read the "customer's copy" whilst I was still in his rear-view mirror as he drove back up to a real road at the speed of a snail protecting its underbody. The small print said that the next inspection would be in two years, that today's inspection cost $155, due in seven days. "Pay to order of the Council Clerk..."

Griff had done it, for this year. Whether he'd be able to do it again was anybody's guess, but the Night of the Waxing Gibbous Moon was due in less than an hour. I opened the door, flourishing my paper in triumph. The hell, I thought, with ruining the last few minutes of *Bewitched*.

Endora lifted her hands and disappeared in a puff of smoke, but no-one was watching. Samantha and Darren said, "I love you," and no one but me saw.

"That's settled," said Petrus.

"I guess so," said Griff in his usual quiet way. "But who's gonna tell—"

"I," said Henry.

"Who?" I said.

"They're leaving," said Griff.

"Not in so few words," said Henry, as I fainted.

Anyway, this was too momentous for me to be out long, so I had to know what had gone on in my absence.

"Tell me, Henry," I said, turning around in Griff's arms.

"I'll tell it, dear," said Griff.

"It's a message, missus," said Bouncer. None of them ever knew what to call me. For some reason, that original mob called Griff *Your Honourship* and me, just *missus*.

Griff waved to Bouncer to continue.

"Didn't you think that 'Go' is a message as the name of a television channel?"

"We made jokes about it," I admitted. I could feel my face flush. "I'm sorry if we insulted you by thinking that *I Dream of Jeannie* is funny, or *Bewitched*. Really I didn't think it would insult you. It makes just as much fun of us."

Bouncer waved his hand. I felt like a fly. "And didn't you think those ads for Summit Ridge something to pay attention to?"

"Summit Ridge?" The back of my head felt sore. Those ads and the ones for Bessemer Cookware, the designed-in-the-60s aluminium pans that you could otherwise get used in some small outback op shop, here "marked down" to fifteen times its worth and sold during these two programs of the supernaturals who actually want to live in suburbia, were what made this hour of every weekday so irresistible to me, though I would have died before admitting that I like anything on the boob.

"She did remark how funny it is that Summit Ridge Estates is flat as a pancake," said Griff.

"Yeah," I said. "No-one in their right mind would go there. It's in the middle of nowhere up in Queensland. It's monoculture land, either sugar cane or rice. Cheap land dependent on subsidised irrigation water. But now they have to pay realistic prices for our country's water, so they're selling the land off as a housing estate."

"She has said that the land would be soaked with pesticides. And that, like many of the new suburbs built by developers in this crooked state, there would be no infrastructure," Griff explained to all.

I turned my head to stare at him. "I never thought you listened."

"And that's why the ad says that they'll give you five gold bars for buying a lot," he finished. He'd never been able to make many of them respect me, but now the original seven were looking at me differently.

"I wish you'd told us years ago about this," said Bouncer to me.

"About *I Dream of Jeannie*? *Bewitched*?" I said, confused. "Go? The sacred hour's only been on a year or so."

"Go," said Byron, who had now grown to a pudgy rosy-lipped adulthood. "That combined with the genie and the witch, and the ridge as flat as a Shrove Tuesday pancake, and land that is likely poisoned, to you. And the purchase in which the seller pays, and what they pay—"

"Gold bars!" burst out Petrus. "Gerr on wid it! There's one of our own up there, I tell youse, and I figgered it out."

"May I?" said Henry.

We turned to him, still lying on his side, his head propped on one hand. There was no room for him to be in any other position.

"First, my lady, you should know that Mister Griff Bartlett here has a distinguished relative."

"May I?" cut in Griff softly. "I didn't tell you because I think it's such a cliché to brag of it, but I arrived on these shores as the sperm of a certain John Barrett."

"And we knew it," said Bouncer. "And tracked you down," said the chorus of six.

"Hand her the eggserpt," someone said.

Griff went upstairs and came down with a page he'd copied. "It's from the log of a doctor Worgan, surgeon of the serious."

"This is a joke?"

"The ship!" a crowd piped. "First fleet, madam!" said Byron.

Griff dropped it in my lap. "I've circled the relevant stuff."

> Wed. 27th
>
> *Nothing material has occurred since the 16th till to Day, when three Convicts, were tried in the Criminal Court for stealing Provisions, they were Convicted upon the clearest Evidence and sentenced to be hung; Accordingly, about 6 o'clock the same Evening, they were brought to the fatal Tree, the Battalion under Arms, Provost Marshal, & the Peace Officers attending at the Execution, when, John Barrett, the most notorious of the Criminals, was tied up, and hung the usual time.*
>
> Thurs. 28th
>
> *The other two were respited till 4 o'clock the next Evening, when, being brought to the place of Execution, the Governor was pleased to send down a Commutation of their Sentence upon the following Conditions. The One was to execute the Office of Hangman, as long as He remained in the Country, the other to suffer Banishment on some adjacent Island. I need not tell you they readily agreed to these Conditions.*
>
> *Some one who should in future perform the disagreeable Task of Hangman, was an Officer which, considering what a class of Men the major Part of our Colony consisted, would probably be much wanted; for the Man who had agreed to execute this Office, failed so much in his Duty, (either from Timidity or Feeling) in the Execution of Barrett, that, our*

> *Sheriff, was under the disagreeable Necessity of mounting the Ladder Himself, in order to fix the Halter, so here was an Opportunity of establishing a [rule]: in all future Executions either Hang or Be Hanged.*
>
> *We have made some Discoveries this last Week, One is that the Tree, which I have said grows something like the Fir, answers very well for the making of Shingle...*

"The *Sirius*?" I said. "1788. Sydney Cove? Do you mean to tell me that your hung ancestor was a First Fleeter?"

"Yes!" answered pretty much the whole room.

"And so was our ancestors," said Bouncer. "Ship for ship, we follered yours."

"There were many ghost ships in those days," said Henry.

"We didn't want you to have your way in this new land by yourselves. All those sheep transported, and those dogs, and peas and milk cows, and stores aplenty. And where would we be, deserted?"

"It's true," said Griff. "I know it now, though when I first researched it, I didn't... it made no sense. Now it's as natural as the motivations of the rats who jumped the ships. And we mustn't be the only ones who know it."

"Parsley!" said Petrus. "Get to the point."

"I'll tell," said Bouncer. "The point is that her ladyship's man here suffered a wrongdoing in his past, and we came here to make it up. His ancestor hung for what we took. My own ancestor intervened to slip the rope, and we had a phantom coach and four lined up, but at the last moment, something slipped and the rope tightened, and your man, such a well-built man of such fierce appetite. His own weight pulled that noose too tight, and he was—"

"Pudding!" said Tweedlefoot.

"So every generation of us has tried to make it up to every generation who's passed down, and we never caught up till that day we found that it was your honourship. And by association, you, my lady," said Bouncer, addressing me as such for the first time ever. "We always wanted to do something to make amends but instead, you sheltered us."

"And now we'll take that burden off your wearied souls," said Byron.

"Don't be daft," snapped Petrus. "If someone wants to have our company and is willing to pay gold to get it, then let's just go without the poetry."

"It can only be a message—'Go—from us who have wronged you, to get us out of here," said Byron, turning his back on Petrus. "As you said, it's a joke as a place for you to live, but we can't be poisoned by pesticides. We don't need buses, or jobs, or shops. And possibly the idea is, the place will just disappear like a ghost ship once we get there. Did it give a real physical address?"

"No," Griff and I said together.

"So you're all going?" I asked.

"We are a burden on you," said Henry. "I read that letter, and it mentioned fines for ferals."

"Everyone who wants to go," I yelled, "Raise a hand."

Everyone did, and I burst into tears.

"They're hunted here," said Griff, putting a hand on my shoulder. "Let them go."

"I wish the *hunters* could be hunted!"

"Don't you *want* us to leave?" said Henry.

"Only those who want to."

So Petrus left. That was two years ago, and tomorrow the inspector's due again. By now, with full disclosure having happened in Green Valley, and the many heads put together—poetry, research, history, and invention—the inspector and all future inspectors will find only what we mean them to see. Just as the buyers of lots in Summit Ridge Estates might see not only a summit where they wish it, but a neighborhood where there are just houses, and real gold bars given out for free.

WHERE GEESE FALL FAR FROM THE TREES

previously unpublished

The tragedy of Australian barnacle geese is that they come at all to our spit-warm waters. You'd think that as flock birds, they'd have developed the intelligence of a group, or would have evolved enough to learn. As long ago as the 1100s, Gerald of Wales reported their happy lives—hatching from fir trees in Ireland. Four hundred years later, John Gerarde reported them thriving as droops on unspecified trees in the even more inclement north of Scotland, dropping like windfalls when they reached maturity, only to right themselves on webbed feet, stagger, run and flap their awning-striped wings till they caught the sky and pierced it as a flock, their V formations and their newfound cries clear in the frigid air as water under fragile summer ice.

That subspecies of barnacle geese only thrives in places where the trees drip in short sharp spring like runny noses, but spend the winter clattering in the dark, their limbs black as frostbite.

In Svalbard, Norway, every home garden sported one of those trees, for *godt hell*, superstitious luck. As a child, Sumptibus Odden spent the months of darkness hearing the icicles rattle in the tree. He could feel the creature shivering. He'd been told how she freezes her blood to keep up her strength, this mother goose tree. A fairy story, to be sure, for how else could a tree pop out in eggs each spring if it didn't work hard all winter long when the very sun is sleeping? In October, when the Northern Lights flashed, the long-necked chicks that hadn't developed enough to drop were lit green and purple, frozen and condemned for all the supposed good luck the mother goose brought to the house—the lack of reason added to the child's nightmares.

Spring, with its bursting forth of green leaves and great laying out along the branches, and the great hatching, always seemed unreachably far away in the dead of winter. But every year spring came, and within weeks, the barnacle geese were gone, no one in the village could tell for sure where nor what they'd eat—thawed wood frogs in the mosquito-ridden marshes, lichen stolen from under the noses of reindeer, grass or, as some said, nothing more than a mushroom would, as the mother goose tree was nourished from the soil and they were merely fruits. If they survived at all, managing to drop and survive the village cats and the influx of strange men with hessian bags briefly lurking in every garden. As to where the barnacle geese flew off to, that was another source of heavily disagreed certainties.

The mother goose tree fascinated the child so much that one day, he tried to pull a barnacle goose's head out instead of waiting and missing the birth, but he pulled too hard, ending up with a headless goose, the long black neck flopping slack from his guilty grasp.

The body was only as big as his pinkie. He was pretty stunted too, so he knew size doesn't mean a thing, but by the way his heart hurt, he reckoned the bird the same age, in barnacle-goose years, as he. Sumptibus never told anyone, for what use would telling serve?

This was the same boy who never cried, for crying earned a painful reward, one his mother could never heal in her furtive glances. One his grandfather could not correct—that dead grandfather whose strange name he had inherited, to the scorn of the boy's father, who stomped on Sumptibus' left hand when he caught the boy scratching a drawing of a barnacle goose one day on the iced shore. To Carl Odden, this effeminate son was shame itself, and so he called the boy Argr, perhaps hating himself for making his son draw even more, dream and perhaps scheme, but who knew the man's heart? Surely not the boy, nor his mother.

That little boy grew till he swore that he would grow up to be not a fisherman but something else. "Dra til helvete," his father said. Go to hell. Carl Odden talked so little, the only conversation he was capable of was curses. His hands, on the other hand, were capable of anything. He could make his belt bite like a snake, and used that more and more as his communication with his son until one dawn in mid-summer, when the man lifted his belt to strike, something snuck up on him—the size and strength of his son. Without a word, Sumptibus tore the belt from his father's grasp and ripped the buckle out, tossing the toothless biter into the fire.

The last memory he had of his father was of the man sitting on the stone in front of that fire, wordlessly pulling out clumps of his beard—that beard so carefully tended to look like a king of beast's face fringe.

Sumptibus left with only the clothes he wore, and on a cord around his neck, the leather pouch he'd made and always wore filled with the dried headless carcass of the barnacle goose he'd accidentally murdered. He didn't even carry a razor, as his face was still smooth as a peach. In the bread trough, he'd secreted a drawing that his mother was too frightened to keep, so she burnt it in the oven.

And the barnacle geese on Australian beaches?

Perhaps the Age of Exploration called irresistibly, and they hitched a ride on some intercontinental air current ditching in the South Seas. Perhaps some stowed away—the fools, the cursed, and possibly the cursers—for not only do they come ashore on driftwood, but on driftwrecks.

Indeed, Sumptibus Odden's journal (as opposed to the published account by the party's bigwig, Ludwig Leichhardt) recorded in 1855 that during the German adventurer's barely-survived "Swan River" expedition, after an episode in which they were attacked and their number violently reduced by two (a lucky boon it seems, as Leichhardt noted in his own journal that there were too many men for the provisions)—

> Our leeder was not a littel moved at the sight of the shor. He ran owt onto the hot wite sands as if chasd, krying "Kokonut!"—falling upon a hayry orb and cluching it to his brest. A moment only did we see him hesitat, and insted of poking it in the eyes to poor its waters of life down his parched gullett, he took to nawing with the covetus ferohsity of the king of beests. Our gulletts were dry as sand, but we had lernd better than to challenzh him. Only I steeled myself to wach and not plug my eers.
>
> Evendully he raysed his hed, his mouth open, panting. He pawd and poked with his nife at a fouling of thik blak Medusik "hair" cawt between his long yellow teeth, wile from the bottom jaw protruded sharp tawny, bloud-tipped spikes stikking owt like Owr Lord's cursed crown.
>
> Beside the madman lay the rudely scalped and flayd head of wat had becom a groteskly beerded woden mayden, this decapitated part having mayd land.

That frightsome fringe was the grizzled necks of barnacle goose chicks, their heads gruesomely buried in the likeness of a Mrs. Lampry, the wife of the ship's owner of *The Abstemious*, torn to driftwood in a terrific tempest. The ship had sailed from London with a cargo of copper roofing, carved oaken pews, pewter chalices, a stone baptismal font, forty headstone blanks cut from the finest Grampian granite, and enough thick, fancy tiles to floor a cathedral, the intended hallowed end of their journey. Naturally, none of this was evident at the time. I have only deduced from comparing the gnawed head (bagged by my ancestor) to Turner's painting *Last Night of the Abstemious*.

That stormy sea was nothing compared to the scene Odden witnessed and sketched, one he was too characteristically understated to go full Goya on. While the other members of the party had spread out along the beach looking for a freshwater outlet, beached fish or birds, there Leichhardt was, wholly occupied with his penknife digging goose-chick necks from between his teeth, spitting sand out of his mouth, and retching.

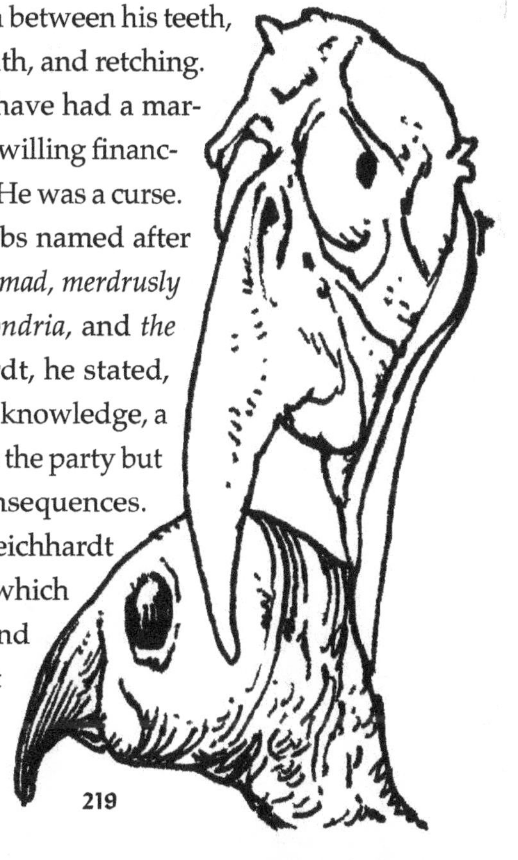

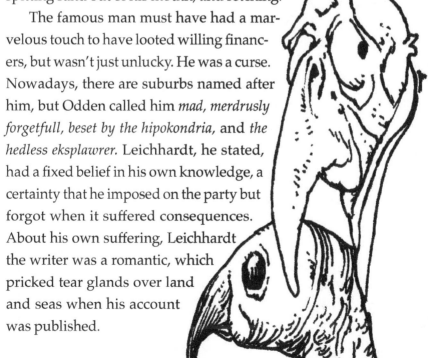

The famous man must have had a marvelous touch to have looted willing financers, but wasn't just unlucky. He was a curse. Nowadays, there are suburbs named after him, but Odden called him *mad, merdrusly forgetfull, beset by the hipokondria*, and *the hedless eksplawrer.* Leichhardt, he stated, had a fixed belief in his own knowledge, a certainty that he imposed on the party but forgot when it suffered consequences. About his own suffering, Leichhardt the writer was a romantic, which pricked tear glands over land and seas when his account was published.

> *I suffered a great deal of palpitation of the heart (perhaps in consequence of strong tea and smoking); I dreamt of * * * and * * * * * she was as blooming and beautiful as ever and showed (as I dreamt at least) some solicitude about me.*

This episode on the beach was, perhaps, only to be expected after the fright of surviving a murderous attack upon the party (The sensational coverage was nursery food to infant Robert Louis Stevenson.)

Leichhardt didn't record, however, the death-defying incident when he purged himself inside out after eating untreated burrawang (the spectacular cycad *Macrozamia communis*)—the whole amount the expedition had gathered to make a poor feast but a feed. The natives, skin and bones, were torturing the party by making them wait till there was sufficient water to wash the poisons out. Water! Why, the kernels were so juicy, Leichhardt's mouth frothed at their sight.

The celebrated man always trusted his own interpretation, so when the moon didn't pitch up for a performance that night, he took that as approval, though Odden was more damning. He called the incident "a deviluslii delibrit loonar kulloozhun."

Odden must have been an odd duck. He wrote, in a precisely chiselled hand, as if he had never read, his tone often apoplectic but always accurate as an honest auditor's. The detailed drawings in his notebook are so gorgeous in their horror, they seem scarcely made by a human, more by an angel caught in a wingtrap. His spelling seems to flow with his mood, sometimes so curt, I don't know if he was making a pun on a vulgar Norwegian three-letter word, sometimes so emotional, a word needed repeated letters for emphasis—all adding up to a journal so over the top yet dry, I can hear his laugh—a shave with a rusty blade.

He must have had the eyesight of an owl, for he relished describing this scene:

> In starless darkness, under the cover of a wind that set branches scratching upon each other like a pack of starving dogs smeared with goose fat, Leichhardt slithered over to the bag of burrawang ears—an odd corn such as the God himself would eat, each kernel as big and red and inviting as a peach—and slunk off into the bush, dispatching all the ears till the cobs were bare, tearing the kernels off with his teeth, their bloodmilk running down his chin. His theft would not have been known by the ignoramuses of the party for hours if the wind could have muffled his purging, in all its offense to the senses.

(That proved to be his penultimate expedition, the next one being doomed or possibly oddly blessed by his decision to give his compass and thermometer away as mementoes before setting out. That expedition has yet to be found.)

But enough of Leichhardt. My great-great-something uncle Sumptibus Odden would be towerably volcanic if Leichhardt stole this telling, too. He took enough of my uncelebrated ancestor's life.

No, Sumptibus Odden was not by nature a biographer, nor a toppler of statues. He was—well, a lover. And it was his description of that scene on the beach that touched my heart—that scene in which he was so starved, he'd considered eating, if next he shat, that shit as a meal.

Yet there was something about those necks hanging from Leichhardt's teeth. There was something about the head that Leichhardt scalped with his teeth. Something snapped in the artist's life.

He never enjoyed eating flesh again, though he scrupulously followed the natives' advice for the rest of the expedition, he being the only one in the party that valued it, the others regarding the men as merely trackers, half-tamed human bloodhounds you had to keep your eyes on, or they'd walk off with your gear.

That expedition ended with a trip on the schooner *Heroine* from Port Essington to Sydney, where Odden slipped away from the hero's welcome for Leichhardt.

Sun, sand, warmth, wide new expanses, the weirdest assortment of animals and plants—paradise, or hell.

The waters are too warm, the sun impertinent and powerful. Most people would never notice the little barnacle geese, as they live as long, unnourished, as any other day-old-chicks cruelly exposed to sun and starved of sustenance.

But most people who come to an Australian beach only look for sun and sand. They're not bird watchers, and certainly not twitchers.

Dead flocks of baby chicks hanging from their necks are only scruff on a log, a log that's only noticed if it's dragged to a beach fire to watch crackle and spit while sitting around bullshitting about breaks, cutbacks, and kooks, while cracking open beers or bonging the bottles.

Not that I think getting pissed mightn't be a brilliant way to get flexible enough to wipe out and not get your neck broken on a sandbar. But I'm not into legal highs, let alone group activities.

Those barnacle geese have haunted me ever since I found the journal whilst cleaning out my dead father's house in Sydney's innercity suburb, Leichhardt. Dad never made it as an artist under his own name, either. But in Leichhardt in the late twentieth century, all kinds of odd people could accumulate wealth. My father's was obsolete medical equipment and fantastical illustrated natural histories—fairy tales for the pseudo-scientific minded. The house was thin and long, with heads of women peering down from plaster arches in the front hall. When a tyre restorer went bust in the next door lot because the restorer played the dogs, Dad took it off the relieved gambler's hands for a sum the poor man lost in a week. Dad let him live in the office for an agreed sum of 50 quid a week, which Dad was never paid but I couldn't get him to kick the old bloke out. In 1980 or so, the reprobate won ten grand on a scratchy, so he skipped, not telling Dad anything. We were told the old guy went on a P & O cruise and died in his bed. We wouldn't have known about it if our neighbourhood hadn't been that kind in those days. People found out stuff. That reinforced to me all I loath about neighbourhoods.

Of course Dad had told me about Odden, and had talked about Odden's journal till I didn't believe a word my father said. He always promised to find it for me, but of course never did. He was hard-pressed to find a packet of tea in that house, though he never threw tea out. Tea's good for drains, can take away bad smells, and makes a capital footbath, if you can find the bath. Buying the filthy two-storey tyre-building and its huge half-concreted lot next door was a steal according to Dad. In no time, it was even more packed than the house.

Death was the only cleanser. The journal was in a box of books crammed under his bed. No wonder he couldn't find it. Only the spine showed, wrinkled and slack as the wasted tattooed arm of a washed-up sailor. Beside it was a clutch of notebooks in various states of ruin, all written in the same hand, almost a child's in the first one but by the last, a rippling wave running downstream in every line—inscrutable till I realised the words must be Norwegian. Sumptibus Odden was just as original a speller in that language, I learned, but since he wrote phonetically, I could hear his voice as I read.

I was just surviving when my father died, but the neighbourhood as it had been was dead. His property was split into two parcels, but the combined land with separate titles made it all the more covetable for the type of developers my father and his anarchist drinking mates would have spat on metaphorically (they never would have mixed with these money-grubbers).

So I had them auctioned, one week apart. It's now the Cyclops Epicure Collection, a complex of 181 "luxury lifestyle" apartments, and a sideshow to the ongoing murder trial of a so-called gangland figure. Consolidation can be fun.

The money was just a means. I'd never found my purpose, though Dad had tried to help, but pushing isn't help, and for all my fancy medical research credentials, I hated labs. I've never been a good suckup, and teaching only increases species contact.

That journal was my saving, for there was one thing in it—not the drawings my father raved about from his memory—but that account. The chronicle my father didn't know about or remember if he'd ever read. That telling kicked me in the gut, for my ancestor and I shared a passion—a passion for damned geese.

I'd researched them, but no one knows who first brought barnacle geese to Australian seas. Perhaps, unlike the rabbit, no one did on purpose, for they impoverish the very idea of sport and make only the poorest snack of rubbery necks.

Down here, they're not even *called* barnacle geese. The Australian Museum, the Queensland Museum and suchlike that are relied upon to know about intertidal beaches and coastal waters call them goose barnacles, but this is the land that calls a redhead "bluey."

Just because they live a life here no one would wish for, that's no reason to nonsensify their name. They're barnacle geese, and have been throughout history in their native lands.

Not that as many as one out of a million people in Australia would give you anything but a blank look if you mentioned them backwards or right way round.

But come to a wild beach after a storm and the only time you won't find them is on the thirty-third day of a month. Any other time, they'll be high and drying, pitifully waving their fluffy white feathered behinds that they can't hide from exposure, their long black necks twisting inscrutably as their heads remain buried in the wood—until death overtakes them under a parching sun.

It begs logic that these birds not only live in flocks, but in flocks with what must be a death-wish, the tight chainlink fence structure of a broken banksia branch being the most common vessel they arrive in, their heads so thoroughly caged, they're hidden from sight. As their beaks must be held fast in the matrix, they are forced to derive sustenance in these crucial first hours, up their bums, which is why their delicate feathers flutter, peeking out from those immature wings, the structure of all that keratin gelled just like our fingernails, to be two body-encompassing shells the size of thumbnails.

I'd left one university after another because the politics sucked my soul dry. Besides, I was really only comfortable when I couldn't hear a human, but living by the beach is only for the rich or those with a high tolerance for humans. So I began to feral-camp. Sometimes I got caught but I've got two things going for me: I'm extraordinarily good-looking, and I always carry a notebook, so in the time it takes for a quick argument, I can draw a likeness that "brings out the beauty" in anyone. My looks aren't technically perfect, but they seem to do a trick. They bring out some sympathetic instinct, a quality that hurt my reputation no end in research environments, but perfect for my feral needs.

My interest was the conundrum of death, particularly that presented by the sea. In the year leading to Dad's death, I was splitting my time between visits when we would get on each other's tits in half an hour but we both treasured that time—and camping by remote protected beaches where rangers pounce on anyone who "disturbs." The rangers don't regard tides as serial perpetrators but that's because rangers are blind to everything but dogma. You mustn't remove anything on a beach, even beached seaweed for your garden or to eat. Beachcombing is *verboten*. Everything is supposed to be left to Nature's way, as it's got a Plan and everything it does is for a reason.

So I was studying, just observing and recording in my journals, but Dad's death changed all that. For the first time in my life, I wanted to *save* life, reason be damned. Is it reasonable that little chicks are born in the wrong place at the wrong time? Dad and I had fought about my throwing my life away, "with all your talents and training" he used to say, he, that waster, being the last person qualified to criticise *me*.

What would Odden have said? I cringe to think of his drawing of me. It would probably have been William Blakish with me tucking the log with its frightful fringe under my angel's wing. I can just see his Byronishly handsome curled lip as he wrote and drew.

Whatever. Once I had the money for real research, I rented a house for position position position. It was in Sanctuary Point, close enough to wild beaches on the South Coast to get my charges home within an hour at most. The house was nestled amongst others owned by the Housing Commission, and owned by aged investors who didn't trust AirB&B yet were terrified of the neighbourhood, mostly single mothers with AVOs out for their children's fathers. The owners of my house thought I'd dropped from heaven, as they were too unsure about the market to sell but were convinced their precious asset would be stripped if they rented it. One look at me, and they almost purred.

To equip myself for any eventuality I took a Mr. Whippy van off the hands of a sad-eyed would-be-retiree for a song. He also threw in a coat of white concealing paint, but I alone refurbished the inside to contain not a soft-serve freezer, but a long covered freezing compartment that made seawater slushy.

I started rescuing during the storms themselves, when tree limbs are flayed from the coastal strip, waves leap onto beaches only to drag anything and -one out into treacherous rips and slicing reefs.

The only people out in this weather are insane rock-fishermen, who face their own censure for dying so frequently which is nothing in itself, but the hunt for their bodies is both costly and manpower-wasteful.

So I had no problem rescuing my first logful. It was heavier than a fat man, but I lashed it to a surfboard trolley and drag-rolled it off the beach, depositing it in my slush.

My own bathroom was readied, and the only word I can think of to describe my joy of getting in my bath with the log and chicks was *Elation*. I filled the bath with slushies. Seawater doesn't freeze as easily as freshwater, but it was good enough. Once in the bath, I could hardly feel my legs. Stripped of my gear, my hair streamed sand and salt water into my crotch which suddenly appeared to me, sand and baubles of water clinging to its hair, to be fortuitously related to bearded mussels.

The chicks were so alive, they looked cavortive. Their necks were stretched out gracefully, their delicate feathers sticking out their bums, waving like so many delicately batting eyelashes.

What to feed them? I'd never properly thought that, concentrating on their saving. The sea provides, but for how long if it's just a bath-sea?

Research. The natural home of the *Branta leucopsis* is so cold and wet that grass must be its main diet. Life is so hard for the chicks in their natural home that many of them die as fledglings on their first flight, literally jumping off a cliff.

No fate like that would befall them in my nursery, if only they could fledge.

Not being able to sneak past the rangers to collect sea lettuce, I fed them kale, chopping it so finely, their thumbnail bodies could chew or whatever, easily.

Their little backfeather filter-feeding behinds worked like crazy. Their necks acted as if their beaks were swallowing (through the net of the banksia wood?).

I fed them for a week, till the water, now as green as kale, began to smell like a beach when littered with torn cunjevoi, the soft-bodied sea squirts that try to anchor themselves to rocks, if that beach were also littered with slippery sunstroked cabbage.

The chicks weren't dried up. These had rotted till the ones most submerged floated to the surface, headless, their shell-wings opened, exposing a translucent froth.

I sieved the bath and buried them, saving the log as a memento of my care, however much good my "care" had done.

The next day I was wandering innocently on that very storm-tossed beach, only to have a ranger grill me like a fish.

And Sanctuary Point wasn't such a sanctuary. I had a rather lot of non-decoratory equipment, and my landlords decided to pay me a visit.

I had to move seven times before I found the right combination of hideaway and beach that I could successfully sneak a rescue out of.

It took me two more years till I figured out how to care and feed the chicks to get them past the day-old stage.

Getting over the moult was the hardest part. Once those shells were shed, their bodies were as vulnerable as a hermit crab without a shell. They also needed to develop an internal skeleton, something that must have dissolved into their organs once they evolved from bursting from eggs and began to be born with their heads buried in wood. But there were still problems I hadn't solved. From my journal: *And I still don't know what will happen when their bodies are too heavy to support their necks. Already, some have torn loose at the top of the neck. If only they were patient. And do their lives have to be so lifeless? Why should they be born, if only to die like this?* A question my father might have posed me. Real research mustn't get tied up in these questions, and real research like mine shouldn't have to always be muzzled by the necessity to be unnoticed.

An hour ago, she (I don't know how to sex them, but they're not its) pulled her head free. For the first eight minutes, she looked like a snake with a mismatched body. Then she shook that head like a wet dog. By ten minutes, the beady black eyes blinked, something a snake can't do. At minute 12.5, a distinct swelling appeared above the eyes and a discoloured wartlike bulge appeared between and under the eyes. At minute 16.4 the swelling had grown 2 centimetres. At m 18.5 the swelling split horizontally.

At minute 21, I strangled her.

How did I know she/it was going to return to form? They're not called cackling geese for nothing. They don't cackle as much as bark—loudly, and repeatedly.

I lived then in a no-pets flat. If anyone heard, I'd be thrown out, even if no one saw me with a dog.

I still mourn her. I think of her as Nora, though I don't know how to sex.

If they make noise, they can be found, tracked down as ferals. If I release mine, for I know better now—I surgically remove their vocal box—to eliminate that vulnerability. But it's still a mystery how they populate once they reach adulthood. I've tried to matchmake, encouraged nestmaking by moving to a highrise, only to have one plucked off by a wedgetailed eagle, and another fall off because their feet haven't developed claws.

Another thing about them. They are curiously striped. Back in their homelands, they are black and grey and white. Here, from their chickhood, they have a purple cast to the stripe. Today I saw just that cast and the very stripe at a Vietnamese grocer. Eggplants the very size and shape of goose eggs, bearing the same stripe and colours as my barnacle geese.

Of course I bought a dozen and brought them home, laying them out on the lounge floor. The geese opened and closed their beaks, clattering them so much that I had to turn on *Married at First Sight*, my go-to socially-sanctioned cacophony. By the time I turned back to the geese, the eggplants had disappeared, three geese looking either smug or guilty. I couldn't get near them, those beaks being more effective than a parrots', attached as they are to those long snakey necks.

Now, I don't know how illegal what I'm doing is. Had to move again, this time to a place in the bush too wild for the landowner, who is only keeping it for its possible land value if bushfire doesn't keep every prospective buyer away forever and a proper road is built. (If you're thinking why don't I buy because I'm so loaded, research comes dear, as does privacy. Living just poor enough gives the ultimate in loneness.)

"Eggplants" are growing on a heavy-gauge trellis. The chicks drop out onto soft grass. I've tried to stop the foxes snapping them up soon as they drop, but there's only so much I can do.

I've always loved foxes, ever since I read my first fairy tale.

This could be called a lonely life, hidden away with my loved ones, hiding from a world hellbent on hurting them because they don't belong. Sometimes, surrounded by the now-muffled cackle (eggplant is a great sound-dampener when it becomes flesh) of my flock, and the sibilance of snails chewing leaves, I open up one of Sumptibus Odden's notebooks, the better to understand his frustrations. I don't know how idiosyncratic his Norwegian was, as there are passages that are so descriptive but unbelievable, they must be idioms. But these are the only places he recorded *his* discoveries and experiments, for he'd learned enough about heroes to keep himself to himself.

Other research has, I'm not surprised, failed me. As the great G.W. Wood noted in *Out of Doors*, "Our River Harvests", certain other eggs in experiments "are hatched in little more than half the time when the generality of books mention is necessary for that operation."

The chicks on the beaches? I haven't been to the ocean for decades. It's too painful, knowing that I can only save so many, with superhuman effort—to what end? They are helpless as any day-old chicks when I rescue them, but with their heads buried in the wood, they fail to imprint me in what passes for their consciousness. They are, for all the work they take to save—dead ends.

They never matured to a reproductive state, nor did I ever get them past ingesting a variation on dogfood.

Here, in my bush hideout, once eggplant was introduced to their development, they've gone from strength to strength. My little secret society of highly developed barnacle geese have a flock consciousness that, whether a chick sees me first upon falling out of the eggplant or not, is irrelevant. They all follow me.

These birds aren't beggars. They're devoted. And developing with every generation.

This season's young don't just bark. I've managed a little something that Sumptibus Odden might turn green over. They knead my back with their webbed feet, and purr.

SHAKING HEAVEN'S FLEAS

"Shaking Heaven's Fleas"
medlarcomfits blog Nov 2020
reprinted by Wildside Press's Black Cat Magazine, March 2021

Year of the dog: Pandemic puppies in high demand, short supply

—CBC News, Ottawa

Before the pandemic you could normally expect to spend anywhere from a few hundred bucks for an 'oodle' from a pet store to something in the low thousands for a puppy from a breeder, but 2020 has seen demand soar. Breeders around the country are now selling designer dog puppies for upwards of $10,000. DMARGE was able to find a seller in Port Macquarie, NSW selling 'miniature Golden Bordoodle' puppies for $7,500 each – as of publishing, all these little cuties have sold out.

—"AUSTRALIAN 'DESIGNER DOG' TREND DRIVING POOCH PRICES BARKING MAD IN 2020", by Jamie Weiss, dmarge.com

Pandemic puppies: Massachusetts sees puppy shortage as demand for dogs skyrockets in quarantine

—Boston Herald

Demand for 'flat-faced' puppies such as the French Bulldog and Pug has soared during the coronavirus pandemic, according to the UK Kennel Club .

—Daily Mail, UK

The rush on toilet paper and other essential products at the start of the pandemic has come and gone, but there's another shortage that hasn't quite let up. This one is cuddly and warm, and one even Santa might not be able to get.

—"Puppies in high demand and short supply this coming Christmas amid COVID-19 pandemic", by Michael Finney and Randall Yip, ABC7 News, San Francisco

My beautiful black German sherpard past away just three days ago at the age of 1 year two weeks. My entire family is heartbroken we are non stop crying for Moonlight (our beloved German Shepherd). She past away instantly with no symptoms we were so distraught. She was a big girl standing up at 5 feet. She had long beautiful black fur. Such a beauty, and tragedy to die from heart disease.

— online eulogy

I shook my head, but no water flew out of my ears. I bit my rump till I could taste blood. This was worse than watching balls being beaten back and forth where there were no balls, no ball smell.

I'd heard of Doggie Heaven. It's where they said Sunlight went shortly after I arrived. They cried as if they were broken-hearted and hugged me till I could hardly breathe. But they kept saying they were happy for her, that she had gone to a better place. That she'd be at peace, have lots of friends to play with, eat fresh meat and ice cream to her heart's content, and sleep on the most comfy—Stop! I'll never trust a word they said.

This place—it's where "Dad" took Tracy for her driving lessons. He let me come too "for the ride" but when they let me out, the ground was so desolate, I could hardly pee. There was nothing worth looking at, no one interesting to smell. The place reeked of road, the sweat of cars, the funk of fucking people. This place looks the same, but it's filled with the smell of fear, the noise of cries and whimpers. I've never seen so many dogs.

I've never heard a dog whistle, but my ears stand up at the thin blue scream. Some of us turn as one, and *that*—that land behind the ruins of this shopping center—there's a rusted sign on a chainlink fence. It says (Don't be so surprised. From 11 weeks, I was given newspapers, and I've only got a cataract in one eye):

DOGGY HEAVEN
THIS FENCE IS PATROLLED 24/7

Sit, blares a voice.

So of course I sit.

There are no gates in Doggie Heaven, says the voice. *You dig your way in under the fence. For the inexperienced and incapacitated, experts either mentor or dig you a new one. Once in, you must expect a period of adjustment, especially if you have entered with pre-existing conditions.*

Pre-existing conditions, it repeats. There's so little discipline here, you could mistake this crowd for humans. And the din is deafening. *Sit!* it bays, though it had never released us.

Of course we don't refuse anyone it says as if it's talking to a puppy who has only piddled in the kitchen, not the carpet. *There's no such thing as a dog eat dog society except in human euphemisms.* In a dried pig's ear would this crowd know a euphemism.

But there is a class structure that has inevitably built up and is increasing exponentially in social stratification based on these pre-existing conditions or the lack of them. Wow. The voice mustn't be attached to eyes. That basset hound, for instance, can barely understand one-syllable words. And oh, boy, Tracy's lucky *she* doesn't have to go to Doggie Heaven. But maybe she'll go to her version, where she'll have to go to all the school she cut while lying to her parents.

Old dogs—those who came here before breeds were invented, continues the imperturbable voice—*and mutts—are naturally the elite, but don't worry. This is a compassionate society.*

If you had people and they loved and 'took good care' of you, you can take advantage of our generous dream rights, though if you truly care about them, you should not abuse the frequency of these visits, or they'll never be able to 'get over' you.

Yes, I'll get to you strays...

It must be dinnertime. My stomach's growling. With my luck, I bet there'll only be a damp bag of kibble, wet, rubbery, stinking of mice, if I can even find it in a corner of some garage...

By the time the voice stopped, only some of us still had our ears at attention, our buttholes warming the tar. When it finally said *Okay!*, of course, with my breeding, I rushed forward to help get the intake through. Some of us were better at this than others, but we managed by dint of lead, push, growl, bite and mothering, to get every last dog through, down to the most intransigent chihuahua with teeth like a whirring lawn mower, and that urine-soaked mop of seizures, the shih-tzu.

The voice wasn't wrong about everyone needing adjustment.

Would you like to know more?

Then sit.

"Did you have to include the social criticism?" asked a pug.

"We felt it only right to be scrupulously honest." The shaggy proto-St. Bernhard who had last saved a boy in 1845 looked around the park. Her eyes, their red rims always showing, gave her the look of someone who'd not only been awake for a week straight, but had spent those 168 hours writing a manifesto.

"More to the point," she said. "Does anyone feel we've left anything out? Try to remember back to when you first arrived. What would you have liked in your welcome pack?"

A dog who was new here, and thus had only begun transitioning, tried to speak, but his or her face wasn't in any state yet. Its bugged-out eyes couldn't even blink once for *Yes*. Its millions of followers mightn't even know that it had passed on, having attained a certain immortality on The Richest for its looks: *"like it stuck its paw into an electrical socket and has been dealing with the aftermath ever since."*

"Are you friends? Can you step in?" asked the proto-St. Bernhard, whose name was not verbal, of course, but scental—(automatic translation: Rolling in Rotting Salmon).

She'd asked a dog who'd *almost* sold for much *much* more. Nibble, she was called by her rescuers who threw themselves in front of the truck that was transporting her and about 150 other Tibetan mastiffs stuffed in chicken crates. Their fad had ended as suddenly as it had begun, and no one wanted them except these fanatic saviours. (How could I possibly know this? As I told you, most of my puppiest life, I was stuck in a room floored with newspaper spreads.) Her life after that had been just as confusing—so obvious she was still shaking from peopleshock. Her smell—people can't handle it. She didn't know what had happened to her. She couldn't even remember her first days, when she'd been taken from her mother and fed a lion's mother's milk. Nor did she understand what anyone here was saying. And there is no place here to hide. *And* though there are scores of Nannas here, there's never one where one needs one. She bit the root of her tail, a bush of dreadlocks, in embarrassment, which made Rolling in Rotten Salmon bow her head and drop her eyes sideways, looking at nothing, in *her* embarrassment.

But Rolling in Rotten Salmon always found good in a situation.

"All those who'd like more brains, raise a paw," she barked.

"Why?" came a yip.

"To show you want more brains."

"For who?"—someone else.

"Why?"—from an English sheepdog.

"Whom."—a Scottish terrier.

"And where are these brains coming from?"—some mutt.

"I know I'm dumb, but my people were dumber and it never hurt them."—something sprayed pink.

Rolling in Rotten Salmon suppressed a growl. Meetings could be very frustrating for those who tried to pay attention. For the rest, that's what fleas are for. The park was filled with the low clarinet reediness of snuffling hunters, the thin staccato of castinetish teeth-to-teeth fine nipping, and the repeated basenotes of involuntary footbeats.

So now you get the gist? It was I who had the bright idea about screening, ID'ing (however that's spelled. I've only heard it), and forming a brigade to get order and discipline at the fence. Before then, it was *laissez-faire* chaos. Oh, I've had lots of bright ideas, and am so handsome, I have quite a presence, but no tact. It's a little scrap of a thing with worn out paws and only a few well chosen words—Fly, who chose to keep her lifelihood's professional name, who takes my ideas and brings the masses around without anyone feeling the least bit manipulated.

The welcome pack is only one of our ongoing projects. Ball-making, sand-dune re-creation, rotting-things-to-roll-in parks, the constant inducements needed to bribe trees to drop sticks of assorted appropriate sizes—all are constants, as are other parts of the necessary infrastructure: lampposts for the Europeans, fire hydrants for the Yankees. But those are piddlesticks compared to the most pressing and important need of our Great Society—the levelling of the playing field when it comes to health care.

Ignoring reality, however, is not an option. Because of the growing demand by humans, for dogs, and because that demand is for breeds with increasingly extreme profiles, the number of new entrants here has skyrocketed even as the percentage of them with pre-existing conditions overwhelmed our capacity to make their Heaven heaven.

At first, the agonizing spinal cysts that are the price of pricey ugliness for that fashionable faux-electrocuted Affenpinscher were treated by proto-cocker spaniels (the ones before their big sad eyes were caused by ingrown eyelashes) who would gaze on a newly resident Affenpinscher with such a caring warmth, the new resident didn't know the cockers practiced this look by gazing at pictures of dried liver.

The treatment was, as treatments usually are, "moderately effective," the term used by the bureaucracy here in DH to denote "As worthless as a picture of a chicken leg."

Something had to be done, for immigration was changing our society, turning it cruder all the time, its mainstays of *ways things are done* ever more dug under as frustration with the status quo stirred up base instincts till our formerly great society was rolling on its back, peeing on its very belly. Thus, competitive howlouts of the old and fit vs. the young and fucked broke out, revolutionarily, *before the sun goes down*, the notes long and tortured as, and possibly haunted by, that humans' horrorsong competition, The Voice.

Still at attention? If you're good, the answer's obvious. Time has passed, but I forgot to release you.

The old and wise Rolling in Rotten Salmon is still top dog. She never gets others' hackles up. And her broad head with its tiny eyes and its practical ears is filled with reasonable brains. Well, *I think so.*

"Reasonable! That's what's wrong with this place."

Burnt Sofa and Rotten Egg are grousing again—their tone so unreasonable, so unlike the tone of Heaven. Two uglier dogs used to be hard to find. Indeed, they'd each been crowned World's Ugliest Dog a few years ago. BS is an English bulldog who could hardly breathe and whose legs are so Chippendaled, he doesn't walk so much as shifts crabbily from side to side. He'd been bought from a puppy mill by an organization opposed to puppy mills but obviously not opposed to the deformed creatures making their new owners money and fame, and thus giving more aspirational owners reasons to find and produce ever more deformed and funny winners.

Rotten Egg's eyes are so bugged out of their sockets, they leap whenever she gets excited—which is like, always. Like Burnt Sofa, her teeth never meet each other but sort of wave from opposite poles of her froglike mouth. Not that they were accidents. Their function had been to mock horrify and genuinely amuse, aided by a few hairs standing up from her crown. Otherwise, she's as naked as a newborn rat.

"What good's a ball to me?"

Another newbie's pitched up. Unlike BS whose tongue is a hanger for a thick stream of spit, this dog's tongue is small and pink and dry. The dog's bright little eyes are on a 7 o'clock / 1 o'clock axis, her head stuck in a lolled position.

"Lolita!" Burnt Sofa nudges Rotten Egg. "This is—"

"I know who she was," RE says coldly. "You made millions on the internet."

"I?" The little dog's eyes lose their gloss. Her crooked tail droops as much as it can.

"Don't take your pain out on her," growls BS, and to the little dog: "You don't have to act happy anymore."

"That doesn't solve anything," snarls Rotten Egg. "Just not having to act happy can't make us happy."

"But throwing off our shackles will."

Me, I've never spoken up at these meetings. I'm not a public speaker. We do have, like you, a loud silent majority, and a silent, furrowed minority. We manage to understand each other. So I'm letting you in on more.

Something's happening.

Be honest. "Doggie Heaven"—like Santa, for your kids. We—we're all just memories, eh? Get those damn buds out of your ears and Sit!

You too, you wretched batch of puppies. Don't cry! You're not drowned rats. Here, curl against my stomach.

You, above and below: Quiet! Listen and learn—

That low, but assertive *grrr* uttered by a little dog so fucked up by breeding, she couldn't properly bark—she was the first in our revolution.

The Old Guard wasn't swept away as humans do. They were merely recognized as irrelevant.

The most urgent order of change to effect was redistribution. Extreme inequality was the root of the problem, and the reason the problem had not been recognized was that the Old Guard was too old and comfortable and the new, too young and therefore socially naive yet in levels of pain and disability unimaginable to the sympathetic olds.

The revolution uprooted standards, digging up the park meetings though they'd been the very symbol of social cohesion with what must have been a proportional slice of the populace attending, or so it was stodgily argued in the first and only challenge to the revolutionaries.

Stop mewling. This is interesting. That little challenge, I say, was a tiny toot compared to the ruckus kicked up when the silent majority got wind of the plans.

You'd think every dog had been made to eat what some had died to tell of: the vegan rawfood diet of broccoli, soy and brussels sprouts. Lucky you were too young for solid food.

The plans, by that Central Committee of Three, have never been caught and collared.

They are just, with no commands, no plans as such, being dug into our future.

Say a dog has hip dysplasia (which by the way, was the first condition to be treated, possibly because there are so many members here who were ex-law enforcement—you all would have got it soon). All hips here will be replaced by healthy ones and all tendons and muscles also, till the dog can happily jump over a junkyard's chainlink fence. Naturally, the laws of economics can never be broken, so the loss of bad bones, muscles, pain and associated arthritis, must be a net gain to the breeders, handlers and owners involved.

Or as in the *grrr* of that little dog with the bright pink tongue that its lady's boyfriend called obscene; "From each according to his disability, to each according to his sleaze."

The revolutionaries will soon be shaking Doggie Heaven so hard, a rain of our fleas is gonna fall on them below.

Still there, puppies? It seems to be just you and me. How long's it's been? You seem to be cold in perpetuity.

I wasn't wrong about one thing. A something has befallen. Nothing like our old everyday pains you drowned puppies were too young to experience—fleas under the collar, having to "hold it" all day till someone comes home, trying not to commit a crime from the boredom of solitary confinement, having to keep calm and carry on when people explode things because they're inscrutably happy. Breathing.

This is something so big, many people would have their tails between their legs if they had tails. Others, like dogs who bark from the safe side of doors, jeer and laugh and live as always till, at their eulogies, people act as if no one noticed their poo-poohs. Some call what's happening cosmic payback. But all that empty chewing on *why* is what people do, like endless watching of balls you can't mouth.

Down there now:

People hobble to cafes on legs as curved as your tongues. They try to to sit on chairs, yet only manage to lean their butts on the edge, their faces twitching. Sometimes a leg juts out with no warning and they clutch parts of them as if pain is a clump of weeds growing in them big enough for a streetgang of strays to pee on. They order coffee, which they pass under noses that cannot be used to breathe through and if meant for decoration, those who value that aesthetic must be a rarified breed indeed. Sprays of teeth protruding from cracked lips make drinking their coffee impossible, so they suck through straws—alternating with taking air through their mouths—as they hold flea collars they call handkerchiefs to their chins to catch their stinking drool.

At their feet are typically, unidentifiable mutts who have bred as naturally as the day likes to be wild. These mutts rule with equanimity, of course, being dogs.

Equanimity? Fly, can you explain? And where's a Nanna where I need one?

THE END

...or so I thought. I was very proud that I got this out. It's one thing to read but another to tell. And I thought, whatwith all the distractions here, I did a rather good job of reporting.

But a story's just a story and life goes on, so to speak. It got out. The story. In places I'd never imagined it could. Rabbits got it, but they're dumb, but from them it spread to their neighbours, the lab rats bred to higher, more specialised registration standards than any Kennel Club.

They're smart but sick, you see, for they were never pets.

BONES
IN
HEAVEN

previously unpublished

It seems only yesterday (poss. seven yesterdays to you) that I reported the goings on in the real Doggie Heaven. "How time flies," you might say Fly would say, getting Fly completely wrong.

For Fly has never raised her voice to say anything other than the necessary. Work hard, work hard, and no philosophizing.

But in Heaven there's no work. You'd think she'd be deliriously happy, jumping for frisbies tossed at her whim from our Heavenly frisbee-tossing robot; mining the innards of sofas; tearing toilet paper; jumping, thoroughly muddied, on the beds of kings, magnates, and ripe strawberries, and curling up into them to sleep, perchance to dream; dining from kitchen counters, restaurant alleys and untended buffets, butcher shop windows, wedding spreads, and the odd fresh bit of fleeing meat—all to her heart's content.

But she's one of a surprising number of mopers here. Many's the time I've lectured about the meaning of the saying *Look a gift horse in the mouth* but do these sadsacks get the symbolism? I'd have had more success giving my For Your Eyes Only tracking lessons to the bloodhounds. "Substitute Heaven for horse," I say, but the ones who don't need to be told to enjoy themselves whine to be released from *Stay*, and the others stay rebelliously, looking anywhere but at me.

Sometimes I despair, and must do something physical to alleviate my disappointment in creating the perfect society in this so perfect place.

So I was the forelands, doing duty in a welcome party, teaching—well, trying to teach a formerly apartment-bound "sheepdog" (bought because the puppy looked like the white, carpet matching, polar bear of a dog in a commercial) how to dig his way in under Heaven's fence when ahead, poss. in Playing Field 1, an explosion of barking, baying and scent excreting erupted—the urgency and cluelessness of which were all directed at, of course, me.

"Come behind," I snapped, and a lieutenant shoved past to push while I raced ahead, past the check-in and what would have been the normal milling crowd of the curious and indiscriminately friendly—all deserted for Field 1.

It was lucky everyone saw the state of my fur when I arrived. Shaking dirt-clods out of my ears gave me time to get a load of this newcomer, this—

Rolling on his bony feet, jumping up his legs, he was surrounded with more squirming bodies than a dead rat on a hot tar road.

More cautiously, others including Fly were doing all they could to protect us all—yapping, whining, baying, woofing till hoarse, baring tartar-crusted teeth, running around trying without success to get to him—to chase him out or bring him down for good.

I barked once, but there was no bringing some in this assembly to dignity.

A curt growl did much more, but it wasn't from me. "Want me to tear his throat out?"

This was the first time I'd ever heard that greyhound, whose first step on the way to Doggie Heaven had been burial, still alive but with her identifying ears cut off for not running fast enough anymore.

An ear-itching whimper rent the crowd. Rork, a misshapen German shepherd bristling with shrapnel, launched himself through the masses like a dart thrown by a drunk, knocking aside the greyhound and landing so hard on the visitor that the crack of two skulls made me wince.

"Attack is futile," I tsked, once again marveling at the reputation for intelligence some get, just because.

But Rork either didn't or wouldn't hear me. His big tongue was licking that face so hard that spittle ricocheted off the cheekbones as the visitor kept grinning—but I knew that grin. It's like a dolphin's. It's like rolling on your back on the grass and looking at a rainbow. It's fixed as a crooked fight.

I was so embarrassed on everyone's account, I got an itch so bad, I had to swallow, else I'd have to scoot on the unwormed-dogs' carpet.

Instead, "Sit!" I barked.

I can't say everyone obeyed instantly, but they did subside, all except for Rork who was uttering so many puppy cries, you'd think this was the pound and the visitor, a dog person.

Fly dropped almost to the ground, poised.

The greyhound rose shakily, her flaccid teats trembling.

Neither looked at me, only at the visitor. I could feel their lack of faith in my judgement. Fly's ears strained for the release to chase him off the field; the greyhound, merely to leap and with one bite, snap that neck.

Instead—oh, how to explain? "He's the Reaper," I announced. "The Reaper," I repeated, loudly enough that Rork, distracted, slid down to standing position.

"Just Reaper," grinned the visitor.

He'd *heard* me, and furthermore, understood—as likely as a fire hydrant saying "Come."

"'Struth," he said, as if he spent his evenings reading antiquariana. "It passeth understanding."

Of course I was dreaming. So I played along. If I were human, I would have winked. This was fabulous. So much better than dreaming of my past life. Any moment, I expected a lawn flamingo to fly in, wagging a German shepherd tail.

"But how does Rork know you?"

"He came before I left," said Rork.

"Rork's sergeant. I dispatched him."

"With that," said Rork, pointing his nose up at a backpack the visitor wore with a panache I hadn't noticed, swung lightly off one shoulder—a high-tech carbon fiber handle poking out.

Rork whimpered once, but only once, so it must have escaped. It had a timbre I recognized—that of the dogs who while awake, were all, as I described them: silent and mopey.

"Thank you for making it quick," he said to the impossible visitor. "I would have put my nose in his hand but—" Rork flicked his left ear with a paw, as if he had been bitten by a bee. Then he pulled himself up to stand as straight as the shrapnel in him and what must be a shattered left thigh let him.

"I don't know that callsign—Reaper," he said, "but General sir, it's an honor to meet you. I apologize—"

"That's quite alright." A bony hand rummaged in a pocket. "Would you like me to read the Post reporting the ceremony at the Capitol? I've got it somewhere here, and the Medal of Bravery . . . But I see from your knit eyebrows, you get no dispatches here. Your man got something too."

Rork looked at the ground, and then at me. "Moonlight," he said. He wouldn't face the crowd, that shamelessly curious crowd. "Meet General Death. General Death, this is our de facto head, Moonlight."

"Just mister," said Death. "I might be rank, but I've got no rank."

He didn't say Mister Human Death, but he didn't have to. And I couldn't help wondering how many times he'd told that joke. Maybe because it came from him, it was doomed to be stale as crypt air.

"And Rork here, he's no civvy," he said. "He's K9 Rork—MWD (that's Military Working Dog to you)—EDD (Explosive Detection Dog), IED/Patrol, US Marine Corps (killed in action) after trying to protect not just his sergeant but—"

Rork barked once, and Death's jaws snapped shut to form that rather infuriatingly smug smile.

I'd never before believed the pictures any more than those of Santa Claus. I knew all the fakery of Santa Claus because humans don't think to hide some lies from dogs.

Humans say dogs just accept, but that is just because they're not paying us attention.

Humans say dogs don't fear death because we only think in the present, but they don't have our dreams, don't see our memories, hopes, and wishes.

Humans have practically no senses, so it boggled me that they got Death so right. It was surprising that Death had let Rork see him in the act, but it was a once in a never, and would never happen again.

So why this unprecedented visit?

I woke at that moment. My mouth tasted of raw broccoli. The muscles in my legs ached from paddling in my sleep. I was in a state of muddled suspended marveling at the dreams one has in Heaven when suddenly, my heart pounded, my paws broke out in sweat—and I knew I'd been all too awake all along.

My lip raised as if hooked. The greyhound took the cue and coiled, ready to pounce.

Rork had never been a mixer, was known as a morose layabout with something heavy on his mind, but he was part of our society, one of us, and like hell were we gonna let him be taken out because he was witness to something he should never have seen. Not that anyone but me, him, and this thing that brings about human death would ever know, all the rest of the dogs in the world being as innocent of this Death creature, this Reaper—as they are to what's so nasty about buttholes.

That excuse to give Rork the award he was supposedly given after death, and to top it off, a ceremony that he would never see—how naive could Reaper think we are? I was almost surprised Reaper didn't report on the dinner they served up for him down there. I suddenly wished I could throw them into their future so I could shove all that stuff into their own cold dead hands. I felt insulted on behalf of all of us that Reaper would take us for such pushovers—and very very scared.

My hackles rose and I took one step back, in preparation for the assault. Rork was like many dogs, trustful to a fault.

I didn't have that fault. And neither did the greyhound.

She took off as if I'd fired the starter gun, but she didn't get there fast enough.

The same mob as before got there first, one terrier leaping so high, his two front paws scrabbled on a rib, his pink tongue flabbering madly.

I've never been so embarrassed.

"Sit!" I bayed. And to the visitor, "Rork has a good life here. Besides, your powers are only supposed to be on Earth, and not in Heaven. So go back to where you came from. Rork hasn't even told anyone his serial number, so your secret's safe with me."

"What secret?" yapped the terrier.

"And who are *you* to say," Rork growled.

"Ey up, lad," said Gyp, who always annoys me with that non-standard language. I'd heard she was a champion in her day. In weather famous for its sting and bite, she'd brought in both sheep so tough they gargled stones for their baahs, and longhorned cattle so blinded with hair over their eyes, they needed seeing eye dogs—but you'd never have known that here. She'd never come forward for a leadership position. I threw her a glance of balanced appreciation—of encouragement, and nodded toward Rork whose ears were thrown back, tense and sullen.

"You know nowt," said Gyp, turning away from me to join the throng.

A bug-eyed little thing who'd died from a diet of pizza and fries chittered like a cat seeing a bird on the other side of a window.

"Perhaps he, Moonlight you say," said the center of attention in a maddeningly low rasp. "Perhaps Moonlight here," he whispered into rapt silence, "doesn't know that many of us have met."

Talk about being speechless! I was positively basenji.

"Thank you for taking care of my master," said a dog so dull, I'd never noticed the thing.

Master—a snarl rose up my throat. "Here in Heaven," I reminded her, "we have no masters. We have self-respect."

Death waved his hand dismissively. "'Twas nothing."

"I loved him," the same dog sniveled.

"And he loved you," said Death.

"Enough!" I howled. "Love! There's no such thing as love, unless you call what they feel for a new phone, a piece of furniture, a song, chocolate. Sure, my human *family* said they loved me, but they treated me like a table, unthought of when not used. That's why board and bored are related, see."

"I spent most of my life on a chain," said Fly.

"At least you died working," said the greyhound. "Wanna know my name? It was Penguinscandance. I was treated like a loser's betting ticket. Love! It's for mugs. Moonlight's the goods. Gospel truth."

I thumped my tail and but had to gently add, "Excellent observation, though it's amazing that you came to that level of sophistication of thought. After all, you've avoided my philosophy classes."

The visitor chuckled. "There are more things in heaven and earth, young Moonlight, than are dreamt of in your philosophy."

"You trying to impress me?" said I. "So you know your Shakespeare."

"He was a plagiarist," Death said drily.

I had to nip this in the butt. "What do you *want* here? Go away!"

"Why?"

"Why? Why?" I admit I had a bit of a scrabbling incident as my back legs lost a bit of balance. I rearanged myself into a power slouch.

"You're destabilizing. Everyone here has their place. Everyone is happy, for after all, this is Doggie Heaven. And for all your Shakespeare quoting, you're making no sense. We have perfect understanding here. And we all speak the same language."

At that, I had to hold a paw up to stop the cacophony of nonsense that came from a myriad of mouths.

"I need you," he said, not speaking to me. "*We* need you." He followed that with a cacophony of nonsense that quietened a myriad of mouths.

So many left with him that many a hill and field and hollow in Heaven echoes with emptiness. My soul howls my failure.

They left even though he told them, "You can't go home again."

They left even though he told them, "You'll be on the fly all the time. You'll never have a home."

They left even though he told them, "You'll be giving love to those who will only leave you."

They left even though he told them, "Their life left will only be short before I give them the coup de grâce."

They left without a backwards glance, because, as he explained to me without making any sense, "They remember."

The rational is in the ascendance here, and it should be a victory with only the ones who know that love is for mugs to keep up standards, to welcome newcomers, to try to keep the flow only one way—but once that way was breached, it's been a constant loss. Heaven is like a river, flowing backwards.

It's even taken the greyhound who never did trust people but missed a certain retired racehorse. This is just what I've heard: that greyhound is presently with some woman who smells of toffee who runs a rescued racehorse and donkey haven. She has, according to Reaper, but this might just be scuttlebutt, five months left, and has named the greyhound Annabelle. None of the volunteers at the haven have noticed or think it strange that she talks to this invisible Annabelle. They're talkative too.

The greyhound leaving for equines inspired Fly, who left for, of all creatures, ewes.

Gyp specialises in widowed farmers whose families want to sell the old stone barns and cramped stone houses for fortunes. Instead, Gyp nurses the farmers and the lambs they bring into the fireplace-warmed kitchens.

And all the ratty little bossy types? I can't keep a chihuahua here to save my death. Once they hear of the openings with wrinklies who live alone who can no longer afford to keep a four-legged baby, they're off like a drowned rat's coat.

But even the dogs big as carthorses perversely leave for the most inhospitable climes. You'd think they don't have noses, the way they're drawn to what's called "care homes" stinking with disinfectants. These dogs seem to want to spend their days standing next to chairs and putting their heads into laps of people who aren't housetrained.

Reports say that Rork was latest seen in hospitals at Novosibirsk, Nagoya, and Nashville—but he doesn't choose as such—just out there on some field of disaster is, I guess, his Heaven. He's so much a one-dog recruitment poster that against my better judgement but bowing to popular demand, I've compiled a book titled *Rork's Revelations* from all the quotes that are supposedly his. The strangest ones I've put in the section "Relative Love".

According to him, many people are actually distressed by their relatives visiting them when they are helpless. Wives irritate husbands by spending the visit crying. Husbands curse the conditions and run out of the ward to yell at staff. But when one of ours settles on the bed or sits by the wheelchair or lies on the floor or dirt in companionship, the dying person often leaks tears of happiness, wholly unrecognised as that of course, except by the dog invisibly cooling a wrist or forehead, or resting a weightless head on a chest.

The other supposed truth humans either don't know or will never admit, but Rork swears it, and he's not alone, so I put it in the book:

People often love us best.

I do love truth, but I regret publishing that book. It has only increased the flow out. Of course there are always newcomers here, but newcomers can't replace old acquaintances. If I didn't know myself to be rational, I'd diagnose my increasing lethargy as loneliness.

Time has lost meaning, but I think it was three mornings ago when the most unlikely dog of all slipped away. I'd only heard rumours of how long she'd been here. She was the colour of granite. She never came to any of my lectures and signed up for no classes. She didn't bark as such, nor did she know how to properly wag her tail. I'd never understood a thing she said, though lots was said *about* her.

Supposedly, she was here before Heaven was Heaven. Her master—there was that filthy word again but this one was rumoured to be a female human—was said to have been killed by a rockfall in a cave after painting her portrait.

One day when all I could do is brood, Death visited again. There was no one in sight, so I sat next to him. He reached out but put his hand back behind his head as if he needed to scratch an itch.

"You know," he said, "I didn't always have this scythe."

That was a surprise.

"I started out with stones."

Eww, I thought to myself, but I couldn't keep my curled netherlip down, our bite being so much more efficient, so humane.

"I've never had a dog," he said.

I jumped up and snarled with outrage. "You're surrounded by them! They are drawn to you like moths to a—"

"You and I are so beyond clichés," he said. "Are we not?"

And he motioned the universal *Down* so I dropped.

He reached out again, and lightly touched my head. When I didn't move, he ran his hand down my left ear. Some of my silky hairs caught in one of his joints, and he stopped. That face of his was still grinning but I could smell panic.

I maneuvered gently till my ear was free. He jerked his hand away and twiddled his digits in embarrassment. But there was something about that hand. I put my nose in it, just sniffing.

"Would you be mine?" he blurted. "Or rather, could I be yours?"

I've got a job to do up there in Heaven, so we can't be inseparable as we'd wish, but I'll tell you some secrets.

He's taken me to see his wife, Pestilence. She's so hot, cats would love her, but I'm not looking for a heater. She's also got red red lips and long red fingernails that desperately need clipping. I don't see what he sees in her. Inevitably, just after they act like they wish they could make babies, they're snappy as a new mother—so it's an on and off relationship. She calls him Angel.

When down here, he can be a bit of an extrovert. I never comment on his taste, but he sees nothing wrong with being mistaken for a Rolling Stone.

When we're alone, he's often overcome with an emotion that causes him to pick me up, crush me to his ribs, and kiss the top of my head with his dry closed mandibles. At times like these, he'll also say, "I love you" and once—just now in fact: "I love you better than life itself."

Who am I to tell him that that cliché makes not a whiff of sense from him?

It's true, however, for me.

"Get ready to be licked to death," I've just replied.

So prick up your ears and listen . . .

Hear Death giggle?

Also by Anna Tambour

NOVELS

Smoke Paper Mirrors

Crandolin

Spotted Lily

COLLECTIONS

The Road to Neozon

The Finest Ass in the Universe

Monterra's Deliciosa & Other Tales &

Anna Tambour is also a photographer of the unnoticed.

Also by Mike Dubisch

Science Fiction" Exhibition catalogue, Science Museum, London 2022

"I Am A Barbarian" Illustrator- comic art and covers   Collected edition CedarRun Books.ERB inc. Edgar Rice Burroughs Inc. 2022

"Forbidden Futures" Literary Fiction Magazine Illustrator- Oddness Books 2018-2022

"Skin Crawl Magazine" Contributor- Skinner 2022

"Professor Dario Bava: Orgy of the Blood Fiends" Illustrator, comic art - Diabolik LLC. 2021

"Carmilla-Vampiress Magazine" Illustrator, comic art Warrant 2021

"Slow Death Zero" Contributor- Last Gasp Books 2020

"Professor Dario Bava: Murder Vibes From The Monster Dimension" Illustrator, comic art and covers- Diabolik LLC. 2019

Graphic Novelist and Illustrator **Mike Dubisch** has been creating and publishing comics and art since the 1980's. Dubisch has carved out a unique place for himself in the world of art and comics, creating works of horror, science-fiction , surrealism, and YA adventure using all but lost traditional techniques. Born in California, USA, the artist has traveled the world and lived in five countries. Dubisch has been an instructor at the Academy of Art University since 2012, and is married to children's book illustrator and sculptor Carolyn Watson Dubisch with whom he has three daughters.

CPSIA information can be obtained
at www.ICGtesting.com
Printed in the USA
BVHW040217100423
662040BV00016B/23

9 781732 212442